SPECIAL
VICTIM

SPECIAL VICTIM

THE DEVINE TRILOGY

TOM COFFEY

LEVEL
BEST BOOKS

Author Photo Credit: Thomas Monaster

First edition

ISBN: 978-1-68512-814-2

Cover art by Level Best Designs

This book was professionally typeset on Reedsy.
Find out more at reedsy.com

To Beth, Eileen and Andrew

"There is a crack, a crack in everything
That's how the light gets in"

—"Anthem," by Leonard Cohen

Praise for Special Victim

"Possessing a distinguished career as a journalist, and the ability to write compelling fiction, Tom Coffey has made his mark. *Special Victim*, loosely based on a horrific crime that grabbed the attention of not only New York City, but the country as well, will keep you reading nonstop."—Harriette Sackler, Agatha Award-Nominated short story writer, Grants Chair - Malice Domestic, Ltd. Board of Directors

Chapter One

Michael Devine

1

July 15, 2013

T he verdict was guilty. The spectators whooshed, and his assistant clenched her fist in a small sign of triumph, but Michael was surprised by his reaction while the word was uttered, over and over, until it seemed like the only sound he had ever heard or would hear again. For more than a year, he'd assumed he would sense the jubilation that swelled inside him on the pitcher's mound whenever he threw a shutout, but all he felt, as he listened to every defendant being convicted on every charge, was a tiny sense of relief.

I never want to go through anything like this again, he said to himself.

After the criminals were led away, Judge Iffath Khan thanked the jurors for their service, banged her gavel to announce that the trial was over, and strode through the door to her chambers.

Lucky woman, Michael thought. She won't have to deal with the fallout.

Reporters rushed forward, screaming for comment. His assistant's eyes opened wide, as if she were a beachgoer who couldn't believe the size of the approaching tsunami. He guided her by the elbow to a vacant conference room, where she searched for something to say before coming up with, "We

1

won."

Her name was Jackie Williams. An up-and-comer, just as Michael had been, way back when.

"We have to face the media," he said. "I'll do the talking. Stand to my right."

Five minutes later, he was on the courthouse steps in front of a battery of microphones and video cameras. The sun blazed a few feet above his eyebrows.

"Are you happy?" a reporter asked.

The question was ridiculous. He had anticipated it.

"I'd give away everything I own not to be here today," Michael said. "A woman was brutally attacked and beaten within an inch of her life. Now four teenagers who've never had a serious problem with the law will spend the best years of their lives in prison."

He shook his head. He hoped he looked as rueful as he felt.

"It's all such a waste, and none of it had to happen."

* * *

When he walked through the door at home, his wife nibbled his ear and said she was proud of him. He put down his briefcase and wrapped his arms around her. The kids rushed up, calling, "Daddy, Daddy, Daddy!" They'd seen him on TV. It was really exciting.

Behind them, he saw his in-laws, and he wondered what they were doing in his living room until he saw the bottle of Champagne in Jacob Meyer's hand.

"Congratulations," the man said as he popped the cork.

"I don't feel like celebrating," Michael said.

"You mean that horseshit you said at the news conference? Don't tell me you meant it."

"I did. And please don't swear in front of the children. They hear enough of it at the playground."

Meyer filled four flutes and proposed a toast to the best prosecutor in

New York. Michael had never cared for Champagne but told himself to be gracious, so he lifted his glass and tried to smile.

Meyer asked if they could talk in private. Michael felt like saying No. He wanted to spend time with his wife and children, whom he had barely seen for months.

"Sure."

They lived in a classic six on Central Park West, so he steered his father-in-law to his little girl's bedroom and cleared away several of her stuffed animals before sitting on the edge of her bed.

"What is it?" Michael asked.

Meyer folded his arms across his chest and rocked on the balls of his feet. Michael recognized the power pose.

"We're all impressed," Meyer said.

"Who are 'we,' and what are 'we' impressed about?"

"People I know. People I work with."

Michael had difficulty figuring out exactly what his father-in-law did for a living. Mostly real estate, although he seemed to have a hand in almost everything that went on in the city.

"This was the toughest case to come along in years," Meyer said. "You dealt with it flawlessly."

Michael was not used to hearing compliments from the man, so he sputtered some thanks.

"You hit all the right notes at that press conference," Meyer said. "The men I know are asking me, 'What does he wanna do next?'"

"Next? Rachel and I get away with the kids for a couple weeks. Somewhere in New England. I'm being vague about the location because I don't want anyone to bother me."

"What happens when you return?"

"I go back to work."

"Yeah, yeah, yeah. Public servant and all that crap."

Michael rose to his feet. He was several inches taller than his father-in-law, and sometimes it felt good to loom over him.

"It's not crap, Jacob, and you know it. What's your point?"

Jacob Meyer nodded. Men who pushed back always impressed him.

"Have you thought about how far you wanna take this? How far you wanna go? You could run for any office in the city right now, and I could get the right people behind you."

"I'd hafta talk to your daughter about that."

"I already have."

"What did she say?"

"'Talk to him.'"

There was only one job Michael truly wanted, but he had never admitted it to anyone, not even his wife.

"Most guys woulda screwed it up today," Meyer said. "They woulda stood on those steps and gloated."

"I didn't feel like gloating," Michael said.

"Now you sound soft. I dunno what I think about that."

He's baiting me, Michael told himself. He likes to irritate people to see how they handle it.

"Those kids we convicted aren't thugs," Michael said. "They're weak, but they're not bad."

Meyer made a noise that sounded like bile rising in his throat. "That makes them even worse. You know what we oughta do with all those animals in that part of the city?"

"I don't wanna hear it, Jacob."

"I'm tired of this politically correct horseshit. Let's say it like it is—they're savages. We oughta do to them what we did to the Indians—slaughter most of 'em and put the rest on reservations. Isolate 'em from civilized people. The men who built this country weren't afraid to do whatever was necessary. Now we're run by wimps."

"For the record— " Michael said.

Be selective in your outrage, the district attorney had told him years ago. You can wrap yourself in the cloak of righteousness once a year, so you better pick the right time.

"—none of those kids had even been arrested for littering."

"That one kid," Meyer said. "The big one. He had juvie stuff. You shoulda made that public."

"Juvenile records are sealed."

Meyer snorted. Michael went on.

"Any problems at school were minor. One of those guys was bound for the Ivy League. You know how the Ivies like to admit three or four disadvantaged kids every year so they can talk about how much good they're doing for society."

"That diversity crap is destroying the country."

Michael glanced around. Now he wanted alcohol of any kind and regretted leaving the Champagne in the living room.

2

April 24, 2012

He was used to seeing people who had been mauled by criminals, but when he first glimpsed the victim, he suppressed a gasp. Two weeks after the crime, she was still hooked to machines and tubes. Her face was purple, her eyes swollen nearly shut, arms and legs encased in casts. A bloody bandage covered her nose, which had been broken in several places, and her breathing reminded him of the rattling sounds his mother emitted as she died from cancer.

The doctors said the victim's recovery so far had been remarkable. They were amazed at her strength. Left for dead in Riverside Park, she refused to succumb.

He crouched beside her and said, as softly as he could, "Ms. Antolini."

He detected the slightest nod a person could manage.

"My name is Michael Devine. I'm with the district attorney's office."

Another nod.

"Do you recall what happened to you? Anything at all?"

"I was running." She struggled with the words. "Then I blacked out. And then I was here."

He debated with himself whether to put her on the stand. Although he wanted to limit her trauma, he believed the world should see what they had done to her.

"Get better, Ms. Antolini."

"I don't know how much help I can be."

"Just keep on living, Ms. Antolini. That's all the help I'm asking for."

Chapter Two

Sheila Devine

September 12, 2023

She was surprised by his email and even more surprised when they talked on the phone, but she needed a project, and Rolando Ortega was the best lawyer in the city, and he had a matter to discuss.

His office was on 125th Street near the Lexington Avenue subway station. The location sent the message that he stood solidly with people of color who were being oppressed by authority, but she suspected he had received tax breaks.

Security theater in the lobby. Hand sanitizer just past the turnstiles. An elevator whisked her to the top floor, where she encountered Ortega's receptionist, a dark-skinned, fortysomething Latina with fierce eyes. Hair fell in ringlets past her shoulders. Some people still wore face masks most of the time, and hers said Black Lives Matter.

"Hola," the woman said.

"Hola," Sheila replied. "Que tal?"

"Bien."

Sheila engaged some rarely used brain cells. "Estoy aquí porque tengo una cita con Señor Ortega."

"I'll tell him you're here."

A few minutes later, Sheila sat across from the man, whose glass-encased space offered a rolling view south toward the behemoth-sized buildings ascending in midtown. Sheila looked at him warily. Rolando Ortega had just passed his seventieth birthday, but he still had a full head of salt-and-pepper hair. Since the beginning of the pandemic she had become good at reading people's eyes, and his smoldered with the remembrance of every slight.

"Why do you wanna see me?" she asked.

"We were impressed with your last film."

Sheila Devine's documentary about her father, a disgraced NYPD cop wrongfully convicted of murdering a sex worker, had been a hit at Sundance and did well on the art house circuit before landing on Netflix, although it failed to receive an Oscar nomination.

"Who are 'we,' and what are 'we' impressed about?"

"People I know. People I work with."

Sheila spit out her next words. Perhaps she should have worn a mask. "I remember our meeting at the prison. You represented the man who murdered my father."

After agreeing to testify against the people who had persuaded him to kill Terence Devine, Octravian Murray's already lengthy prison sentence was extended by twenty years. The trail of evidence indicated a conspiracy that included Adam Fishman, the former district attorney who committed suicide rather than face charges, and Aaron Grubb, a multimillionaire real estate developer who copped a plea to obstruction of justice and got three years at a medium-security prison. But the jails were overcrowded and still full of Covid, so after ten months, New York State agreed to let him do the rest of his time under house arrest.

"You reopened a case everyone thought was closed," Ortega said. "You were persistent and clear-eyed, and you got to the truth. Very few people can do something like that."

Sheila sensed the light bulb flicking on over her head. "And now you have a case like that, and you want me to take a look at it."

"I heard you had a quick mind."

"What's the case?"

"The Riverside Runner."

Sheila gulped.

"I represent Manuel Fuentes," Ortega said. "One of the convicted men. He's appealing his conviction."

"All those guys have been appealing their convictions since the verdicts came in."

"There's new evidence."

A voice inside Sheila's head began to shout that she should leave immediately.

Ortega cleared his throat, as if he were about to address a jury. "One of the prisoners in the penitentiary where my client is incarcerated told him something interesting. This man said that while he was at Attica, he talked to an inmate named Jose Ramos, who has been convicted for both drug possession and sex offenses. Ramos told this prisoner that he alone had assaulted the Riverside Runner. According to the man who talked to my client, Ramos laughed while he discussed the attack, which he described in clinical detail."

"With all due respect, Señor Ortega, I am deeply skeptical."

"As you should be."

Think, Sheila told herself. Rolando Ortega always has an angle. Usually, more than one.

"Are you working pro bono?" she asked.

"For the time being."

The metaphorical light bulb above Sheila's head began to flicker more strongly.

"Which individual or entity do you plan to sue, and for how much?"

"The City of New York. Twenty-five million dollars for wrongful imprisonment."

Sheila did the math. If Ortega was successful, he stood to make about eight million.

"You seem perturbed, Ms. Devine."

"Of course, I'm perturbed."

"Why?"

"Don't you remember who prosecuted the case?"

"That's why I wanted to talk to you." Ortega clasped his hands on his oak desk. "Merely winning our appeal isn't good enough. The media, many members of the public—they'll say I used lawyers' tricks. Technicalities. They'll always believe that Manuel Fuentes and his companions are guilty. That's why I need to change the public's opinion about this case. My assistant Dolores—"

He pointed to the reception area.

"—came up with the idea of approaching a filmmaker to work with us."

"Why me?" Sheila asked.

"Many Latinos and Blacks in this city feel those young men were railroaded."

"I attended some sessions of the trial," Sheila said. "They weren't railroaded."

Ortega nodded, agreeing to disagree. "A film about this case by a Black or a Latin will be dismissed as agitprop. And if the moviemaker is a man, there will be criticism that he doesn't understand the awful realities of sexual assault."

"But I'm white—" Sheila said.

Ortega smiled.

"—and a woman—"

His smile grew wider.

"—and the sister of the prosecutor who sent your client and his buddies away."

"Which is why your conclusions will have credibility."

"What if I conclude your client is guilty?"

"All lawyers gamble sometimes. This is one of those occasions."

Sheila leaned back in her chair and blew out some air as if she were doing a breathing exercise in yoga class. I need to stay Zen, she thought, but right now, that's really hard.

"Men... " she said.

"What about us?" Ortega asked.

"They don't realize how traumatic that case was for every woman in New

York. We walked around for weeks looking over our shoulders. Didn't feel safe anywhere, at any time. Even though only one woman was attacked, all of us felt violated."

"I am a man," Ortega said, "so I will not pretend I understand how you feel. But I do understand the sense of violation, and Manuel Fuentes has been violated constantly since the day he was arrested."

"I'm no fan of the prison system," Sheila said, "but your point about your client is debatable. The trial was run by the rules."

"Sometimes the rules fail." Ortega leaned toward her. His voice acquired an end-of-meeting, time-to-make-a-decision tone. "I will give you complete access, Ms. Devine. You will talk to my client, and he will try to persuade the other defendants to cooperate with you. I imagine they will retain lawyers, perhaps even me, once word gets out."

Sheila shook her head. "I doubt I can do this, Señor Ortega. For many reasons."

The lawyer walked to the window and waved his arm, as if he were trying to sprinkle pixie dust over every section of Manhattan.

"Your brother will be elected soon. To a term in his own right."

Sheila nodded. After the governor appointed Michael Devine as the interim district attorney, Jacob Meyer lined up the power brokers behind him. Now Michael was campaigning to win the only job he had ever wanted, and the latest poll had him ahead by three-to-one over his closest opponent, who was running as an independent but had a surprising amount of money. The Republicans hadn't even bothered to nominate a candidate.

"I've gone up against your brother in the courtroom," Ortega said. "A worthy adversary, always."

"My brother prosecuted your client and his friends because he thought they were guilty," Sheila said. "He doesn't send innocent people to jail."

"Inevitably," Ortega said, "over the course of a career, at some point, a prosecutor will convict someone who was guilty only of being in the wrong place at the wrong time."

Sheila stood. "I'll consider your offer, but I'll tell you right now that my answer will probably be 'No.'"

Ortega nodded. "You are my first choice. I'll give you until Thursday. After then, I may have to swat away potential collaborators with a club."

"What happens Thursday?"

"I file my motion."

"Motions get filed all the time."

"I have new evidence."

"That statement from your jailhouse guy? Good luck with that. For openers, it sounds like hearsay."

All that time with her brother had given Sheila a decent working knowledge of the legal system. She stepped toward the door. She doubted she'd see Rolando Ortega again.

"There is DNA," Ortega said.

Sheila stopped. "What DNA?"

"From the crime scene."

Sheila rummaged her mind for details about the case. She recalled that no DNA from any of the perpetrators was recovered, which most observers thought was curious but ultimately irrelevant because they all confessed. Their statements were written down and then videotaped. When they were shown in court, the cumulative effect was damning.

"DNA was gathered that did not match the victim, or any of the men convicted in the case," Ortega said. "My motion will ask for that DNA to be tested against Jose Ramos."

* * *

Wesley McBride kept a file of Jamaican recipes that Sheila dived into whenever she had time to cook, so after meeting with Ortega, she put together a dinner of jerk chicken with rice, beans, cabbage and, in a touch she thought inspired, plantains.

"This is really good, Mom," Bethany said.

"Thanks," Sheila said before exchanging a glance with her husband. They both suspected the second shoe was about to drop.

"I like it when you're not working," Bethany said. "You make better dinners."

Sheila resisted the urge to engage in a teenage-style rolling of the eyes, although her daughter had latched onto a point: Whenever Sheila was involved in a project, most of her efforts to create meals revolved around boiling water.

"I keep telling you," Sheila said in what she hoped was an even tone, "you're a big girl now, so if you don't like what I'm making, you can cook dinner for the family."

Bethany rolled her eyes.

Wesley turned to Dylan, their son, who seemed intent on hoovering up as much food as possible.

"What do you think?" Wesley asked. His eyes sparked with the light touch of a born prankster. As far as Sheila could tell, just about everything in the universe amused her husband, except for his efforts to engineer the perfect cup of coffee.

"Think about what?" Dylan replied between mouthfuls.

"About what your mother makes for dinner."

Dylan swallowed. "It's all good."

His parents laughed. Sometimes, Sheila thought her son had diplomatic skills and should consider a career in the Foreign Service. He was a senior at Brooklyn Tech, so they were close to a decision about college. Around the house, he was acting like a soldier near the end of his tour in a war zone.

"As a matter of fact," Sheila said.

She took a slug of pinot and became aware of her husband and children turning to her with the undivided attention she always enjoyed.

"I got a job offer today," she said. "It was strange."

"What's the offer?" Dylan asked. He reached for the rice and beans. He'd always liked rice and beans, even as a baby.

"It was from Rolando Ortega," she said. "He wants me to film him while he pursues his latest case."

"Didn't he represent the guy who killed Grandpa?" Dylan asked.

"Yup," Sheila said.

"Fuck him," Dylan said.

13

"It's a good thing I don't believe in hitting my children," Wesley said.

"What am I supposed to say?" Dylan replied.

"Something that doesn't involve profanity."

"You've studied the Constitution," Sheila told her son. "In this country, everybody has the right to a lawyer. Even the scum of the earth."

"But why did he have to represent that assho—that piece of scum?"

"Because he got paid," Wesley said.

"You didn't tell us what the case was, Mom," Bethany said.

"The Riverside Runner."

Her kids looked blankly at her. The crime had occurred when they were small. So many awful things had happened since then.

Sheila briefly explained the details.

"I dunno, Ma," Dylan said when she was done. "Sounds like bullsh—sounds bogus to me."

Sheila turned to Bethany. "What do you think?"

"You should do what you want. You will anyway."

"I left out one important thing," Sheila said.

"What's that?" Bethany asked.

"The case was prosecuted by your Uncle Michael. It made his reputation."

Dylan shook his head so forcefully his 'fro started swaying. "Uncle Michael doesn't send people to jail just because he feels like it. If he prosecuted those creeps, they deserved it."

Sheila smiled. "My son, the Fox News conservative." She turned to her husband. "You've been strangely silent."

"We'll talk about this later," he said.

*　*　*

Sheila, propped in bed, did one last look through her emails. She hoped to find an offer better than the one Ortega had dangled, but her inbox was clogged with spam.

Wesley called out from the bathroom: "Have you talked to Joel?"

Joel Moscowitz distributed Sheila's films. If there was a way to screen, televise, stream, or hype a movie, he had probably thought of it first.

"Not yet."

"Why not?"

"'Cause he'd tell me to do it, and I'm not sure I want to."

Wesley finished his ablutions and lay down. His brown eyes burned straight through her.

"What's wrong?" she asked.

Nothing, she expected him to say. Nothing at all. Why do you think anything is wrong?

Men always reacted that way. They never wanted to admit they felt anything about anything.

"I want you to do the film," he said.

Sheila shut off her iPhone and put it on the nightstand. After persuading her to have a second child, Wesley had rarely lobbied her.

"Go ahead," Sheila said.

"When the crime first occurred, I was horrified. Also ashamed. Young men of color marauding through the park like a pack of wild beasts—it fit every stereotype that's ever been laid against us. I've always been proud of my background, and of who I am. Except then."

Sheila tried to remember if they had ever talked about the case. They must have, but their children were little. Just about everything from those years blurred together.

Besides, the guys confessed. Their guilt was obvious.

"As time went on," Wesley said, "I read some stories. And people talk. You know—Black talk."

"Keep going."

"When you look at it closely, the prosecution's case is flimsy."

"Why do you say that?"

"Consider the physical evidence against those kids."

"There was no physical evidence against them."

"Exactly." Wesley started ticking off points on his long fingers. "Supposedly, they attacked that woman within an inch of her life. Supposedly, they did all kinds of unspeakable things to her. But none of them left even a hair behind. How is that possible?"

"I saw those so-called kids up close," Sheila said. "A couple of them were as naïve as Kanye. Or whatever he's calling himself these days."

Wesley yawned. Sheila realized he was as tired as she was. Maybe more. But this was a conversation he was determined to have.

"Growing up," he said, "I knew lots of guys who thought they were the world's biggest badasses. But when they went up against the police, they found out who the real badasses are."

Sheila rolled onto her side and closed her eyes.

"Look at me," her husband said.

She did.

"How many guys were in the park that night?"

"The cops never knew for sure. Fifteen. Twenty. Maybe more." Sheila's voice sounded far away in her own ears. "The reports never specified an exact number."

"They arrested five," Wesley said. "They convicted four. And do you know why?"

"I forget." Sheila thought she might drift to sleep at any second.

"Because the fifth guy never confessed, and they had no physical evidence against him, so they didn't indict him for the attack. Does that sound like a prosecution that's absolutely confident in its case?"

I'm sure Michael had a reason, Sheila said to herself. Although, right now, I can't think of what it could be.

"Have you ever pictured Dylan in that situation?" Wesley asked. "Have you ever asked what you would do if the police charged him with something?"

If he ever got involved in a rampage through a park, Sheila thought, once the cops were done with him, I'd kick his butt to Jersey and back. Then, I'd ground him until he was eligible for Social Security.

"Dylan would never take part in something like that," she said. "He's the only kid in Brooklyn who doesn't cross against the light."

"You never know when somebody's gonna be in the wrong place at the wrong time."

That phrase again, she thought. And then she was asleep.

* * *

In the morning, Sheila created a Word file and poured in facts, notes, questions, and observations about the Riverside Runner. She searched for video clips about the crime and the trial, discovered a trove, bookmarked all of them.

Public domain, she said to herself. I could use as much of this as I want. If I agree to do it.

She ate lunch at her desk and finally logged off in the late afternoon. She rubbed her eyes and stretched. Long sessions on the computer always left her feeling stiff and sore, especially in her back, neck, and forearms.

Yoga, she thought. Gotta do yoga tomorrow.

She texted Wesley: **We have 2 talk**.

While she waited for a reply, she tried to work out some of the kinks in her body. After five minutes, she picked up her iPhone and called her husband, but it went straight to voicemail. Wesley was working from his Fort Greene store, which was closest to their home, but sometimes he ignored his cell for hours.

Sheila looked at the clock. Four p.m. The kids would be home soon. She needed to start dinner by five. Rolando Ortega wanted her decision in the morning.

She texted her husband again: **Coming 2 see U**.

The air was pleasant and dry, already hinting of autumn. After spending the best part of the day staring at a computer screen, Sheila was glad to be outside, even for just a ten-minute walk.

The coffeehouse was dark and woody. The aroma made her think of mornings and the slow battle she waged to get ready every day.

Why doesn't coffee taste as good as it smells? she asked herself. Maybe I could do a short about that. Get a grant or something. Then I wouldn't have to take this job from Ortega.

She saw Clayton, her husband's longest-tenured employee, pushing a broom across the shiny oak floor. After all these years, she still didn't know his last name.

"The Divine Ms. Sheila," he said. He looked happy to see her, but he always looked happy to see everyone. "What's going on?"

She asked where her husband was. Clayton's normally sunny expression turned neutral. He blinked a few times, leaned on his broom, and said, "Well, Ms. Sheila, I think he's around here somewhere, but I'm not sure exactly—"

"I'll check his office."

"I dunno if he's—"

But she was already heading there, re-slinging her shoulder bag in the sign of a professional woman with no time to waste.

Wesley's lair was past shelves of Caribbean pastries, cakes, and cookies. The hesitance in Clayton's voice made Sheila think that something might be going on, and she imagined the type of scene that prompted catfights on trash TV, barging into the room to find her husband engaged in an intimate act with a twentysomething barista.

Wesley's not the type, she reminded herself. Way too introverted.

She pushed open the door.

"I said I didn't want to be interrupted. I need to concentrate on this."

She stood in the frame a few seconds. Wesley stared at his computer as if it had magic powers.

"I texted you," she said. "Left voicemail, too."

He looked up, startled. "This can't wait?"

"What are you doing?"

"Inventory. You know—running a business."

She stopped by his desk. "We need to talk now. While I'm thinking of this. While everything is fresh in my mind."

He turned his body away from the computer. "Go ahead."

"I spent all day looking up the Riverside Runner case. Reading. Watching. I've got information overload."

"And?"

She swallowed a few times. "I'm gonna do it."

"Why?"

"There's more to it than I thought."

"Is that the only reason?"

"I kept looking at the guys who were convicted, and I started asking myself your question. The one about Dylan. It hits home."

"He could wind up in prison for something he didn't do."

"Or for not having enough sense to walk away from a bad situation."

Wesley shook his head. "They didn't do it."

"I'm not sure about that."

"The DA needed scapegoats."

"That DA is your brother-in-law."

"I'm aware of that."

"Michael doesn't scapegoat people."

Wesley's voice grew softer, the Jamaican lilt more pronounced. "I'm not saying he did anything maliciously. Michael is not a malicious man. But he was under a lot of pressure. I'm not a babe in the woods. I realize what he was facing."

He looked over his wife as if he were seeing her after a months-long separation. He stood up, closed the office door, and stopped only inches from her.

Keep talking, she thought. Say anything. It doesn't matter what.

He wrapped his arms around her and brought his head down to her shoulder. Even now, twenty years married, she still enjoyed feeling this close.

"Thank you," he said.

Chapter Three

Michael Devine

1

September 13, 2023

T he applause from the members of the Detectives Endowment Association was respectful but not thunderous, and Michael knew why. The union had endorsed him because he was going to win, but during his time in office he had stressed new approaches to both crime-fighting and prosecutions, and cops believed the old ways worked just fine.

This is Manhattan in the third decade of the Twenty-First Century, he felt like telling them. I can't run on a law-and-order platform like it's the Bronx in 1985.

Of course, he reminded himself, for the members of the NYPD, it's always the Bronx in 1985.

He looked out at the audience—about one hundred people, almost all white men. A mix of active duty and retired, they skewed old. He had dealt with many of them on difficult cases over the years. By now, most had forgiven him for the sins of his father, although their clemency was reluctant since many of them were of Irish descent and they cherished their grudges.

As he talked, a part of his brain asked why he was campaigning so relentlessly. His main opponent was barely known, and Michael had the support of all three newspapers, which never agreed on anything. They weren't as important as they once were, but they still had some clout.

Then he heard Jacob Meyer in his ear. His father-in-law had been around forever, it seemed. Known everyone, it seemed.

"I met Tom Dewey a few times when I was young," Meyer said. "He started out as a special prosecutor. Went after the Mafia and then became Manhattan's DA. Best one ever. Governor for twelve years and damn good at the job. He shoulda been president. But he lost to Truman. You know why? He told me once."

Michael made no reply. He knew Meyer would continue.

"He said: 'I sat on my lead. Everyone told me I couldn't lose, and I believed them, but that sonuvabitch Truman outworked me.'"

Michael wrapped up his speech by lauding the detectives for making New York so much safer over the years. Always praise the people you're talking to, his consultants told him. Everybody likes to hear how wonderful they are.

As the audience cheered, Brendan Haggerty, the head of the union, walked out from the wings. Michael expected pro forma words like "Nice speech" and "Good luck." He and Haggerty had worked closely together for a long time.

"After I talk to the guys," the detective said, "I need five minutes of your time."

Michael looked at his watch. His handlers were waiting. He had three more events before dinner and didn't want to be late, the way the mayor always was. But there was an edge of concern in Haggerty's voice that made Michael uneasy, so instead of leaving right away, he waited offstage and checked his iPhone. Fourteen texts and twenty-seven emails, and he'd been off the grid only half an hour.

Michael heard a final surge of applause that meant Haggerty had finished. When he looked up, the man was bearing down on him.

"Rolando Ortega has filed a motion," Haggerty said.

"Rolando files lots of motions."

"It's the Riverside Runner," Haggerty said. "He's representing one of the scumbags who did it. Ortega claims he has new evidence, and he wants to do DNA testing."

2

April 12, 2012

A damp river mist had spread over the West Side. It was chilly, too, so Michael wore a battered overcoat, an old scarf, and his fifth-best pair of shoes. He'd been awakened before dawn by a call from the DA—check it out, report back to me, wear crappy clothes because the place is a mess in every sense of the word.

The yellow crime-scene tape was familiar. So were the uniformed cops on the perimeter, glaring outward as they fended off the curious. Despite the police presence, four news crews had already started filming. Michael ignored shouted questions.

Haggerty walked out of the trees. He was a no-nonsense pro's pro who acted like a veteran, although he'd had his shield only three years.

"Waddya got?" Michael asked.

"Worst I've ever seen," Haggerty said.

"She dead?"

"Not yet. She's at Columbia-Presbyterian, but it's only a matter of time. I've never seen anyone lose so much blood." He motioned to Michael. "Follow me."

Michael ducked under the yellow tape. The detective walked him a few yards before stopping at an asphalt path.

"She was along here," Haggerty said. "We figure it was sometime after nine p.m."

"Kinda late to be running," Michael said.

"She's a grad student. They keep weird hours." Haggerty pointed toward the river. "We think the perps were there, outta sight. We're not sure yet which direction she was going, but we're pretty sure she didn't hear anything.

She was wearing an iPod."

"That was dumb," Michael said. "Running in the park at night, not being able to hear what's going on around you—"

"You should be able to go jogging without being attacked by creeps," Haggerty said.

"Fair point. What happened?"

Haggerty pointed to a spot on the path. "They got her here. See that trail?"

A line of matted-down grass the width of a woman's torso led to the trees. Michael looked for footprints, but the dampness must have wiped them out. The detective led him into the thicket, and Michael noticed the narrow path the runner's body continued to make as her attackers dragged her deeper into the night.

Haggerty pointed ahead. Two dozen detectives and technicians scoured the ground, making notes and occasionally placing items in clear plastic bags. Michael stopped a few feet away.

Dried blood covered the ground. The runner's tights, exercise bra, and long-sleeved T-shirt had been shredded, with pieces scattered over nearby bushes. A torn nylon Adidas shell was half-buried in the dirt, and a battered iPod lay at the base of a tree.

It was easy to figure out what had happened, but Michael asked the obvious question: "Sexual assault?"

"We recovered semen," Haggerty said. "Some clothing fibers. There was skin from another person under her fingernails and traces of silver in her hands. They might be from a piece of jewelry one of the attackers was wearing."

"The media is already going crazy about this."

"Vultures love a new carcass."

"Tell me about the kids in the park."

The detective reached into his jacket, took out a notepad with a Mets logo, and flipped a few pages.

"Last night, about nine-fifteen p.m., the Two-Six Precinct began receiving reports of disturbances in Riverside Park. A group of young men was moving south, harassing and, ultimately, assaulting various people they encountered—bicyclists, passersby, homeless."

"The Two-Six gets these reports," Michael said. "Then what happens?"

"They send a squad car. When those officers see what's happening, they ask for backup, and lots of it. By ten the precinct was flooding the zone. They were joined by officers from the Two-Four. Cops from both precincts swept through the park on foot, and around 102nd Street, they encountered a group of young men. The perps had accosted a homeless woman who was pushing a shopping cart. Several of them were standing on her, pinning her to the ground, while the others took turns dumping the contents of the shopping cart onto her head."

Michael shut his eyes. Hearing about human beings' creative cruelty always disheartened him.

"When the officers moved in," Haggerty said, "the perps scattered and fled. One of the cops said it was like watching cockroaches run when you turn on the kitchen light. Five of the young men were apprehended and brought in for questioning. At first, we were concerned solely with the assaults that had been reported. One vic was stopped and questioned, but he didn't wanna cooperate. Said he just wanted to get the hell outta there. He was scratched and bruised and bleeding, so they let him go. Anyway, around midnight, officers from both precincts began a thorough search of the park to see if they'd missed anything, and at one in the morning, they came across Marie Antolini. At first, they thought she was dead."

"Before the cops found her, did any of the perps say anything about her?"

"No."

"What were they hoping—that she'd get up and walk away?"

"That's one of the things we're asking right now."

"Were all of them involved in the attack?"

"We're not sure."

"Do any of them have lawyers?"

"Nobody has asked for one."

"Have they been Miranda-ed?"

For the first time since they started talking, Haggerty directed a you've-gotta-be-kidding look at the prosecutor.

"For Christ's sake, Counselor, we're not amateurs."

3

April 26, 2012

A few of the victim's bandages had been removed, and by now, the doctors believed she would live. But the attack had left her with brain trauma, and the medical people kept saying they had no idea how well she would function once they discharged her.

Michael heard the beeps and blips of life-preserving machines in an intensive-care unit. Her eyes were open a third of the way.

"Ms. Antolini?" he said as softly as he could.

Her eyelids fluttered a bit.

"I don't know if you remember me. I'm Michael Devine. From the district attorney's office."

"I think I do." Her voice sounded a little stronger than it had the last time.

"How are you feeling?"

"Better. I keep thinking that I'd like to go home. I know that's what I'm supposed to say. But then I can't remember where home is."

"That's all right, Ms. Antolini. It'll come back to you someday. Everyone is impressed with your recovery so far."

She said nothing. Michael cleared his throat. He was unsure of how he was supposed to bring up the topic he needed to discuss.

"We're preparing the case," he said. "Against the men who did this to you."

Still no response. The blips and beeps grew louder. Or was that just his brain amplifying every sound?

"After the trial starts," Michael said, "after I've made our opening arguments, we'll want you to take the stand."

"But I don't remember anything," she said. "Certainly not about the attack. I couldn't identify anybody, or describe what happened."

Before coming here, Michael had raised his objections with the district attorney, who cut him off by saying:

"She has to testify. And you hafta get her ready."

Adam Fishman was all business all the time. Michael respected that, even when they disagreed.

"The doctors say she has no recall of the events," Michael told his boss. "She can't ID the perps, so what's the point?"

"She'll generate sympathy," Fishman said. "The jury will see her, and hear her voice, and they'll wanna punish someone. It doesn't matter if she can't remember what happened. In some ways, it's better. The defense won't trip her up on cross-examination. If they have any sense, they won't ask her any questions at all."

"Can't we cut a deal?" Michael asked. "It'd be better for everybody. The city can move on, and she won't need to testify."

He felt like saying: *Putting her on the stand would be like violating her all over again.*

"Some situations require a public spectacle," Fishman said. "You'll understand that yourself someday."

Now Michael was gazing down on Marie Antolini. Her rib cage fell and rose with the labored breathing of the badly injured. She looked so fragile he feared that anything could break her.

"I barely remember the details of my life," she said. "Where I grew up, or went to school. What my mother and father look like. I don't even recall if I have brothers and sisters. Sometimes a memory comes, and I ask myself if it really happened, or if I'm just imagining it."

"If you decline to testify," Michael said, "I'll understand." *Although I don't know what I'll say to my boss*, he thought.

"Do you think it's a good idea? I wanna help."

It'll help us win the case, he said to himself. But I don't know if it's a good idea.

4

September 13, 2023

Michael let Brendan Haggerty vent about Rolando Ortega for three minutes, but when the detective said the man was planning "some bullshit defense lawyer's trick," Michael tried to steer the conversation to a conclusion.

"I've gone up against Rolando lotsa times," Michael said. "There's nothing bullshit about him."

"Haven't you heard what he's planning to do?" Haggerty asked.

"I'm running for office," Michael said. "That means I live in a cocoon."

"He's gonna work with a filmmaker while he does the appeal. So this isn't just a legal battle—the bastard is launching a P.R. offensive. He'll probably have a goddamn Facebook page about it by the end of the week."

"I'm not worried," Michael said.

"Maybe you should be."

"Why?"

"From what I hear, he's lined up your sister to do the film."

Michael tried to say something, but nothing came to his mind, and he prided himself on never being blindsided by anything.

"I thought you two were close," Haggerty said.

"So did I," Michael said.

* * *

For once, he was going to bed before midnight, so when his iPhone rang, he was tempted to let the call go straight to voicemail. Out of habit, he looked to see who was calling.

Sheila.

He unlocked the phone. "Hey."

"Hey, yourself."

"Wazzup?"

Don't let her know you've heard, he told himself. Make her say it herself.

"I have something to tell you."

He wanted to say: *I know.* He wanted to ask: *How could you?*

"Go ahead."

"I've received a job offer."

Sheila never lied. As far back as he could remember, she always spoke about the absolute importance of telling the truth. But whenever she was uncomfortable with being straightforward, she entered the temple of honesty through a side door.

"What is it?" Michael said.

"You sound like you already know."

They never could keep anything from each other.

"You'll be working with Rolando Ortega," Michael said.

"Your nemesis," she said.

"Incorrect," he replied. "Sometimes, my adversary. A worthy one. I've always respected the man. He doesn't pull stunts." Michael resisted adding, *Until now.*

"So you know what he's planning to do?"

"People tell me things."

Sheila sighed. He wanted more from her, and he suspected she'd tell him. Like all lapsed Catholics, she still needed to confess. When they were teenagers, she had left the church, so instead of talking about her transgressions to a cleric, she'd tell them to Michael, who, unlike the priests, was always ready to absolve her.

"I've drawn up a contract," she said. "It gives me complete access to him, as well as total independence in pursuing the project any way I want and coming to any conclusion I deem appropriate."

"What if he doesn't sign?"

"Then I'll be looking for work again."

A thousand responses ran through Michael's head. This was different from their adolescence, when Terence Devine, their father, was imprisoned, and Bridget, their mother, worked horrible jobs and wallowed in self-pity while she smoked herself to death. Back then, while breaking the rules that kids always break, forgiveness was easy.

"I'm not gonna pretend I'm happy about this," he told Sheila in what he hoped was an even tone.

"I didn't expect you to be."

"Everything we did on that case was on the up-and-up."

"Are you willing to say that on camera?"

"Of course."

He waited for her to speak. After a long minute in which he could almost hear her thinking, Sheila said: "It's like this, Michael—Ortega's gonna get this movie made anyway, and there are plenty of people who'll be happy to do it. If I don't work with him, he'll bring in somebody with an ax to grind, and you'll wind up looking like a Klan member."

"This is something I never expected from you," Michael said.

"What's that?"

"Rationalizing."

* * *

The next morning he was introduced to the Lenox Avenue Civic Association by Lonette Smith, a Black businesswoman with graying hair and the demeanor of a middle-school principal who took no crap from the kids. Applause bordered between tepid and polite. Michael raced through his talking points but half his head was still occupied by his phone call with Sheila, and he could tell from the way the audience murmured and squirmed that he was failing to connect.

When he stopped, Lonette Smith came back onstage and asked if he could stay a bit to answer questions from the people. Michael looked at his watch. His speech had been so mechanical he had finished ten minutes early, and for the first time in months, he was running ahead of schedule.

"Sure."

Hands flew up. Michael took the microphone and began pacing around the stage. The baseball pitcher inside him said it was time to raise his game, so he pointed to a dreadlocked young man in a three-piece suit.

"What are you doing about all those police officers who use excessive force against the people?"

"If it's shown that a member of the police uses excessive force," Michael replied, "my office prosecutes him or her."

This prompted the loudest round of applause he had heard all morning. The young man, implacably grim, remained standing.

"With all due respect—" he said.

Which means I'll get no respect at all, Michael thought.

"—we hear that all the time. The police routinely brutalize the people, and many times, it's caught on camera, but nothing is ever done about it. Frankly, we are fed up with this state of affairs, and the people will no longer tolerate it."

Michael was grateful for the raucous cheering that followed, because it gave him a few seconds to come up with an answer.

The police will say you don't know how hard it is to be a cop, he thought. Which is true. And you'll say the cops don't know what it's like to be disrespected all the time for being Black in a society dominated by whites. Which is also true. The biggest problem in the world is that everyone believes everybody else's life is problem-free.

"As you know," Michael said after the room quieted, "I've been with the district attorney's office a long time, and I know its ins and outs. I can't run as an outsider, but I have a strong idea of what works, and what doesn't, and what needs to be changed. After the governor appointed me as the interim DA, I implemented some new policies and procedures.

"Having said that, I want to add this: Everyone should obey the law. That goes from the poorest person in Manhattan to the billionaires living on Fifth Avenue. And it certainly goes for public servants. We have to lead by example.

"I've listened to the critics of the way law enforcement has been conducted in this city and this country. Nobody has a monopoly on wisdom, and I try to learn something every day. After leading the operations of the DA's office since I was appointed, I've decided that, if I am fortunate enough to have a mandate to work for the good people of this borough for the next few years, I will set up a separate unit in the public integrity office to investigate allegations of misconduct by both police and prosecutors."

He had bounced this idea off Rachel and his media adviser, who both suggested saving it for a moment he needed it. Now Michael received the warmest applause he'd heard all morning.

The dreadlocked man sat down. Michael glanced around. Dozens of hands were raised, and Michael settled on a middle-aged woman, slightly overweight, who wore a housedress and beaded necklace.

I'd like a hanging curveball, he thought. Something I can hit out of the park. I should stop using sports metaphors.

The woman wobbled a bit as she stood, but her voice was firm and clear.

"I don't know if you remember me, Mr. Devine. My name is LaToya Crawford."

Michael blanked. If he had ever met this woman, it had occurred a long time ago, and both of them now looked different.

"I'm sure you remember my son," she said. "His name is Roberto Linares."

Oh shit.

"You persecuted my son," she said.

"I prosecuted him, ma'am."

"It was that Riverside Park case," she said, her voice rising, "and you *persecuted* him." Those last words rebounded around the room as if they were small but hard balls being fired from an air cannon. "He was arrested by the police for something he didn't do, and he wasn't allowed to talk to a lawyer, and they made him say things that weren't true, and then you *persecuted* him at his trial."

Michael tried to keep the image of Marie Antolini, body wrapped in bandages, out of his mind.

"Your son confessed, ma'am. It was on videotape, and we used it at the trial, and the jury found it convincing."

I certainly did, he said to himself, but he kept that thought private.

"My son is still in prison," she said. "Up in the Catskills. It gets cold there. He gets sick every winter, and then there's the Covid, and jail is turning him hard, even though he was the sweetest boy. Now the parole board says he can get out if he shows remorse, but he won't show remorse for something he didn't do."

Rhythmic clapping swept the auditorium. Michael felt like an unbeliever at a revival.

"My office will never persecute anyone," Michael said. "We look at the facts, and we reach a conclusion based on the evidence."

"There was no evidence!" LaToya Crawford's voice was rising. "The only evidence you had was his confession, and the police tricked him into giving it."

"Your son was in the park that night—"

Michael began to hear an undercurrent of boos, whistles, and catcalls.

"—with a bunch of his friends, and they were committing illegal acts—"

The jeers grew louder.

"—and they were apprehended by the police, who followed the correct protocols, and the young men confessed to the crime."

The hostile noises were in crescendo while LaToya Crawford shook her head so vigorously she reminded Michael of the dolls the Mets gave away on promotional nights at Citi Field.

Goddammit, Michael said to himself. How long before all of this is on YouTube?

"You put young men in prison for crimes they did not commit," LaToya Crawford said. "Thousands of our young men are in prison, and their lives are ruined, and men like you just don't care."

He felt like asking: What about Marie Antolini? Her life was ruined, too.

"Men like you are what's wrong with this society."

LaToya Crawford was spilling out words she had wanted to say to him for years.

"All of you are interested in gaining power so you can oppress the people and deny us justice."

She pointed her finger at him.

"I've got news for you, Mr. District Attorney. We are tired of the way we've been treated. Tired of having our rights denied. Tired of being disrespected, and being told our lives are worthless. We are rising up, and we are demanding that you take us seriously."

CHAPTER THREE

The applause from the crowd as it rose to its feet sounded like the booms of a thundercloud that was close to the ground. Michael felt a presence beside him, and when he turned, he saw Lonette Smith.

"I think you're done here," she said.

Chapter Four

Sheila Devine

1

September 14, 2023

She walked into Rolando Ortega's office just as he was getting ready to head downtown to file the motion asking for a DNA test on Jose Ramos. In one hand, she held her camera, and in the other, a memorandum she had written the night before laying out the conditions under which she would undertake the documentary he said he wanted.

She still thought there was a good chance he'd say No. Perhaps kick her out of his office. He might even put the paper through the shredder by his secretary's desk.

Instead, he examined it slowly—just like a lawyer, she thought—before placing it on his desk and smoothing it out.

"I see nothing to object to," he said. "Shall we sign it?"

Holy crap, she thought, I'm in.

They took a black car to Foley Square. Sitting next to Ortega was Manuel Fuentes' mother, Paloma Santiago, a sharp-featured Latina in her late fifties who wore a conservative navy blue dress, a Black Lives Matter pin, and the implacable look of a woman who was convinced she had been wronged by everyone she had ever met.

The back of the car was roomy, with seats that ran both ways. Sheila rode backwards, facing the lawyer and the mother of his client.

"Do you mind if I record you on this?" Sheila asked as she took out her iPhone.

"Why don't you use your camera?" Ortega asked.

"The space is too tight. Besides, the iPhone footage will look edgy." Sheila motioned to Paloma Santiago. "Go ahead and talk. Pretend I'm not here."

"But you are here," the woman said.

"Do your best," Sheila said.

"English or español?"

"Whichever you prefer. Although my Spanish is shaky."

"English, then," Ortega said. "We'll make this easy for the greatest number of people."

Sheila began recording. "Tell me about your son."

"He was a good kid." Paloma Santiago fingered the small crucifix pressed against her neck. "I use the past tense when I talk about him. I wish I didn't. But it's almost like he's dead, away in that place."

"How has prison affected him?" Sheila asked.

"It has made him tough. Insensitive. That's how you have to act if you wanna survive there."

"You said your son was a good kid. So what happened that night? How did he wind up with that pack in the park?"

"A friend took him to play soccer. Manuel didn't know the other boys well. When it got dark, some of them—the ones he didn't know—said they should go into the park and raise some hell."

"Boys will be boys?" Sheila asked. An often-uttered sentiment that she had never regarded as valid.

"He should have walked away," Paloma Santiago said. "He was el stupido for going along with them. But he was young. We all do stupid things when we're young."

"Why did he confess if he didn't do it?" Sheila asked.

"He didn't have a lawyer. He was scared. He told me the police promised he could go home once he signed the statement they gave him."

Do I believe that? Sheila asked herself. Will an audience believe it?

Paloma Santiago raised her voice, almost as if she knew the questions in Sheila's head. "He did not attack that woman. I did not raise him that way. I taught him to respect everyone, especially the girls he went out with."

Sheila pointed the iPhone at Ortega. "What will you do if the DNA isn't a match?"

"It will match," he said.

"What makes you so certain?"

"I am confident about the information I've received."

Paloma Santiago spoke up. "Even if it doesn't match, there are so many things the police never checked out."

"Like what?" Sheila asked.

"Her old boyfriend. Did you know that girl had an order of protection against him?"

"I wasn't aware of that." Sheila was surprised by the surprise in her voice.

"They said he had an alibi. But it's pathetic. I wish I'd been able to afford my own investigator." Paloma Santiago shook her head and looked out the car window. Morning sun glinted off the glass high-rises going up on both sides of the East River. "By then, they had their scapegoats, so they didn't look anywhere else. When you get right down to it, the police are lazy."

My brother worked eighteen hours a day on that case, Sheila thought. The cops worked those kinds of hours, too.

"They try to keep us afraid," Paloma Santiago said.

"What do you mean by that?" Sheila asked.

"The police. The authorities. They want the citizens to be scared all the time so they can get away with their nonsense. I bet somebody high up, like in the government or something, dreamed up this attack so everyone would go into a frenzy, and then the authorities could start screaming about how they need stop-and-frisk and all this other law-and-order mierda." She nodded vigorously, pleased to agree with her own theory. "That's the way they work, you know."

Sheila pointed the iPhone back at Ortega, who looked like a man trying to persuade himself that the woman sitting next to him was not as loca as

36

she seemed.

"What do you think?" Sheila asked.

The lawyer flashed the briefest smile she'd ever seen. "I think the court will order a DNA test, and the test will reveal the true perpetrator."

* * *

Crews from TV stations and podcasts gathered at the foot of the courthouse steps, joining photographers from what was left of the print media. Sheila decided to stand apart, under the columns that held the building's weight, filming down on Rolando Ortega's back while he addressed the swarm.

"Today," Ortega said, "I have filed a motion to reopen the case of my client Manuel Fuentes. We have new evidence in the matter of the Riverside Runner. A man currently in prison has confessed to the crime, and we are demanding that New York State engage in DNA testing to determine if he is, in fact, the perpetrator of that heinous attack that occurred more than ten years ago."

This led to a chorus of shouted questions. Sheila smiled to herself. As they usually did in these scrums, the reporters stepped on each other, so Ortega could answer the easiest question, or just say what he wanted.

"All of us who lived in New York when this crime occurred remember the hysteria that gripped the city," Ortega said. "Somebody had to pay the price for what happened, and my client was in the wrong place at the wrong time." When he paused, Sheila recognized him for what he was—the star defense attorney ready to wow the jury with a zinger. "What this case is about," he said, "is a rush to judgment."

This prompted more shouted questions that Sheila couldn't decipher. Christ, she thought, what's wrong with these people? Even preschoolers learn to take turns.

"Yes, I respect the police and the district attorney," Ortega said. "They were under an enormous amount of pressure to produce a quick result. But pressure is no excuse for injustice."

A blond reporter for the local Fox station asked Paloma Santiago if she had any theories about who had assaulted the victim and why the authorities were so intent on punishing her son. Sheila noticed Ortega nudging the mother of his client as if she were a scatterbrained actress who had trouble remembering her lines.

"I don't have anything to say about that," Paloma Santiago told the media.

"You must have thought about those things," the Fox reporter said. "So much time has passed."

Sheila wondered if the reporter had heard rumors about Manuel Fuentes' mother, or seen something on social media.

Ortega leaned into the woman's ear. Sheila picked up the whispered word "alocada" and realized he was trying to get her to stay on message. In Twenty-First Century America, everybody eventually turns into a politician.

"I have my beliefs," Paloma Santiago said into the microphones. "But my firmest belief is that we need the DNA test. It will prove my son and the other boys are innocent."

Those so-called boys are not innocent, Sheila said to herself. At best, they're not guilty.

* * *

She began typing into her desktop at home:

NOTES ON THE RIVERSIDE RUNNER CASE

The Defendants

(1) Manuel Fuentes

17 at the time of the crime. A high school junior way more interested in sports and girls than school. Never in trouble with the law until that night. Sometimes flagged for being late to his classes, or skipping them entirely. Not much direction in his life; spent most of his time hanging with friends. (Typical teenager?) In prison he got a GED and enrolled online in community college courses, mostly concerning the law and criminal justice.

No sign of a father.

(2) Roberto Linares

18. High school senior at LaGuardia who aspired to a musical career. Deejayed parties in Upper Manhattan and self-produced a rap CD that he hawked illegally on the subway. Those were his only run-ins with the law. Decent grades. Wanted to attend SUNY Purchase. Chances of getting in were fifty-fifty.

Nothing about a father.

(3) Ulysses Watkins

16. High school junior. Showed promise as a football player. Physically the biggest defendant. Some stories called him "hulking." No priors on the public record. Off-the-record allegations of problems as a juvenile. Barely old enough to be charged as an adult.

No word about a father.

(4) Howard Baines

17. The star of the bunch. Tested into Bronx Science. Near the top of his class his senior year. Drew interest from every Ivy League college. Absolutely no trouble either from school or the law. Many stories called him "articulate." (Good God, spare me.) In prison, he earned a bachelor's degree in chemistry. Now pursuing a master's as best he can. Warden allowed him to set up a makeshift lab to perform experiments.

Father abandoned the family when Howard was 6.

The One Who Got Away

Felipe Huerta

19. High school dropout. Not clear how he made ends meet. Had priors for breaking and entering. The only one arrested that night who refused to talk to the cops until he lawyered up. Admitted being in the park, but never confessed to the assault on the runner. Pleaded guilty to three misdemeanors related to other parts of the rampage. Never charged in the

attack on the runner. Got off with probation and time already served in Rikers. Since then, arrested at different times for drug possession, drug dealing, larceny, grand larceny, simple assault, assault and battery, assault with intent to kill, attempted murder. In and out of prison numerous times. No indication he is currently incarcerated.

No mention of parents at all.

Where Are They Now?

Manuel Fuentes: Clinton Correctional Facility, a.k.a. Dannemora

Roberto Linares: Sullivan Correctional Facility (Catskills)

Ulysses Watkins: Attica. 'Nuff said.

Howard Baines: Walkill Correctional Facility (Hudson Valley; medium security)

Felipe Huerta: Currently off the grid, although he has spent time in Southport Correctional Facility, the worst prison in New York.

One More Thing

Bookmark July 16, 2013, column in the *Daily News* headlined "What Really Happened?" Talk to the writer.

2

September 15, 2023

"You were fucked by the Oscars," Jamie Quinn said as soon as he saw her.

"Tell me about it," Sheila replied.

He pushed his walker toward his favorite chair while Sheila closed the door behind her. The Tribeca loft was the way she remembered—open and airy, exposed brick, soft colors, warm afternoon sunlight giving the room a comforting glow. There are worse places to wait for death, she said to herself.

Jamie Quinn was talking. Jamie Quinn liked to talk. "They wouldn't know a good documentary if it bit 'em in their private parts. Goddamn

Hollywood. Their brains are mush. It's all those idiotic superhero movies."

"My son and his friends love the Avenger series," Sheila said. "They saw the last one five days in a row."

Quinn eased into his chair. "Are their brains mush?"

"They're different from mine, that's for sure."

She sat down without being asked. Despite her mixed feelings about Jamie Quinn, she liked the sense of old acquaintances reconnecting. The man had written for the *Daily News* for decades, and her father was one of his best sources inside the NYPD before being exposed as the most corrupt cop in the city's history.

"You're not filming," Quinn said.

"Not yet. If you say something interesting, I've got this." She held up her iPhone.

"Your email said you wanted to talk about the Riverside Runner."

"That's right."

"That case made your brother's career."

"I know."

"And now Rolando Ortega's filed a motion to reopen it."

"You're up on things."

"I love news. You know that."

"Ortega commissioned me to do a documentary about the appeal and his role in it."

Quinn's bushy gray eyebrows surged toward his hairline. "Ballsy move. By both of you."

"I needed a project. I'm not sure what his game is."

"Chess."

"Huh?"

"I'll tell you something about me that very few people know."

I'm not sure I wanna hear this, Sheila thought.

"I used to be pretty good at chess," Quinn said. "Sometimes, I'd go to Washington Square to take on the guys who played there. I held my own. Anyway, it was in the Eighties, and Bobby Fischer was in the news for one of those weird things he used to do after he was stripped of the championship.

I was writing a column—I forget what it was about, I'd hafta look it up—and I needed to talk to Rolando Ortega. Back then, he was a hotshot young Puerto Rican lawyer. I was in his office, and we were shooting the breeze, and we got to talking about Fischer. I mentioned that I played chess. 'So do I,' Ortega said. So he whips out this small board, and we started a game." Quinn licked his lips. "Bastard beat me in fifteen moves. So I asked around about his game, and a guy who ran a chess club in the Bronx said Ortega was the second most naturally gifted player he'd ever run across."

"After Fischer?"

"Ortega coulda been a grandmaster if he'd pursued it."

"There's a lot more money in being a lawyer," Sheila said. "Plus, you don't go crazy."

"Whatever Ortega's doing," Quinn said, "he's thinking at least a dozen moves ahead."

Sheila coughed. Time for business. "I came across the column you wrote when the Riverside Four were convicted."

"My last hurrah."

"Waddya mean?"

"My final big story. I was arguing with my editors all the time, but by then, I'd stopped enjoying it. My wife kept telling me, 'You don't need the agita,' and one day I decided she was right."

"What were you arguing with your editors about?"

"The case against those kids."

"Tell me."

Quinn took a few wheezy breaths. "My editors went batshit when the runner was attacked. I did, too. It was our kinda story. Horrible crime, gal's left for dead in the park, it looks like these punks did it, string 'em up by their gonads, don't even wait for a trial."

Sheila nodded. "That's how I felt."

"That's how everybody felt. But then I started doing some legwork—you know, reporting."

"Nobody does that anymore. Today, they just aggregate."

"Don't get me started." He hacked vigorously for thirty seconds. When they first met, Sheila was convinced he'd keel over dead at any moment. Now, she believed he'd make it to a hundred because he wanted to outlive his enemies. "The more I looked at it, the less sense the prosecution's case made. With all due respect to your brother, the current and future district attorney."

"Last night, I read the column you wrote right after the verdicts came in. How did your editors react?"

"They hit the roof. Most of them were Brits. I wish I could do a British accent. 'Bollocks, you can't say these things. You're suggesting these darkies didn't do it.' And I said, 'That's exactly my fucking point, you fucking limeys.'" He shook his head. "I'll never figure out why you have goddamn Brits running a New York newspaper. What the hell do I know about London?"

Sheila let his anger linger a few seconds. "What was it like?" she asked.

"What was what like?"

"The atmosphere in the newsroom when that story broke. The night of the attack and the day after."

"Frenzied. The only other thing that compared was Son of Sam. And he was killing people."

"So everybody wanted to hang the defendants."

"Absolutely."

"But eventually, you decided they didn't do it?"

"Eventually, I decided there was reasonable doubt."

"At this stage, reasonable doubt isn't gonna cut it. Ortega has to prove they're innocent."

Quinn took in a few labored breaths. Sheila waited for him to say something.

"You ever read their confessions?" he asked.

Their statements were long and sometimes rambling. Sheila had surfed through some of the video clips the prosecution presented at trial, but she hadn't read or watched everything all the way through.

"Not yet." She felt like a high school student who'd been called out for cutting corners on an assignment.

"I'm extremely disappointed in you." Quinn wheezed some more. "Read 'em. Every goddamn word. Watch 'em. Every goddamn second. Take notes while you do it."

"What's in them?"

"Dozens of contradictions. Maybe hundreds. By the time you're finished, you'll have a hard time believing those guys were in the same place at the same time."

Sheila summoned some memories from the trial. "Their lawyers kept making that point. As I recall, nobody paid much attention."

"Your brother's the best prosecutor I've ever seen," Quinn said. "And he kept talking about how confusing the situation was—it was pitch black, a lotta guys were there, it was impossible to keep track of who did what when, it made perfect sense the stories didn't track, in fact, the jurors should be suspicious if everything matched perfectly." Quinn shook his head. "Legal jujitsu. I was impressed."

* * *

Back home, Sheila followed Quinn's instructions. While she watched and read, she banged more notes into her desktop:

The Confession of Manuel Fuentes

The pack was heading south, intent on more mayhem, when it encountered the victim. Ulysses Watkins grabbed her first. She didn't see him until he was on her. He knocked her out before she could say anything, and then he dragged her across the grass to the trees. Everyone else followed. At that point, nobody knew what they would do with her. In fact, Fuentes asked Watkins why he had hit her when she wasn't bothering anyone.

The Confession of Roberto Linares

By the time they saw the runner, the guys had turned north so they could go home. Howard Baines suggested they run up to her and scare her, just to see how fast she could run. But then Ulysses Watkins wrapped his arms around her and started tearing off her tights and nylon shell. She yelled and struggled, but the other guys swarmed her and hit her and told her to shut up, and carried her into the thicket.

The Confession of Ulysses Watkins

Felipe Huerta saw the girl first. By then, everyone was just standing around. Truth was, they were tired. They'd played soccer and done all this crap in the park, and the guys' legs all felt like jelly. Huerta let out a long wolf whistle, and Manuel Fuentes asked what was going on, and Huerta said he really wanted to do the nasty on that chick. Before anyone could say anything, he ran after her and clocked her. She shrieked, but then Huerta hit her again, and she went out cold, and then he hauled her toward the woods, and the others went along.

The Confession of Howard Baines

Roberto Linares saw her first. By then, they were turning over trashcans and banging them against the pavement. It was all pretty stupid when you thought about it. Anyway, Linares pointed her out and said she was running real slow so he ran after her and tackled her from behind. She tried to fight him, but he was too big, and by then Felipe Huerta and Ulysses Watkins were on her, too, and the three of them took her away. At that point, a couple of guys fled because they said things were out of control, but Baines went toward the woods because he knew what they were going to do, and he wanted to stop them.

The Testimony of Marie Antolini

She was running along her usual route. Her iPod was on. She didn't hear anyone approach. She blacked out, and then she was in a hospital bed, encased in bandages and attached to tubes.

She wished she could provide more information.

Expert Witnesses on PTSD

Ms. Antolini's lack of recall was typical. Many people who have been through this type of trauma fail to remember even the most basic facts about the events. The human memory can be extremely effective at blocking out the worst things that happen.

Loose Ends

- None of the defendants admitted having sexual contact with the victim.
- None of their DNA was found at the scene.
- Not even a shred of their clothing was recovered.
- Baines said the victim was jogging slowly, but actually, she ran distance races several times a year and was considering training for a triathlon.

The Accusations Fly

- Howard Baines said Roberto Linares had intercourse with the victim, who was unconscious by that point.
- Roberto Linares said Ulysses Watkins penetrated her. She was drowsy, but pleading for help. (Wouldn't she remember?)
- Ulysses Watkins said Felipe Huerta first "did the thing." The woman was "glassy-eyed, like she was on drugs or something." Some other guys "did it, too, and she went all limp, like a rag doll." By that point, Watkins "didn't wanna do that shit no more."
- Manuel Fuentes said he wasn't sure who raped her. By then, he wasn't looking anymore because he felt sick to his stomach.

How Many Attackers Were There?

The four defendants (plus Felipe Huerta) were not the only ones who took part in the assault. Howard Baines said at least ten guys were there. Manuel Fuentes said twelve. Roberto Linares put it at fifteen. A cop asked Ulysses Watkins to give a number. Watkins said he couldn't count that high.

* * *

Sheila logged off and pushed herself away from the desk. A dull ache had drilled into her temples, and she contemplated Tylenol, although she disliked taking pain-killers, because she preferred knowing precisely how her body was operating. While she was growing up, she had been lied to constantly, and by now she had a nearly spiritual belief that it was always better to know the truth about everything.

Wesley will be home any minute, she thought. Gotta get dinner started. Keep it simple. Pasta and salad. That way, I just hafta boil water and wash vegetables. Christ, I hope my husband stashed a bottle of Chianti somewhere.

Her iPhone rang. She thought about letting it go to voicemail, but the call was from Rolando Ortega.

"Hola. Que tal?"

"That is a difficult question to answer, Ms. Devine."

"Por que?"

"Because something very strange has happened."

Chapter Five

Michael Devine

September 15, 2023

Rachel kept staring at her Android. "It's been more than twenty-four hours. I've gotten dozens of texts asking for your reaction. *Daily Beast* says your refusal to comment indicates you think Ortega's on to something."

"*Daily Beast* is wrong," Michael said. "And I'm still working on my reaction."

"Tell 'em all to go fuck themselves," Jacob Meyer said.

"That would not go over well, Dad," Rachel said.

They were in Jacob Meyer's pied-á-terre a two-minute walk from his Fifth Avenue office. Years ago, when Michael first started dating Rachel, it had struck him as strange that the old man kept a separate apartment in addition to the penthouse he owned in the Majestic. Eventually, Michael realized it was a good spot for meetings that his father-in-law didn't want his business associates to know about. It was also the place where he entertained his mistresses.

Rachel scowled at her phone as if she were afraid a cockroach was about to crawl out of it. "Your reaction should be that you are confident in the original verdict rendered by the jury. That verdict has been upheld through numerous appeals."

"That goddamn spic is on a fishing expedition," Meyer said.

Years ago, Michael realized it was pointless to argue with his father-in-law about using ethnic and racial slurs (although G-d help anyone who uttered something anti-Semitic). Instead, he said, "Rolando Ortega does not go on fishing expeditions."

"Those scumbags are guilty," Meyer said. "Why do we hafta jump through these goddamn hoops?"

Two days after the attack on the Riverside Runner, Jacob Meyer took out a full-page ad in the *Post*. In big, bold letters, he urged New York State to reinstate capital punishment and extend it to sexual assault so the perpetrators of the outrage against that poor girl could get the sentence they deserved. The ad provoked a torrent of comments, mostly from people who believed Jacob Meyer should run for governor.

Rachel put down her phone. "We can't put it off any longer—we've gotta feed the jackals in time for the nightly news cycle." She looked at her husband as if he were on a window ledge fifty floors above Rockefeller Center. "What do we do if the DNA matches?"

* * *

Michael straightened his tie and smoothed his jacket just as Jackie Williams walked into his office. She had been his lead assistant on the Riverside Runner case, and he had brought her with him as he worked his way up the ranks in the DA's office. Now, she had his old job of chief deputy.

"Waddya think?" he asked.

"You look fine."

So did she, with her understated business attire and the casually upright stance of a slender woman who did Pilates twice a week. If Jackie's courtroom career ever stalled, Michael believed she had a great future as a legal analyst on cable news, but he kept that thought to himself. He kept many thoughts to himself, and never understood why most people blabbed whatever came into their heads.

"Time to face the vultures," Jackie said.

"My wife compared them to jackals," Michael said.

They headed for the media room.

"We could have an interesting debate about that," Jackie said. "Which scavenging animals do reporters most closely resemble?"

"The problem isn't that they're scavengers," Michael said. "The problem is, they're professional second-guessers. We're gonna be questioned by a bunch of people who've never had to make an important decision."

In the room now. Burst of noise. Cameras snapping. Michael behind a lectern. Jackie to his right. Without saying anything about it, they both understood the optics of a Black woman appearing in the picture.

Michael's iPhone vibrated. He was inclined to ignore it, but sometimes he felt he knew who was calling him and why, just by the way the thing moved, so he looked at his device as surreptitiously as he could.

Haggerty was trying to reach him.

Michael mouthed the words "I hafta take this" to Jackie, who slipped into his spot as he stepped away. While he walked into the wings, he heard her say, "The district attorney will be with you in a minute, and he will address the matter that was raised yesterday by the attorney for one of the perpetrators in the attack on the Riverside Runner."

Away from the crowd, Michael answered his phone by saying, "I'm about to use a news conference to tell Rolando Ortega, in polite, legal language, to commit an act that is anatomically impossible."

"That's why I wanna talk to you," Haggerty said.

"Go ahead."

"I've been double-checking my notes ever since Ortega filed that bullshit motion."

"And?"

"Tell those media whores you're gonna support it."

Chapter Six

Sheila Devine

September 16, 2023

Sheila had emailed Haggerty several times and left a number of increasingly terse voicemails, but he had not responded, and she was becoming convinced he never would. So she was surprised at lunch when he texted her to call him at two.

He picked up on the first ring. Sheila got to the point: "I'd like to interview you. On camera and on the record."

"Not yet."

"Then why did you want me to call you?"

"I know you're working for Ortega."

His rapid-fire Queens accent reminded her that few New Yorkers talked that way anymore.

"I'm working with him, not for him."

"I don't see the difference."

"He's giving me a lotta access, but I have final cut."

"He's playing you."

"Filmmakers are biased toward people who cooperate with them."

She heard Haggerty breathing on the other end. He still hadn't told her why he wanted to talk.

"You saw what your brother did yesterday." Half statement, half question.

"I did, but I haven't talked to him about it yet."

"I'm gonna tell you something, off the record," Haggerty said.

"I don't like doing things that way, but go ahead."

"I was the one who told him not to oppose Ortega's motion."

"Why'd you do that?"

"The DNA won't match."

"You sound certain."

"The night Marie Antolini was attacked, Jose Ramos was smoking crack in the Bronx."

"The Bronx isn't far from the park."

"He was on a binge. Believe me, we checked him out, 'cause he kept telling every junkie on Willis Avenue that he'd attacked her. But eight different people told us that Jose Ramos was in a crack den in Mott Haven from five p.m. that night until noon the next day, when he staggered off to another shithole."

"He's a sex offender," Sheila said.

"He's in prison for a reason. But he did not attack Marie Antolini."

Time to shift gears, Sheila said to herself.

"What about Rocco Cantone?" she asked.

"The ex-boyfriend?"

"Yeah. Him. The guy she had an order of protection from."

Haggerty cleared his throat. "I'm gonna say something here, and I don't want you to take it the wrong way."

Which means I will, Sheila thought.

Haggerty went on: "Whenever people like you or Rolando Ortega start looking into a case, you assume we're stupid and that we overlooked evidence that was sitting around in plain sight."

"Okay. Tell me what you know about Rocco Cantone."

"Within twelve hours of the crime, we knew all about him. His buddies call him Rocky. Like half the Italian guys in Philadelphia. All because of those godawful movies."

"You find out anything else? Besides his nickname?"

"It isn't relevant."

Sheila cleared her throat. "I'm gonna say something here, and I don't want you to take it the wrong way."

"I'd forgotten how much of a ball buster you are."

Sheila waited a beat. "In my films, Detective Haggerty, I am God. That means I decide what's relevant and what isn't."

The cop chuckled. Haggerty was one of those hard-assed men who respected any woman who stood up to him. "Here's what we found out about Rocco Cantone. The ex-boyfriend. You're not gonna like it." Pause for dramatic effect. Sometimes Sheila thought Haggerty should be a regular on a Dick Wolf show. "Cantone and the vic had dated, on and off, for years. At the time of the attack, he was in Philadelphia, where they both grew up. She went to college at Temple, where she studied journalism—though why the fuck you gotta study that, I'll never know."

Sheila waited for more.

"They're both Italian, blue-collar, not a lotta money, that's why she didn't go away to school. But she's ambitious, a real go-getter. He's more of a slacker—drops outta community college, works at a bar—"

"Bouncing or tending?" A question that came naturally to people of Irish descent.

"Both."

"So he can use his fists?"

"Wouldn't surprise me. He also drove a truck and worked for some construction companies. Nothing ever stuck."

"What about their relationship?"

"Everybody said he had a temper, but he was also really sweet with her."

"What did she see in him?"

"He was a good-looking guy. Some people thought he should try to become an actor, but he wasn't interested."

"So they dated, on and off, even when she was in college?"

"That's right. And then, just after she gets her degree, she lands a job at a local cable station, doing a bit of everything. It's a start, but she's set her sights really high, so she looks at graduate school and gets into Columbia."

"Big break for her," Sheila said. "But not for him."

"It's only an hour and a half away," Haggerty said. "The relationship didn't end right then."

"How did it end?" Sheila asked.

"One night, he was at her place in Graduate Housing." Haggerty sounded like a guy looking at his notes. "They got into a big argument. One of the neighbors told us she heard Marie say, 'Will you show some fucking ambition just once in your useless life?' Which did not go over well."

"Did he hit her?"

"We're not sure. No report was made, no charges were filed, but the neighbors heard stuff being broken inside the apartment, so they called 911."

"Domestic dispute," Sheila said. "Just what you guys hate the most."

"You'll always be a cop's daughter."

"Tell me what happened next."

"Patrol car reaches the scene. Marie and the boyfriend are both really worked up. You know how Italians are."

Ethnic stereotyping will never end, she thought. "Keep going."

"The cops ask if she wants to press charges. She says, 'I just want him outta here.' So they order him to leave. He stomps around a bit, but eventually leaves with the officers. On the way out, he says, 'You haven't seen the last of me.' And she says, 'Oh, yes, I have.'"

"Sounds like my kind of woman," Sheila said.

Haggerty's voice turned rock hard. "Before those bastards raped her and beat her within an inch of her life, everyone who knew her said she had a lotta moxie."

He's trying to hijack the thread, Sheila told herself. Stay on topic.

"Was that the last she ever saw of him?"

"I dunno. But the next day, she filed for that order of protection, which the judge granted right away."

"You can see where I'm going with this."

"We went by the book." Haggerty's voice grew urgent, insistent, as if he believed she'd believe if he talked as quickly as he could. "I drove to Philadelphia with another detective. Jesus, that town makes New York look like the Emerald City. Anyway, we found Cantone real easy and started asking questions."

"What did he say?"

"He denied it."

"That settles it, then."

"He said he was home. He lived with his parents, who both vouched for him. They had dinner and watched TV and went to bed. They all liked to watch *Law & Order* together."

That figures, Sheila thought.

"And you bought that?" she asked.

She could almost see him shrug.

"We checked his credit card records," Haggerty said. "Nothing outta the ordinary that day. No train or bus tickets—nothing that would put him in New York."

"He coulda driven."

"He always took the train or the bus. You drive into Manhattan, you hafta deal with tolls, gas, and parking. Especially parking."

"He coulda paid for a train or bus ticket in cash."

"We checked his ATM records. He hadn't withdrawn any money for a week."

"It's not the most airtight alibi I've ever heard," Sheila said.

"That's why I buy it. If he'd done it, he woulda concocted a story about going out and seeing some people—he woulda been at a bar or a game or a movie—but instead, he just described what most people do most of the time. He spent a quiet night at home with his family. He even described the plot of the *Law & Order* episode."

"Lemme guess," Sheila said. "Somebody committed a crime and then got arrested and convicted."

Haggerty adopted a cop-sticking-to-his-story voice. "We never found any evidence that placed him in New York that day."

"Whatever happened to him? He ever find a real job?"

"Oh, yeah."

"What's he doing?"

Haggerty chuckled. "He's a cop in Philly. From what I've heard, he's doing okay."

Great, Sheila thought. Another guy with an attitude problem joining the police.

"Lemme ask you about the victim," Sheila said.

"What about her?"

"Was she seeing somebody else? She have a new boyfriend?"

"We asked around about that. Like I said, we covered all the bases."

"What did you find?"

"Nothing definite. She did hang out with a guy named Rajeev Dalweet. He's with CNN now."

He was one of Sheila's favorite correspondents—serious-looking, self-assured, unflappable. Recently the suits had given him his own show.

Maybe he'll talk to me, she thought. That would definitely raise the profile of this thing.

Haggerty was still talking: "We touched base with him, of course, and he said they were friends, but there was nothing romantic between them. I dunno if I believe that."

"He have an alibi for that night?"

"He was working on a project," Haggerty said. "Six different people put him in the editing lab until at least ten o'clock. There are surveillance cameras on the campus. He was pictured going from the lab to the building he lived in, which he entered by punching in a key code. He said he had a cup of decaf tea and went to bed, and we have no evidence to the contrary."

Haggerty sighed like a father who can't get his kids to do their homework.

"I'd forgotten," he said.

"Forgotten what?"

"That knack you have. For getting people to talk to you."

"It's what I do for a living."

"I've stayed on the line too long. But I wanna tell you something before I hang up. About your brother."

"Go ahead."

"He followed the book even more closely than I did. After we got the confessions, he insisted we check out everything—all the other possibilities, including the crackhead and the old boyfriend and her classmate and, oh, I dunno, friggin' space aliens beaming down into the park that night. Some of the guys working with me grumbled about it—it's open and shut, what the hell's going on—but I saw what he was doing. He didn't wanna give any bullshit defense lawyer a chance to say we'd blown off a promising lead."

"But you never found a shred of DNA or physical evidence that tied the defendants to the crime. Doesn't that bother you?"

"You wanna know what I think?" Haggerty said.

I do, Sheila thought. I really do.

"A pack of kids was rampaging through the park that night," Haggerty said. "Fifteen, twenty of 'em. The semen we found? Probably from one of the assholes we didn't catch. Same thing with the clothing fibers and the skin under her nails. But the guys we did catch? They were at the scene, aiding and abetting. They were guilty as hell, and I don't feel sorry for them one bit."

Chapter Seven

Michael Devine

April 27, 2012

He grabbed lunch from a halal truck off Foley Square because he had no time to go out to eat. The vendor stuffed a Styrofoam container into a brown paper bag. Michael wanted to hurry back to his office before the chicken and rice got cold. He'd fill the empty plastic bottle at his desk with tap water and eat at his desk, surrounded by documents, paper napkins, and assistants.

"Mike!"

A few feet away, striding toward him casually, as if this were a chance encounter, he saw a lawyer he had met a few times but had never worked with. The man's name was Chris Santangelo, and if Michael remembered correctly, he was now high up in the mayor's legal office.

"I'd shake your hand, Chris, but I've got my lunch."

"I understand, Mikey. Mind if I walk with you?"

Michael disliked being called Mike, and detested Mikey.

"No problem. But I gotta get back quickly."

"I hear what you're saying, Mikey. We all know what you're working on."

Michael stopped at the crosswalk.

"We're all wondering how it's going," Santangelo said. The guy was five-foot-six, with a square body that reminded Michael of a large piece of plasterboard.

"It's going." Michael resisted the urge to flash an insincere smile.

"That's great, Mikey."

Traffic stopped. Michael sprang out as quickly as he could.

"Because we all know how important this thing is," Santangelo said. "And we're all happy it's in good hands."

This is totally inappropriate, Michael thought. You know how inappropriate it is. Who's making you do this?

"We all wanna know it'll be okay," Santangelo said.

Michael gazed straight ahead. The side door he always used was about a hundred yards ahead. He would not invite Santangelo to come up with him.

"We should be all right," Michael said. "But it's complicated."

"Not to rain on your parade, Mikey, but that's just the thing we don't wanna hear."

Michael thought about bursting into a sprint to reach the sanctuary of his office. Santangelo kept yammering.

"'Cause if I go back to my people and I tell 'em that Mikey Devine is saying, 'It's complicated,' they're all gonna say: 'What's so complicated? Those dirtbags confessed. Why aren't they in prison for the rest of their friggin' lives already?' You know what I'm saying?"

Michael stopped, turned, and raised himself on the balls of his feet just to stress the intimidation factor. He had at least eight inches on the other attorney.

"No, Chrissie." Michael hoped Santangelo hated the diminutive as much as he did. "To be honest about it, I have no idea what the fuck you're saying."

Although he did, and he understood why the other guy had avoided putting any of this in an email, text, or phone call. There was no record that this interaction had ever occurred.

Santangelo's voice dropped from meeting-old-friends-at-the-bar heartiness to a conspiratorial murmur. "The big guy is concerned. He doesn't want the bad old days coming back. You remember the bad old days, don'tcha, Mikey?"

The Seventies and Eighties. Even into the Nineties. Crime and drugs and graffiti. An entire city crumbling: subways, roads, bridges, buildings, people. New York as urban hellhole, symbol of everything wrong with modern society.

And then, *mirabile dictu*, the turnaround. Nobody could figure out why, although Michael's theory was that the city embraced money with the fervor of the world's most ardent lover. Money and gravity were the only forces in the world that always conquered every opponent.

"All those media assholes think it's an illusion," Santangelo said. "They expect the bad old days to return any minute, but it's even worse than that— they want the bad old days to come back. Muggings, crack vials, drugs, sex for sale on the streets—that shit sells newspapers and gets ratings, and those are the only things they're interested in. What's the biggest problem in the city right now? Rents are sky high in Brooklyn?" He shrugged. "We'll take that."

Michael wanted to say something, but couldn't. Despite the skin-crawling nature of the conversation, Santangelo had a point.

"The media's gonna use this case," Santangelo said. "They're gonna say: 'See, we told ya. They just kept a cork in it a few years. But now it's all coming back, and it's even worse than before. In fact, it's our worst fears coming true. 'Cause these Black and brown kids are busting outta their neighborhoods, and now they're raping our women, and there's nothing we can do to stop 'em.'"

"Don't go there," Michael said.

"What?"

"There's nothing racial about this case."

"What're you talking about? It's all racial."

Michael wanted to poke Santangelo in the chest with his fingers, but was afraid of dropping his lunch. "If you inject race into this case, it'll contaminate the prosecution, and we'll never get any convictions. Certainly, nothing that'll stand on appeal. And there will be appeals."

Santangelo looked like he wanted to interject, but Michael went on.

"This is a case about a bunch of kids who committed a sexual assault and damn near killed a woman. Period. We don't need to bring race into it. Far from it. There are plenty of Blacks and Latins in this city who are just as sick of criminals as you and I are. Even more, because they hafta live with them."

The barest smile possible played out on Santangelo's face. "You're smooth, Mikey. Really smooth. I'll pass that along. But there is one thing."

Oh Christ, what is it? Michael asked himself. But he didn't say anything. He had already encouraged this conversation far too much.

"How long is this gonna take? The big guy wants it wrapped up quick."

* * *

Michael went to her hospital room late that afternoon.

"Can she see anyone?" he asked the nurse's aide outside the door.

"She's with some people right now. Friends."

This was surprising. As far as he knew, since the attack, she had seen only medical or legal personnel.

"Is she feeling better?" he asked.

"A little." The woman's voice had a Caribbean lilt that reminded him of his brother-in-law's family. "Every day, a little better."

Michael heard a stirring that sounded like chairs being moved. In a moment, three people stepped out of the room—two twentysomethings, a guy and a woman, followed by a man in his mid-forties who looked familiar.

Michael introduced himself and shook hands with everyone. The older man was six-foot-three, with a full head of dark brown hair and eyes so blue they bordered on cobalt. His face had a few faint red welts and blisters, as if he'd been scratched a week before by low-lying branches while hiking through the woods.

"Seamus O'Toole," he said, and Michael realized why he recognized him. A television correspondent for years, he had reported for one network or another from places beset by war, disease, famine, and other forms of global nastiness. Michael hadn't seen him on TV for a while. Of course, being the father of two school-age kids, Michael rarely had time to watch the news.

The woman, a chunky Latina named Gloria Estevez, spoke with the quick and strong cadences of a striver. The younger man was Rajeev Dalweet. Michael expected him to talk like a Robin Williams character just off the subcontinent, but when he spoke, he sounded like a young man who aspired to be one of those voice-of-God anchors. He was a graduate student in broadcast journalism—as was Gloria, as was Marie Antolini—and Michael reminded himself it was always careless to make judgments about people before talking to them.

"You're gonna nail those creeps?" Rajeev asked.

"I expect to," Michael said. He was surrounded by journalists, so he had to be wary.

"We're all shaken," Gloria said. "My mom in Texas was nervous about me coming to New York, but I kept telling her it's safe."

"It's a lot safer than it used to be," Michael said, "but you should still keep your guard up."

O'Toole turned to the younger people with the type of avuncular authority Michael associated with Walter Cronkite.

"This is a good lesson," he said. He had a bit of a brogue. Michael wondered how long he'd been in the States after all that globe-trotting. "You never know when you'll run into somebody who can help you with a story."

Michael thought about insisting that everything was off the record. "I don't know how much help I can be."

"I've heard you're thinking about letting those guys plead down," O'Toole said.

"I'm not thinking about it," Michael said.

O'Toole raised his eyebrows as he turned to Gloria and Rajeev. "Straight from the horse's mouth. That's a good confirmation."

Michael motioned toward the room. "How's she doing?"

Gloria shook her head. "It's sad to see. Marie was a dynamo, but now she's shattered. It's like there's nothing left inside."

Michael detected something insincere in her voice, as if she were uttering phrases she was supposed to say instead of what she really felt.

"Do you have business cards?" he asked. "In case I wanna talk to you about Ms. Antolini?"

O'Toole produced a small piece of cardboard with printing on it. It had his contact information and said he was a visiting professor of international reporting. Gloria and Rajeev had nothing, but they both gave Michael their cell numbers and email addresses. All three promised to help in any way they could.

They left. Michael entered the room. He heard beeping machines and took note of the lines that traced Marie's vital signs. Erratic in the first days, by now they were either steady or rhythmic.

"Can you spare a few minutes, Ms. Antolini?"

She tried to smile, but it looked like it hurt. "Your name's Michael, isn't it?"

He nodded. "I just met some of your friends outside."

"That's what they told me. That they were my friends. That they knew me."

This doesn't sound good, Michael thought. "What do you mean?"

"Everything before..." She stopped. She was looking for words. "Before what happened. It's all fragments. Like a jigsaw puzzle that has too many pieces of sky."

"But you remember me?"

"The people I've met since I've been here—the doctors, the nurses, the police—I can process all of them, even though it's difficult. But what came before..." She shook her head. "The older man, he said he was my teacher. The other two said we took classes together. They said we used to hang out. Work on projects. But I don't remember."

He tried to take her all in. Before he'd always been overwhelmed by the bandages and tubes covering her body, but most of them were gone. She was five-foot-two, with sharp but delicate features, olive skin, dark brown hair that matched her eyes. Michael was sure she was photogenic.

"I've talked to your parents," he said.

She uttered a noncommittal "Hmmmmmmm."

"They're concerned about you, obviously. Very concerned."

"Where do they live?"

"Philadelphia." Where you grew up, he thought.

"I remember..." She glanced out the window. Spring was late this year, but the trees were budding at last. "I remember a house. Red brick, I think. And I remember smells. Especially of food. I remember a woman in the kitchen, cooking. A lot."

Sounds like every Italian family I've ever known, Michael thought. Maybe some of this will come back to her. Maybe she'll regain at least part of her life.

"They'd like to see you," he said.

"Hmmmmmmmmm."

"If the doctors say it's okay, I'd like to talk to all of you together. It might help me."

She turned to him. She looked vulnerable, a word he hated to use about anyone.

"If you say so."

Never get close to the victims, Adam Fishman had told Michael when he was starting out. Respect them and be sympathetic, but keep a distance. It's better both professionally and personally.

Michael had a silent retort to the voice in his head: *You've never met her.*

Chapter Eight

Sheila Devine

September 18, 2023

T he upstate bleakness was familiar, battered wood frames
surrounding shuttered mill towns populated by pensioners and
feral dogs. Whenever she drove through these places she asked
herself, What do people do here? And then, because of the interview she
was about to conduct, the answer came to her:

They work in prisons. We send them our criminals. If there was no crime
downstate, there'd be nothing here at all.

Ortega had arranged the interview. She would talk to Manuel Fuentes.
After their meeting, she'd decide whether to put him on camera. If Ortega
won the appeal he had filed, Fuentes and his mother would make tons of
money from their lawsuit against the city. But after her conversation with
Haggerty, Sheila figured the odds against them were long, although she was
interested in recording how a lawyer like Ortega operated.

At the prison, she went through security and talked briefly to the
communications director, a paunchy woman in her fifties who told Sheila
that Manuel Fuentes was a model inmate who never caused any trouble—
one of those quiet guys who kept to himself.

Sounds like the description of every mass murderer I've ever heard about,
Sheila thought.

In the visitors' room, she sat behind the heavy glass partition that separated freed from captured. When Fuentes was arrested, he was a teenager with hints of baby fat around his chin and belly, but the man she saw had a sagging body and tufts of hair starting to gray. Prison defeats people and ages them quickly, especially when they're forced to wear the orange jumpsuit that has become America's equivalent of the scarlet letter.

Fuentes leaned forward to speak into the voice box. His eyes looked dark and half-dead.

"You the filmmaker?" he asked.

"That's right."

"Mi madre y Señor Ortega—they've talked about you."

"What did they say?"

"That you're making a movie about my case. That you've done this kind of película before."

"Did they tell you my brother was the prosecutor who sent away you and your friends?"

She saw a spark in his brown eyes. "Is that why you're doing this? You hate su hermano?"

"I love my brother. We went through a lot together while we were growing up. Us against the world."

He snorted. "I bet."

It occurred to her that Fuentes was like most nonwhite Americans she'd ever met: He believed every Anglo was a billionaire.

"You have no idea what my life was like," Sheila told him, "so here's the short version:

"My father spent most of his life in a prison much like this one, for a murder he didn't commit. I strongly suspect my mother was depressed, but it never occurred to her to see a shrink, so she found refuge in tobacco and smoked herself to death before she was fifty-five. As a result of all that, my brother and I ate shit sandwiches for breakfast, lunch, and dinner. Comprende?"

Fuentes blinked a few times. "Lo siento, Señora. I've probably been in prison too long. You lose the ability to sympathize with others. But you, too, made a mistake."

"What was it?"

"You talked about me and my friends. Only one of them was mi amigo. Roberto Linares. The others I'd seen around, but I'd never hung with them until that night." He paused. "It was, by far, the worst mistake of my life."

Chapter Nine

Manuel Fuentes

April 11, 2012

Dusk crept westward as Manuel Fuentes and Roberto Linares walked toward the soccer field in Morningside Heights. Roberto knew a guy who knew a guy who said a pickup game was going on, and maybe they'd get to play. Sounded good to Manuel. Blowing off steam and all that. They'd been in school most of the day. On their way, they talked about a party Roberto was gonna deejay over the weekend. Lotsa hot chiquitas. Roberto told su amigo he'd make sure he could get in without paying the cover.

They stopped at the field. Artificial turf. Manuel hated that stuff because it was brutal on his knees, but this was the only place around to play. The lights flickered on as a bunch of hombres kicked a ball around. Roberto went up to one of them and asked if he and his bud could join.

Sí. Claro.

They chose sides and whacked away at the pelota a while and all that running felt great but it grew chilly and after an hour the game wound down. Manuel thought they'd call it a night, and everyone would go wherever. He figured he'd head home. Dinnertime. His madre was working a swing shift, but she usually left rice and beans and chicken that he could reheat.

"C'mon, you pussies, it's early," one of the guys said. Manuel didn't know him. It turned out to be Felipe Huerta. During the game, he'd been a hothead, overreacting to whatever happened and confirming Manuel's belief that in every situation in life, you run into at least one asshole.

A few kids said they had to go home to eat, and left.

"Maricóns," Huerta said as they walked away.

More than a dozen guys remained. Roberto asked Huerta what he had in mind.

"We go to the park, man," Huerta said.

"And do what?"

"Raise some hell. We got a lotta peeps here. It'll be fun."

A few others shook their heads. One or two more walked away. Huerta bellowed that they were mariquitas.

Manuel was hetero and did not want anyone to think otherwise, so he joined the guys setting out for the park. Once they crossed Riverside Drive, it grew even darker, and the gang was swept along by the giddy feeling that all the rules they usually observed had been suspended.

They'd been in the park only a minute when they saw a homeless guy sprawled on a bench. Newspapers and a mud-splattered blanket covered him. A shopping cart filled with cans and bottles lay within reach of his arm.

Huerta nudged his companions. "Let's start here."

He ran to the cart and flipped it over. The stuff inside crashed to the ground, and then Huerta and a couple of other kids began smashing glass on the pavement. The homeless man moved a bit under his papers. He was Black and bearded, and when he started to talk, Manuel noticed he had just three teeth in his mouth. It was impossible to know his age—anywhere from thirty to sixty—but he stank with the odor of a human being who hadn't showered in weeks.

"What the fuck?" Homeless said. Or at least, tried to say. His words were slurred, and Manuel mentally ran through the drugs that could have induced his stupor: crack or meth or heroin or pills, or maybe he was old-fashioned and had gotten wasted on a gallon of Ripple.

"You motherfuckers fucking with me?" Homeless said.

Huerta tossed the newspapers into the air. "Fuckin' A we are," he said. Some of the bros dragged the blanket into the trees.

"That's my shit," Homeless said.

"Not anymore," Huerta said. He grabbed a thick piece of broken glass and pressed the shard against the man's neck. "You stink like a fuckin' animal. I oughta carve you up like one, you useless piece of crap."

A couple of kids told Huerta to go ahead. They wanted to watch.

"Don't, man."

Roberto used his deejay voice. He knew how to get above the noise.

Huerta looked at him with eyes that blazed with hate for the world. "You a pansy or something? What the fuck's wrong with you?"

"If you do that," Roberto said, "you'll kill him."

"So what? He's worthless."

"Nobody's worthless."

Huerta glared at Roberto a minute before throwing the shard away. But then he punched the homeless man all over—head, ribs, neck, groin—and a few other dudes joined in. Homeless groaned, fell off the bench, rolled on the ground. The kids kicked him as he writhed.

Chapter Ten

Sheila Devine

September 18, 2023

The man she was interviewing had delivered his story in an affectless tone, as if he were describing a trip to the dry cleaner.

I need a reaction from him, she said to herself. I need to see if there's anything left inside.

"Did you kick him?" she asked.

"Excuse me?"

"The homeless man. Were you one of the ones who kicked him? Or beat him up? Were you one of the jerks who assaulted a man who wasn't doing anything to you, just because he was sleeping on a park bench and helpless?"

Her voice was rising. Now that she had finally heard about that night from one of the men involved, she was growing increasingly pissed about what they had done.

"I don't remember, Señora. Lo siento."

"If you're gonna give me answers like that, there's no reason for me to continue talking to you. We're discussing the most crucial night of your life—a night you've spent years thinking about, because what the hell else are you gonna do—and now you're telling the audience you don't remember something like that? They're not gonna buy it. I don't buy it."

Manuel Fuentes glanced away and scratched his earlobe.

"I kicked him."

His voice was so soft she wasn't sure she'd heard him right.

"Say that again," she said.

His voice was stronger, but still flat. "I kicked him in the ribs and the stomach."

That's better, she thought.

"Why?" she asked.

He puckered his lips. She wondered how he would look on camera. He struck her as the type of man who would be evasive for as long as he could get away with it.

"No sé."

"Use English when I'm talking to you, por favor."

"I wish I could tell you," he said. "I was there, and we were all yelling, and it seemed like the thing to do. We were all overcome by something, an awful spirit, that made us do things we never knew we were capable of."

People can always reach the heights or depths of their character, Sheila thought. It all depends on the circumstances.

"When I do this film," Sheila said, "I'm gonna emphasize a point that you and your compatriots and your families and your lawyer will not like one bit."

"Do we have a choice?" Manuel asked.

Sheila ignored the question. "You guys weren't in the park that night doing outreach to the homeless. You were in the park that night beating up the homeless."

Manuel puckered his lips again. He reminded her of a kid who had been caught with a crayon in his hand standing beside fresh scribblings on a newly painted wall.

"I should've known better," he said. "I should've done better."

That's good, Sheila thought. You better say that to me when I start filming.

"After you stopped beating up that guy," she asked, "what did you do next?"

Chapter Eleven

Michael Devine

1

September 19, 2023

M ichael looked at his iPhone. Haggerty calling.

"The DNA test came back," the detective said.

"And?"

"No match. Just like I told you."

Michael knew he should feel glad, or at least vindicated, but the only emotion that edged into him was a smidgen of satisfaction.

"I talked to your sister," Haggerty said.

"How's she doing?"

"She's got a lotta questions."

"She always does."

"She got me thinking about the case. I hadn't done that in years."

Michael was at his desk in his campaign headquarters in the Flatiron district. Although he was sure no one could overhear, he stood up and closed the door. On the way back to his chair, he glanced over the latest numbers. Thanks to his father-in-law, he'd hired the best pollster in the country. He could get figures hourly if he wanted.

His support was getting soft, especially among Blacks and Hispanics. A few percentage points had moved from his column into undecided.

"What's your angle?" Michael asked as soon as he'd closed the door.

"Felipe Huerta," Haggerty said.

"What about him?"

"It always bugged me that he skated on the case. That scumbag lawyered up before we had a chance to get at him."

"I remember."

"Your sister pointed out that none of the DNA or clothing matched anything from the perps. I told her that up to twenty guys were there, so the evidence we found musta belonged to one of the shitheads who ran away."

"What's your point?" Michael asked.

"Felipe Huerta's been in trouble with the law almost every day since then. I think the semen is his. So now it's our turn. We go on offense. We've busted that skel a half-dozen times, so we've got his DNA somewhere. We ask for a test."

Michael started to think about what could go wrong.

Haggerty went on: "We didn't test his DNA at the time because he cut a deal with us. But now, with Ortega reopening the case, we have grounds to make the motion. If we get a match, we finally nail Huerta for this thing, and if we can find him, we'll put his ass in prison for the rest of his life, which is what he deserves anyway. Plus, that ties the other guys into what happened, because they all admit they were with him that night. This whole thing goes away for good, and Ortega looks like a putz."

"What if there's no match?" Michael asked.

"I like our chances," Haggerty said.

"When Ortega asked for the test, you were absolutely certain there'd be no match. Are you that confident now?"

Michael heard Haggerty taking a long, slow intake of air, which meant that the answer was No.

"It's like drawing nineteen in blackjack," Haggerty said. "Our odds are really good."

2

April 12, 2012

After visiting the crime scene, Michael went to One Hogan Place. Ordinarily, an attack like the one on the runner would be assigned to the Sex Crimes Unit, but if she died, which seemed likely, the case would be transferred to Homicide, and everyone would have to start over, and Adam Fishman was a political animal acutely aware of how any delay would play out in the media. So, the DA called Michael into his office and gave him the orders he was expecting:

- Drop everything else you're working on.
- Assemble a task force and get on this.
- Above all else, don't lose.

At four p.m., Michael arrived at the station house where Haggerty and his detectives were questioning the suspects. By this point, the media swarm resembled a plague of camera-wielding locusts, and he heard barking questions as he went inside, but it was best to stay silent and adopt the grim-faced look of a dedicated public servant doing his sad duty. Several reporters asked if the victim was dead yet.

Inside the cop shop: cacophony—every computer terminal occupied by a furiously typing officer; cells and landlines pinging and ringing; platoons of paper-clutching clerks running at full speed; shouted commands and profanities.

Michael poked around for fifteen minutes before finding Haggerty in a ten-by-ten storage closet he had turned into a temporary office. The detective had his mobile in one ear and a landline receiver in another, but he grunted the same words into both phones: "The DA is here. I'll get back to you."

Michael liked hearing himself referred to as the DA. "She still alive?"

"Barely. They're all amazed at the hospital. What's the word downtown?"

"This is priority one through one thousand. Waddya got from the perps?"

"They're making statements right now. We've got video cameras recording each one."

"All five of them?"

"Four of them are talking."

This sounded bad. Michael sat down although his overcoat was still on. He had expected to hear everything was jake, so he'd planned to stay just a short time.

"What about the fifth one?" he asked.

"Wants to lawyer up. Says he won't tell us anything unless he runs it through his mouthpiece."

"Did the others waive Miranda?"

"They're cooperating."

This was not the definitive Yes that Michael was seeking. "Why is the fifth guy busting our chops?" he asked.

Haggerty looked over a computer printout in front of him. "Name's Felipe Huerta. Has a bunch of priors—he's been in the system, so he knows how it works. The other guys..." Haggerty shrugged and shook his head.

"What about the other guys?"

"One of 'em has some juvie stuff. For the rest, this is the first time they've ever been run in."

Michael thought this over. "I wanna look at them."

"Why?"

"Humor me."

Haggerty led him through the station house. The perps who were talking were being held in different rooms, but they all had the same body language—slumped forward in their chairs, bloodshot eyes on the ground, clasped hands in front of them while they kneaded their fingers. They reminded Michael of high school kids who'd been caught sharing a joint in the boys' room.

At the end of the tour, Haggerty guided Michael into an observation room with a two-way mirror. They looked into an interrogation chamber occupied by a solitary man who was sitting straight as a board and staring ahead without blinking. His jaw was set in the tight manner of a guy who knew he could take a punch and then hit back harder. Manacled wrists rested on the table in front of him.

"Huerta?" Michael asked.

Haggerty nodded.

"You're making him sweat?" Michael asked.

"We want him to be alone with his thoughts for a while."

"He's asked for a lawyer."

"It doesn't mean we have to get him one right away."

Michael shook his head. "We've seen plenty of guys like this. He's not gonna talk until his lawyer tells him to."

"What should we do with him?"

"The other guys say he was with them?"

"That's right."

"So their statements put him at the scene?"

"That's right."

"Let him talk to a lawyer. He'll stonewall, but we have enough to hold him awhile. Given the victim's condition, we'll ask the judge to deny bail. That means he'll wind up in Rikers with the rest of them. In a week or two, his memory might improve."

For the first time since they'd begun talking, Haggerty smiled. "I like the way you think, Counselor."

3

May 7, 2012

It was ten at night, but Michael knew Haggerty would be at his desk.

"I've watched the confessions," Michael said into the phone. "All the way through. Dozens of times."

"You don't sound happy," the detective said.

"We've got problems."

"What problems? They confessed. We got them on tape."

"We've got different guys doing different things at different times in different places. That's gonna give their lawyers a lot to work with."

"We got them to give their best recollections before they got their asshole lawyers involved," Haggerty said. "As soon as those cretins talked to their douchebag attorneys, they recanted, but that's all bullshit."

"None of their stories jibe," Michael said. "That'll be a tough sell to the jury. And I'm the one who has to sell it."

Haggerty took a breath. "Despite what their shithead lawyers are saying, we did not write a script. Different detectives questioned different perps and took their statements. You remember—you were there part of the time."

"Did you Miranda them?" Michael asked.

"You keep asking that."

"I don't want their convictions tossed by the Court of Appeals."

"We read them their goddamn rights, even though they don't deserve any."

"Don't say that on the witness stand, Detective."

"Look, Counselor, I understand where you're coming from." Haggerty had a rare talent—the ability to play both good cop and bad cop in the same situation. "At the trial, your balls are the ones that'll be on the chopping block. But consider it this way—it was a confusing situation. Nighttime. Lotsa stuff going on. Lotsa guys around. If the perps were telling just one story, their lawyers would say we dictated the confessions. Which we didn't. It makes perfect sense that these guys have different memories of a chaotic event. It's like *Rashomon*."

Michael was surprised. "You've seen *Rashomon*?"

"At the academy, I took a course from a Japanese detective who required us to watch it. A lotta guys rolled their eyes, but it's one of the best movies I've ever seen."

4

September 19, 2023

Michael looked up from his iPhone when he heard the door to his campaign office open. Rachel was the only person who could enter without knocking.

"Good news for us today," she said.

"Haggerty thinks we should stop playing defense."

Rachel perched on the edge of her husband's desk. She spent at least thirty minutes a day on the StairMaster, and after all these years, Michael still enjoyed looking at her legs.

"I remember watching a football game on TV with Dad when I was growing up," she said. "The announcer kept going on about the importance of defense. Dad cut the sound, turned to me, and asked, 'D'ya know what they call people who play defense all the time?'"

Michael shook his head.

"'Losers.'"

Michael smiled. "Our detective friend thinks we should ask for a DNA test." Slight pause. "On Felipe Huerta."

"I never understood why you didn't do that in the first place," Rachel said.

Chapter Twelve

Sheila Devine

1

September 19, 2023

Sheila brought her handheld Sony to Ortega's suite and recorded him talking to his assistant Dolores, the plaintiff Paloma Santiago, and an unpaid intern from Columbia Law named Tamika Riley. They were waiting for a call telling them the results of the DNA test on Jose Ramos, although the DA's decision not to oppose it had flummoxed everyone on Ortega's legal team.

The lab called shortly before ten. As Ortega listened, his face sagged in the manner of a CEO receiving news that his once-prosperous company had gone belly up, and when he hung up, he told the others that the DNA did not match. Dolores shook her head. Paloma Santiago cried. The intern asked what she was supposed to do now. Ortega told all of them that this was only the beginning of the process, not the end. Many options were still available. Sheila asked what they were. Ortega raised his eyebrows and opened his mouth, as if he were about to say something, before silently retreating to his office and locking the door. Sheila slid in that direction and listened for sounds. She wasn't certain, but she believed she could hear him swearing softly in Spanish.

* * *

The next morning, Tamika Riley walked into Ortega's office saying she had pulled an all-nighter doing research into false confessions, and she believed they had a basis for filing a motion on the grounds that the police had coerced Manuel Fuentes into talking by using tactics that violated his constitutional rights.

"Those points were made at the trial and have been made before on appeal," Ortega said. "Unless we come up with something new, the court will throw us out."

"Maybe I'm grasping at straws," Tamika said. She was a chunky African-American whose most striking feature was her straightened hair, which was streaked blond, green, and purple. Sheila was tempted to ask how much time she spent on it every day.

"Maybe you are," Ortega replied.

The lawyer drummed his fingers on his desktop. Dolores poked in her head and told Ortega he had a call. He picked up the receiver, listened a few seconds, thanked whoever was on the line and turned toward Sheila. His face filled the camera frame.

"Your brother, the district attorney, has filed a motion," the lawyer said.

So much for the fourth wall, Sheila thought.

"What's the motion?" Tamika asked.

"He is asking for a DNA test on the semen that was recovered in the Riverside Runner case. He wants to see if it matches Felipe Huerta's."

Everyone understood the implications. If the DNA belonged to Huerta, the case was over. Physical evidence combined with the confessions already on file would be enough to convict Huerta and keep the rest of the defendants in prison until their sentences ran out.

"This could really screw us, couldn't it?" Tamika asked.

Dolores walked into the room and put a café con leche on Ortega's desk. "It doesn't screw us if there's no match," she said.

Ortega sipped his drink and cleared his throat. Sheila marveled at the clarifying power of caffeine.

"Provided there is no match," he said, "a number of avenues become open to us. The police and the district attorney want to finally prove beyond all doubt that they resolved this case properly. But they don't know for a fact that the DNA matches Felipe Huerta's. Were they one hundred percent certain of this, they would have asked for a test while they were collecting evidence after the crime, but they didn't."

Everyone else remained quiet, like students in thrall to a professor's lecture, although Sheila felt Ortega was overlooking an obvious point. So she spoke up.

"If the DNA doesn't match Huerta's, the cops and prosecutors can just say it belongs to somebody else who belonged to that pack of kids. There were as many as twenty guys in the park when the attack occurred."

Ortega was ready. "But then we can make the argument that the request for a test indicates the authorities still have questions about who actually committed the rape. It was not any of the men now in prison for the assault. It was not Jose Ramos. If it was not Felipe Huerta, it could just as easily be the man in the moon."

"Space aliens would get everybody off the hook," Tamika said.

"Waddya do if the DNA doesn't match Huerta's?" Sheila asked.

"We file discovery motions related to the way the interrogations were handled." He gestured toward Tamika. "I may have been too dismissive of Ms. Riley's research. Lo siento."

"Apology accepted," Tamika said.

Ortega continued. "When the initial appeals were filed, the courts refused to look at how the police conducted the questioning. But now, if the DNA does not match Felipe Huerta's..."

The lawyer's voice drifted a bit.

"If we can say the DA's office itself has reopened the case..."

His voice drifted even more.

"If we find a favorable judge..."

His voice faded out.

"That's a lotta ifs," Sheila said.

"Only three," Ortega said.

* * *

She stayed at the lawyer's office all day, so on her way home, she sent a Seamless order to Tandoori Kitchen on Atlantic Avenue. As she walked from the subway toward the takeout place, she texted Michael: "Pretty swift move on the DNA front." She threw in a smile-face emoji. Her iPhone rang a minute later.

"You coulda sent me a text," she said.

"A text leaves way too much of a trail," Michael said.

He was being cagey. All those years of dealing with their mother had made him a master of revealing as little as possible. Bridget Devine was imprisoned by her own problems, so she rarely asked her kids what they were doing as long as they got good grades and stayed out of jail.

"Haggerty's convinced the DNA will match Huerta's," Michael said. "He's usually right about things like that."

"What if he isn't?" Sheila asked. "Ortega was sure he had a match with Ramos, but then science pissed all over him. He was flailing around for his next move, and you may have given it to him."

"We'll be okay no matter what," Michael said. "We showed the jury that those guys were at the scene. Which meant they participated in the assault, even if they didn't commit the rape. That was all we needed to prove."

"I don't think I'm revealing any confidences by telling you that Ortega will file motions if the DNA doesn't match."

Michael sounded dismissive. "I've dealt with Rolando's motions for years."

2

September 21, 2023

Roberto Linares was serving his sentence at a prison in the Catskills that had been built on the site of an old Borscht Belt hotel. Sheila checked the lighting after setting up her camera in the small room the warden had agreed to provide. The severe glare matched the surroundings.

Two guards flanked Linares as they escorted him into the room. When he sat down, he scratched his nose, and Sheila caught a glint of metal from his cuffs.

Sheila filmed him describing what had happened in the park that night. She let him talk uninterrupted until he said that the police had collared him after he slipped on wet grass.

"What did they do next?" she asked.

"They took me to a station house. Did good-cop, bad-cop stuff."

"Were you scared?"

"Oh, yeah. I'd never been arrested before. I was scared of what my Moms would say when she found out."

If Dylan got caught doing something like that, Sheila thought, my son would discover the true extent of my vocabulary.

"What did you think she'd say?"

"She'd call me stupido. I felt stupido. I had a good thing goin', bein' a deejay. Now I'm in jail. I ain't no tough guy, but that's how I gotta act. My life's wasted."

Sheila waited a beat. She reminded herself that she was not making a movie about the prison system. She had to focus on the case.

"Let's go back to that night," she said. "You're in the cops' custody. What was it like?"

"They said they knew what we'd done in the park. Said the other guys were talkin', and if I had any sense, I'd talk, too."

"Did you?"

"Yeah."

"What did you tell them?"

"I said we beat up the homeless guy, and then we hassled a couple of kids who were ridin' bikes. Huerta threw a rock at one of 'em. Hit him in the head. Kid fell off the bike, and he was bleedin', but when he saw us runnin' toward him, he got back on the bike and rode away like he was Lance Armstrong. We laughed. Called him maricón."

"Did the cops ever say anything about talking to a lawyer?"

"Not until the very end."

"Did they ever read you your rights?"

"Not until the very end."

"What did you tell the cops about the runner?"

Roberto Linares scratched his nose again.

Chapter Thirteen

Roberto Linares

April 12, 2012

Roberto Linares, eighteen years old, no previous arrests, sat alone in a windowless room deep inside a station house in Morningside Heights, wondering when the police would let him go home. It was three in the morning.

The door crashed open. Two cops he didn't recognize strode in.

"We gotta talk," one of them said. He identified himself as Detective Haggerty.

"I talked already," Roberto said.

"Not to me," Haggerty said.

Roberto remembered his mother's lecture: If he was ever in a situation with the NYPD, he should be polite and respectful and do whatever the man said.

"Look, Officer—"

"I'm a detective, scumbag."

He's baiting me, Roberto said to himself. Don't let him rattle you. Suck up to him if you have to.

"I'm sorry about what I did," Roberto said. "I really am. I got no explanation and no excuse. My Moms raised me better than that."

Haggerty pulled a chair close while the other cop folded his arms across his chest and slouched against the wall. He identified himself as Detective Boyle.

Haggerty held up a few pieces of paper. "Your statement," he said.

"What about it?"

"It's total bullshit."

With that, Haggerty tore the sheets in half, then in quarters, then in eighths, and then in sixteenths, before sprinkling the bits on the floor.

Roberto didn't know what to say. He'd been as honest as he could with the other police officers, although the park was dark and so many things had occurred so quickly. Doubtless he'd gotten a few details wrong.

"What're you talking about?" Roberto asked.

"The girl," Haggerty said.

"What girl?"

Boyle lowered his head. Haggerty bolted to his feet and kicked over the chair he'd been sitting in.

"The girl in the park!" he screamed. "The girl you attacked! The girl who's nearly dead at Columbia-Presbyterian! Remember her?"

Roberto had no idea what he was shouting about. The guy seemed unhinged, and Roberto's instinct was to tell him to calm down, but that was a bad thing to say to an angry representative of law enforcement.

"We've talked to your friends!" Haggerty was yelling full throttle. "They're all telling us about it! One of them even says you raped that girl!"

"I didn't rape nobody."

Haggerty got in his face. "Bullshit!"

Boyle put his hand on Haggerty's shoulder and gently pushed him away before squatting beside Roberto.

"We've got a young woman at the hospital who's gonna die any minute," Boyle said. "We think you know what happened to her. While you guys were having your fun a few hours ago, you saw her running in the park, and you decided to go after her, and, well, things got outta hand. To be honest, we're not exactly sure who did what. That's why you've gotta help us."

Roberto shook his head. "I'm sorry, Officer."

"Detective."

"I'd like to help you, Detective, but I got no idea what you're talkin' about."

Boyle slowly raised himself to his full height and shook his head sadly. Haggerty let out a string of profanity.

"I dunno know why we're even talking to this fuck," Haggerty said. "We've got enough from the other guys. We can charge him with rape, and then, when she dies, we'll pin the murder on him. He'll be in prison 'til he's ninety."

Roberto tried hard to stop himself from shaking. He needed to talk to his mother. She'd know what to do.

"I want—" He stopped. He couldn't get the words out. That never happened to him when he was deejaying.

"Waddya want, Roberto?" Boyle asked.

"I wanna talk to my Moms."

Boyle squatted beside him again. "I understand that, Roberto. I really do. But you gotta talk to us first. You gotta tell us what went on in the park. With the girl."

"Then can I talk to my Moms?"

"I don't see why not."

"I didn't rape no girl," Roberto said. "I didn't attack her neither."

"Then who did?" Boyle asked.

"I dunno, Detective. I just dunno."

"We're wasting our time with this creep," Haggerty said. "Let's get outta here and go to the DA and get him to draw up an indictment right now. We've got more than enough."

The detectives headed for the door.

"Don't go," Roberto said.

Haggerty had one foot out of the room. Boyle turned around.

"This is your last shot, Roberto," he said. "Who saw her first? Was it Huerta?"

Roberto thought this over before saying: "Felipe. Yeah. He was the... whatchamacallit?"

He hunted for the word. Deejaying was so easy compared with talking to cops.

"Ringleader."

Chapter Fourteen

Michael Devine

1

September 22, 2023

T
hey usually met for lunch twice a month in Chinatown, but his campaign had bollixed his schedule, so they hadn't talked face-to-face for a while. She messaged that they needed a sit-down, and he was tempted to reply that they weren't capos in what was left of the Mafia, but public life had taught him one important lesson: Never say, email, or text the first thing that pops into your mind.

He agreed to meet for coffee, but now, for the first time he could remember, he approached his sister with the wariness he almost always displayed toward others.

"C'mon," she DM'd as they arranged the meeting, "you know I just wanna find out the truth."

That was Sheila's biggest problem—she believed every situation had an objective truth that she would discover if she looked hard enough. But decades in the legal system had taught him that everyone has his or her own truth, and nothing can shake an immutable belief.

He sat in a booth in the rear of a Starbucks near Union Square. He had ordered a venti, although it would keep him awake past midnight. That was okay. He could go over campaign details while nobody was bothering him.

He saw her the moment she came in. She always walked purposefully, like a woman who was late for a train, and today, she toted her camera. It was small, but in a media-saturated culture, everyone knew what it was, and they'd all wonder what she was doing, why she was here, and whether they should know who she was.

She had a presence. The way she moved forced people to notice her, and she had been that way for as long as he could remember because she needed attention.

It was Dad's doing, Michael said to himself. On the rare occasions when he was home, Terence Devine made a show of fussing over her, and she always enjoyed it.

She lay her camera on the table. "Watch this," she said. "I'll be right back."

He watched her go. Skinny jeans. Calf-high boots. All that yoga paid off. As she talked and gesticulated with the barista, he figured she was ordering something frou-frou, like a Frappuccino with a special blend of beans. He knew that as soon as she returned, she'd lament buying something from caffeine's Evil Empire.

"I shouldn't have gotten this," she said when she sat down.

"It's all right," Michael said. "Wesley doesn't have any stores in Manhattan."

"Still. The guilt."

"We're Irish-Catholic. We'll feel guilty 'til the day we die."

"About what?"

"Everything." He pointed to her drink. "What is it?"

"Frappuccino. But I don't like the beans they use. Their blend of the day is from Ethiopia, so I talked the barista into brewing my drink with it."

She took a sip. Michael was more than halfway done with his venti. A Starbucks buzz squeezed his temples.

"You wanted to talk," Michael said.

"Can I film you?" she asked.

"Not yet."

"Waddya waiting for? You know you're gonna talk to me."

"I'm waiting for the DNA test on Felipe Huerta. When we get the results,

I'll gloat. But I'll try to be understated about it."

Sheila sipped. "I don't think it's gonna match."

"You know something I don't?"

"Maybe."

"If it's not Huerta's," Michael said, "then it belongs to one of the guys who got away. And in that case, I'd hafta tell you that I wish we could track him down, but at this late date, it's really unlikely."

She shook her head. "I think it's the boyfriend. Ex-boyfriend. Rocco Cantone."

"You have any evidence for that?"

"His alibi sucks."

"We never came up with anything that placed him in New York that day."

"But in a crime like that, aren't you supposed to look at lovers and spouses first? Aren't they almost always the perpetrator?"

Michael made a noise that he hoped sounded noncommittal.

"C'mon, Michael," Sheila said. "Despite what the news media wants everyone to believe, random acts of violence by strangers are extremely rare."

"Crimes of opportunity aren't," Michael said. "That's what this was."

Sheila swirled her drink with a straw. When she looked down into the cup, Michael knew she was going to say something unpleasant.

"I've been talking to the defendants," she said.

Michael noted that she didn't call them criminals, or even prisoners.

"Yesterday, I interviewed Roberto Linares. He said he told Haggerty and his partner what they wanted to hear. He just wanted to get outta there and go home to his mother. But then they brought in a camera, and they made him repeat what he'd just said. After they turned the camera off, they told him he could talk to a lawyer. He said he didn't wanna do that. He just wanted his mom. After that, the cops finally read him his rights, and they asked if he understood them. He said he did, although he didn't. He told me he never paid attention in civics class."

Maybe he should have, Michael thought.

"Do you believe him?" he asked his sister. "Because it sounds like bullshit to me."

"I recorded him," Sheila said. "This morning, I watched the footage. He's awfully convincing."

"He's had a decade to convince himself of his version of the truth."

"That's why you and Haggerty hafta talk to me on camera," Sheila said. "Otherwise, it's just gonna be him and the other defendants, and they'll make you guys look terrible."

Michael finished his venti. Every neuron in his body was wired.

"It's easy," he said, and then he caught himself. He was buzzed, so he was afraid of saying something he could never take back.

"What's easy?" Sheila asked.

Michael considered his words. "It's easy to sit here, more than ten years after the fact, and second-guess everything we did. You have no idea what we were up against."

Sheila gulped her Frappuccino and shook her head. He could tell that she, too, was beginning to feel a sugar-caffeine rush.

"I do remember, Michael. The city was in a frenzy. Everybody lost their mind; I know I did. But there was one thing I never understood."

"What was that?"

"Why didn't you charge Felipe Huerta in the first place?"

2

April 17, 2012

He tossed the *Post* onto his desk where all his assistants could see it. The front page had mug shots of the Riverside Five, as they were already being called, with one huge word superimposed in red ink over their pictures: "JACKALS!"

"This oughta make it easy to pick an impartial jury," Jackie Williams said. She was working longer hours on the case than any of his other assistants, so Michael was leaning toward having her at his side while he presented the case.

He kept looking at the front page. Mug shots always made criminals look guiltier than they were.

"I hafta talk to him," he said.

"Who?" Jackie asked.

"The editor of the *Post*. Tell him to tone it down."

"Good luck with that."

Later that day, when he met with the DA, Michael raised the problems the *Post* was causing and suggested setting up a meeting with the man who ran the paper.

"You ever deal with him?" Adam Fishman asked.

Michael admitted he hadn't.

"He's a Brit. I can barely understand him, and when I do, I realize he doesn't know the first thing about New York City."

"Maybe we can explain how things work here," Michael said.

"The Brits put a lot more restrictions on the media than we do," Fishman said. "When guys like him come to this side of the pond, they find the promised land. He thinks things work just fine."

They debated about where to see him. Michael wanted to summon him to One Hogan Place, where he could pack a conference room with members of his staff. The presence of all those lawyers might make the newsman reconsider what he was doing.

"He'll never come here," Fishman said. "He'll know it's a trap."

"Then where do we go?"

"He's a newspaperman. As long as we pick up the tab, he'll show up at any bar we want."

The DA decided on the Yale Club. Michael had never been. It was in a nondescript building on Vanderbilt Avenue across the street from Grand Central, with only a small sign announcing its presence.

You're just supposed to know, Michael said to himself as Fishman showed him in. People in the one percent like to keep their lairs secret. How many times have I passed this place and not noticed what it was?

They waited in the lobby, which was tastefully ornate and dominated by portraits of alums who had reached the presidency. A tuxedo-clad waiter brought Michael sparkling water with lemon. Fishman sipped cognac.

"You drink less than any Irish-Catholic I've ever met," the DA said.

"Red wine at dinner," Michael said. "That's about it. I tended bar through law school. I've seen what too much alcohol does to people."

"Sometimes I don't mind what it does," Fishman said.

A minute later, he nudged Michael on the shoulder and pointed to the foyer. A florid and gray-haired man, five-foot-five on a good day, was handing a wool overcoat to the woman at the coat check. She kept nodding as he gave a string of instructions.

"That's our man," the DA said.

He led Michael toward the editor and called out "Nigel" when they were within earshot.

The Brit looked at them. He wore a deeply blue suit, gleaming white shirt, and scarlet tie.

Fishman introduced Michael to Nigel White, editor of the *Post*. Michael shook hands with him. White said something. Michael had no idea what it was.

"Buy you a drink?" Fishman asked.

Michael thought the Brit replied, "Bloody right."

White nodded approvingly at the understatedly posh surroundings and then at his host. This was years before Adam Fishman's disgrace and suicide. Before those events, the powers in New York deeply approved of everything he did.

The DA led his guests to a dark and oaky barroom where billion-dollar deals were made with the slightest of nods. As they took a table, another tuxedo-clad waiter glided by to ask what they wanted. Michael and Fishman said they were fine. White asked for whisky, neat, then pointed to Michael's sparkling water.

"You're not drinking."

It was more accusation than observation, but at least Michael was beginning to understand what the man was saying.

"I still have work to do," Michael said.

"All the more reason to drink."

Michael tried to decode the accent. He had seen enough BBC shows on public television to know that Nigel White was not Oxbridge.

"How's that case?" White asked. "Giving those buggers what they deserve?"

Michael worked his mouth a bit. He hadn't anticipated answering questions.

"I'm not sure what they deserve," Michael said. "That's up to the judge and jury. But I'm confident with what we have."

The whisky came. White knocked back half of it in one gulp.

"I'll tell you what they bloody well deserve," he said. "Those arseholes should have their bollocks sliced off and shoved down their bloody throats."

The classic punishment administered by wise guys. Michael considered the possibility that Nigel White was in the wrong line of work.

"That's what we need to talk about," Fishman said.

White's thick eyebrows shot up, as if he were a coal miner who'd just won the lottery. "If you go medieval on those shites, you'll have our full support."

"They're in Rikers," Michael said. "That's medieval enough."

"We're worried about the media coverage," Fishman said.

"You should worry more about packs of hooligans rampaging through your parks."

"That was a one-off," the DA said.

White slammed his drink on the glass-topped table in mid-gulp. "I started coming to this city in the Eighties. Dangerous as bloody hell back then. But bloody interesting. In those days, I thought: 'This'd be a great town to work in. Don't know about living in it, though.'"

"This isn't the Eighties," Michael said. Guys like my father were cops back then, he thought. The line between police and criminals was almost nonexistent, which was a big part of the problem.

"All it takes is one incident," White said. "And then—poof!—all your precious progress is gone."

Michael glanced sideways at Fishman, who had been elected during the crack era. On more than one occasion, he had told Michael that when he first took office, he couldn't keep up with all the crimes.

White went on: "I grew up with working-class gits in Leeds. Shites like that are the same all over. They sit on their arses in their flats, loafing on the dole, and they relieve their tedium by causing mayhem. Right now, I wager some other dark-skinned blokes in Harlem and the Bronx are drinking their Ripple and smoking their reefer and thinking it's not such a bad thing, wreaking havoc and raping Caucasians. It's like *A Clockwork* bloody *Orange.*"

Michael tossed that morning's *Post* onto the table. "We wanna get convictions in this case. Headlines like this don't help."

"I'm not here to help," White said.

Michael persisted. "The defense lawyers are gonna wave stuff like this in front of Judge Khan. They'll demand a change of venue, and she might give it to them. The trial could be held in Utica. You want that?"

"It'll cost a few quid to put our people up, but we'll pay it. We're balls to the walls on this story. That's the word from the very top."

White downed the rest of his whisky and again thumped his tumbler on the table. Michael wondered if he was getting ready to leave or expected another drink. The editor turned to him.

"Let me say something to you, young man."

Michael hated being addressed that way.

"This is just between us. In confidence. Big boy talk."

This was a first for Michael: a journalist taking a conversation off the record.

"You're a comer," White said. "I can tell. Rising star. All that shite. That's why you were assigned this case. Am I right?"

"I don't discuss decisions regarding my personnel," Fishman said.

"That means I'm right." White looked straight at Michael. His eyes were rimmed with red. "And I'm sure you're an ambitious fellow. Nothing wrong with ambition. That's how I got out of bloody fucking Leeds."

By now, Michael was regretting his decision not to drink alcohol.

"But if you bollix this case," White said, "you'll be chasing bloody ambulances for a living. I'll make sure of it."

He walked out. Fishman finished his cognac.

"That went well," he said.

* * *

Michael's cell vibrated late that night. He was still at the office and wanted to ignore the call, but the number was Haggerty's.

"We hafta talk," the detective said.

"So talk," Michael said.

"Not over the phone."

That sounded bad.

"I'm at work," Michael said.

The detective showed up fifteen minutes later. His clothes were rumpled, his eyelids were drooping, and he reeked of stale coffee. He mouthed the word "alone," so Michael made his apologies to his assistants, who were reviewing the videotaped confessions, although by now they could repeat the perps' words verbatim.

Michael found a small conference room down the hall. When he flicked the switch, the glare of the fluorescent lights made him squint nearly to the point of shutting his eyes. He noticed that he had a profound headache.

"What is it?" Michael asked.

"Huerta," Haggerty replied.

The two men moved as far from the door as they could and kept their voices as low as possible, as if they were plotting a coup.

"What about him?" Michael asked.

"He refuses to talk."

It had been a week since the crime. The perps were still at Rikers. Based on their confessions, four of them had been indicted.

Haggerty went on. "He's been in the system before. He knows his bullshit rights. His scumbag lawyer is gonna file habeas corpus tomorrow. Then what do we do?"

Michael considered the possibilities. Like most judges, Iffath Khan hated holding suspects who hadn't been charged.

"We can oppose the motion," Michael said. "Say we're still assembling our facts. That could buy us a couple days, and then he might start seeing things our way."

"Huerta will plead to third-degree assault," Haggerty said. "But his lawyer claims he never saw that girl. The lawyer says the first time his client heard of it was when we started bringing it up. He says his client will testify under oath that we tried to coerce him into making a false confession."

"Did you?" Michael asked.

Haggerty blinked. He had the astonished look Goliath must have displayed when David hit him with the slingshot.

"What kinda horseshit question is that?" Haggerty asked.

"The kinda horseshit question I get to ask as the lead prosecutor on this case."

Haggerty blinked a few more times. Michael held his gaze. He had grown up around cops, so he knew their methods of intimidating people.

"They did it," Haggerty said. "They attacked that girl, and at least one of them raped her, and the rest of those cretins stood around while she got beaten within an inch of her life. Are we ever gonna know exactly who did what, and in what order?" The detective shook his head. "It was dark, there were a lotta people around, and a lotta things happened in a short amount of time. But we brought in those dickwads for a reason."

"You didn't answer my question," Michael said.

"We did not coerce those murdering sons of bitches," Haggerty said. "Although maybe we should have."

Michael closed his eyes and let out a long, slow breath. He wanted sleep, but rest was hours away, so he ran through his options. While he was sure that Haggerty and the other detectives did not believe they had coerced the suspects, a judge and jury might interpret their behavior differently. Michael pictured what would happen at trial if Huerta took the stand and denied everything. The other suspects had already recanted their confessions, to widespread ridicule. But the trial was months in the future, so they'd have time to get their stories straight, and if they echoed one another in the courtroom, with Huerta backing them up...

"Things could get complicated if Huerta doesn't confess," Michael said in a thinking-out-loud voice.

"They sure could," Haggerty replied.

"And he's not going to, is he?"

"Only if…" Haggerty said.

"Only if what?"

"Only if the DNA matches his."

Michael thought this over. They had taken DNA swabs from the suspects who'd been indicted. No results yet. But Huerta's lawyer had objected to a DNA test, and Judge Khan ruled that the state couldn't conduct one until the young man had been formally charged.

"So we go to the grand jury and get our bill and take Huerta's DNA," Michael said. "If it matches, we're golden. But what if it doesn't?"

"We don't have the results yet. Maybe it'll match one of those other shitheads. We'd be fine then, too. Huerta was with them. Everyone admits it."

"We've got five guys in custody," Michael said. "How many were rampaging through the park?"

"I dunno."

"You better know when we go to trial, Detective."

Haggerty sighed. "At least a dozen. Maybe twenty. My best estimate right now is fifteen."

"With five guys in custody, we have less than a fifty-fifty chance of coming up with a match."

"I think the DNA is Huerta's," Haggerty said.

"You have any proof?"

"Only every instinct in my body."

Michael remembered something the DA had told him early in his career: Be skeptical when cops rely on their instincts.

* * *

Michael plopped into a chair in the conference room that he and his assistants had turned into their war room. Walls were covered with maps and charts. He and his staff were putting together a timeline of the rampage through the park.

"You look upset," Jackie said.

"I'm surprised I look like anything," Michael said.

"What's wrong?"

He gazed at the ceiling and considered the possibility that it contained lethal amounts of asbestos.

"What if we let Felipe Huerta plead to a lesser charge?" he asked.

The room's low-level hum was replaced by absolute silence. Everyone looked at him as if he had just praised Hitler.

"Why would we do that?" Jackie asked.

"Because he hasn't confessed," Michael said.

"All the other confessions put him at the scene. Some of them identify him as the rapist. Or one of the rapists."

"I'm aware of that," Michael said.

"That should be enough."

"What if it isn't?" Michael asked.

"Why wouldn't it be?"

"The four guys who confessed are all recanting," Michael said. "On the stand, they'll say their confessions were coerced. The cops will say that's bullshit. Juries tend to believe cops, so that's a point for our side. However…"

He let the thought dangle. He wanted to see if one of his bright young aides could figure out the problem.

Jackie spoke up. "If Huerta goes on the stand and denies everything and says the police tried to coerce a confession out of him, and there's no physical evidence tying him to the crime…"

Michael nodded. "The jury might not believe any of the confessions. And then it could get awfully complicated for our side."

Jackie pushed her chair into the table as hard as she could and began to pace around. "But Huerta's the worst one of the bunch. He's got multiple arrests before this, and he instigated the whole goddamn thing. If he hadn't been there that night, those kids woulda gone home to dinner, nobody woulda been attacked, and we wouldn't be spending all these wonderful evenings together."

"You're absolutely right," Michael said. "But I'm not sure, in this instance, if being right is enough."

"We indict him," Jackie said. "Then we do a DNA test."

"What if it doesn't match?" Michael asked.

* * *

The next morning, after two hours' sleep, Michael met the DA just as the sun poked over Brooklyn.

"You look like hell," Fishman said.

"That's an improvement," Michael said before laying out the problems caused by Felipe Huerta's refusal to confess. As Michael talked, Fishman began to look like a man sucking a truckload of lemons.

"What day is it?" the DA asked when Michael was done.

Michael had to think about the answer. "Tuesday."

"Okay," Fishman said. "So we stall on the habeas corpus motion, and we give it till the end of the week."

"Then what?"

"If Felipe Huerta has not confessed by four fifty-five p.m. on Friday, we accept his plea, and then you call Rikers and tell them to let him go."

Michael understood. It was best to release prisoners and bad news just before the weekend, when few people were paying attention.

"And there's one other thing, Michael."

"What is it?"

"If you release that subhuman piece of shit, make sure he never testifies in this case."

Chapter Fifteen

Sheila Devine

September 25, 2023

Since nobody knew where Felipe Huerta was, no one objected to the DA's motion, so Judge Iffath Khan ordered the DNA test conducted as expeditiously as possible.

Sheila spent most of the day on her phone and computer. In between setting up interviews with the two remaining defendants, she kept going back to Huerta because she was convinced she'd find him if she just conducted the right Google search.

Shortly before five, she heard clumping sounds that indicated Dylan was home. The knock on her office door surprised her. Dylan rarely interrupted while she was working.

"What?" she said in what she hoped was a mildly annoyed tone.

"You've gotta sign something."

"Why?"

"Permission form. Field trip."

"Where?"

"Washington."

"When?"

"Wednesday."

"How long?"

"Overnight."

"Have we talked about this?"

"Maybe."

"What's in Washington?"

"The White House. Congress. The Supreme Court."

Sheila gave him a peeved-mom look.

"The Smithsonian, mostly," Dylan said. "School set up something with the African American Museum."

He unzipped his backpack and removed a piece of paper covered with dust and crumbs. Sheila read the form and wondered how long it had cohabitated with her son's detritus. She and Wesley would need to come up with one hundred and five dollars to cover transportation and lodging, so she rooted around in the top desk drawer for the checkbook. She liked paying bills like this the old-fashioned way.

Dylan pointed to the computer screen. "Whatcha doin'?"

"Looking up Felipe Huerta. The man who got away."

She signed the slip.

"You're trying to locate him?" Dylan asked.

"Me and a lotta other people."

He pointed to her chair. "May I?"

Sheila slid to the side and began writing the check.

This is why everyone in my generation has kids, she said to herself. In-house tech support.

"I've found something on him from last year," Dylan said.

Sheila looked at him, startled. "When I was searching, my trail went cold in 2018."

"I do stuff like this all the time, Ma."

"What was he up to last year?" Sheila asked.

"Medicinal marijuana."

Dylan pointed to the screen. An article from a micropublication based in Gowanus included a paragraph about a thirty-year-old named Felipe Huerta complaining that the authorities were giving him a hard time about the weed he needed to relieve his chronic pain just because he had a few minor convictions.

"You sure it's the same guy?" Sheila asked.

"He's the right age," Dylan said. "I like that part about minor convictions. Self-serving bullshit."

Sheila considered reprimanding her son's language, then thought better of it. He was nearly eighteen. Almost a man.

"They keep hauling him up on serious charges," she said. "He keeps pleading them down. If it's the same guy."

"I bet it is."

"And what's that stuff about chronic pain?"

"Probably more bullshit so he can get stoned."

The article listed an email address for the reporter, whose name was Bashir el-Hassan. Sheila kicked Dylan out of the chair, typed out a question, and hit Send.

* * *

She left home early the next morning, but this time, she looked forward to the drive. The Hudson Valley foliage was starting to turn, and when she took the thruway exit, she rolled down her window and breathed crisp air that smelled of apples and freshly cut hay. She would have enjoyed a hike and a chance to buy fruit and vegetables at a roadside stand, but her appointment was at ten, and she was on business, so she had to be prompt.

The front of the Walkill Correctional Facility reminded her of every high school that had been built in New York City in the early part of the twentieth century—forbidding stones, enormous and gray, that sent a message to everyone who stepped through the entrance: Nothing enjoyable will happen here.

No wonder so many students feel like they're in prison, she said to herself. That's the way they're supposed to feel.

She found the main desk, produced her driver's license, told the guard why she was there, and was informed she'd have to wait a few minutes. She found a seat and took out her laptop. Most of the emails were junk or spam, so she deleted them quickly, but she was happy to see, in a message timed just before eight a.m., a response from Bashir el-Hassan.

The reporter wrote that he remembered Felipe Huerta because he made an impression, but not in a good way. The guy was bone-thin, and his eyes were sunken and wild, and his matted hair fell to his shoulders. Whenever he spoke, it sounded as if he had gravel in his throat. At the time of the story, he was living in a homeless shelter near the Fourth Street Basin, and he said he made money by collecting cans and bottles for recycling. El-Hassan said the dude freaked him out—and he was a reporter, so he was used to practically everything. He added that he'd had no contact with Huerta since the article appeared, so he had no idea if he was still at the shelter.

El-Hassan concluded by writing that he had never asked Huerta about the Riverside Runner case, and the guy hadn't volunteered anything, so he was unsure if this was the man Sheila was looking for.

She shot back a reply thanking him but saying, in Lieutenant Columbo fashion, that she had just one more question: What was this chronic pain Huerta was complaining about?

The guard called out that the prisoner was ready. Sheila checked her bag at the desk. Security led her down a blindingly lit hallway before pushing open the door to a book-lined room. A Black male in his early thirties sat in a leather chair with no armrests. He wore thick glasses. Had a thick head of hair. His skin was smooth, and his eyes blazed with the intelligence of a man who was convinced he was the smartest person in the room. If it weren't for the orange jumpsuit, he would have looked like an executive at a tech startup.

He rose when Sheila entered before nodding at her. "Ms. Devine."

She was surprised by the honorific, but she responded in kind. "Mr. Baines."

"I saw the film about your father." He sounded like a guy who narrated science documentaries. "It was quite impressive."

"Thank you." Sheila sat in a chair opposite him and waved her arm around. "What's the deal with this room?"

"It's a library." Howard Baines smiled a bit. "The warden and I are the only ones who use it."

"I hear he lets you conduct science experiments."

"I'm trying to get a master's in chemistry. Given my situation, it's challenging."

"I'd like to film you conducting one of them. If it's all right with you and the warden."

"I don't see why not."

Don't let this guy hijack the movie, Sheila said to herself. Don't become another white filmmaker seduced by an intellectual Black man.

"Prison makes people hard," Sheila said. "If you don't mind me saying, you don't look that way."

"I have my niche in this ecosystem." Now, it was his turn to wave his arm around. "Most of these are law books, and everyone in here has legal issues. I help them out, so they leave the nerd alone."

Sheila nodded. It made sense. Although science was his first love, Howard Baines had survived by becoming a jailhouse lawyer.

"Let's talk about that night," she said.

"April Eleventh, Two Thousand Twelve."

"That's the one."

"What do you wanna know?"

"What the hell were you thinking?"

He screwed his face into the chagrined look she usually saw on her kids as they contemplated their latest blunder.

"I wasn't thinking," he said. "That was my mistake."

Chapter Sixteen

Howard Baines

April 11, 2012

Howard Baines, eyes on the prize, paid no attention to the activity on the soccer field as he headed home. His impending decision about college had crowded out all other thoughts, and he'd narrowed his choices to Brown or Cornell. Neil deGrasse Tyson had gone to Cornell, and although Howard was more interested in chemistry than astronomy, he looked at the man as a role model. As for Brown, well, going to a college named for a color appealed to his sense of humor.

When he got back to the apartment, provided his internet was working, he'd take another look at the schools' websites. He had to choose within a week.

All those rich white kids I'll be dealing with, he said to himself. Most of them have never talked to a Black person, except maybe a maid. They'll look at me and freak. Maybe I should play up my Urkel vibe.

Someone shouted his name, so he stopped, turned, looked. A kid named Benji was leaning against a chain-link fence.

"I called you three times," Benji said. "What's a bro gotta do to get your attention?"

"You've got it now," Howard said.

Benji motioned behind him. Howard saw a bunch of kids kicking around a soccer ball. The sun was low, air already chilly.

"Wanna play?"

The question seemed ridiculous. Howard's lack of athletic ability was notorious in the neighborhood. He made that point to Benji.

"We need one more guy to even up the sides," Benji said. "You won't hafta do much. Just hang back on defense and kick the ball up the field whenever it gets near you."

It sounded easy, and Howard was secretly flattered about being asked to join. He took his position and did what Benji had told him. As the game unfolded it was fun for the most part, a friendly match between guys from the neighborhood, although one player on the other team was out of place. He looked Latin, and his eyes burned with the intensity of a man who regarded even the slightest trifle as a matter of life and death, and he ran around the field like he was hopped on the world's most potent amphetamine, and he kept barking at the kids on both sides whenever they did something that angered him, which occurred frequently. At one point, the ball came in Howard's direction, and he ran toward it, but he could see the guy—Howard had started thinking of him as Madman—running his way with the fury of a jihadist. For a second Howard considered just letting him get the ball, then chided himself for being wimpy. He ran toward it and reached it a second before Madman did, drew back his leg, and kicked it as hard as he could toward the other team's goal. He was pleased with how far the ball traveled. He had figured out the angle and trajectory precisely.

And the adrenaline, he told himself. There really is a scientific basis to it.

But then Madman was literally in his face, the veins in his neck and forehead close to bursting through his skin.

"You fuckin' four-eyed maricón! What the fuck you doing here anyway?"

I live near here, Howard felt like saying. Why are you here? I've never seen you before.

An instant later, Madman bolted down the field after the ball, arms and legs flailing in a manner Howard thought wildly inefficient. Benji jogged over and put his hand on Howard's shoulder.

"You okay?" he asked.

Howard pointed up the field. "Who's the jerk?"

"Somebody's friend."

"Whose?"

"Dunno."

"Hard to believe a guy like that has friends."

Benji trotted back to his position. Howard decided not to take the maricón insult personally because Madman was screaming it at everyone. The dude sprinted all over like he was the Energizer Bunny, even as the other guys got tired. Night crept in, and the air went from cool to cold, and when the lights over the field started flickering, the players reached an unconscious but unanimous decision that it was time to end the game.

Howard told himself to go home. His mother worked nights cleaning office buildings in Midtown, but she always left him something for dinner. She'd grown up in the South and was partial to soul food, and Howard hoped to find fried chicken in the fridge.

"C'mon, you pussies, let's keep going," Madman said.

Two kids walked away. Madman called them maricóns.

Howard approached Benji and, in the softest voice he could manage, said he believed it was a good time to get going.

"He's gonna call you a maricón," Benji said.

"Takes one to know one," Howard said.

The two of them cracked up.

"Fuck you laughin' at?" Madman said. "What's so fuckin' funny? Fuckin' maricóns."

"Told ya," Benji whispered.

Howard laughed again. Madman walked straight at him.

"I oughta fuckin' pop you right now, you fuckin' four-eyed fa—."

Benji spoke up. "Take it easy, bro."

Madman whirled. "Stickin' up for your fuckin' boyfriend? You got some queer bullshit goin' on?"

Two more guys slipped from the group and walked into the night.

"Maricóns!" Madman bellowed. He spun around three hundred and sixty degrees. He's a dervish, Howard thought. "You're all a buncha fuckin' pansies!"

A guy behind Howard spoke up. "I ain't no fuckin' pansy."

Madman headed toward him. "Prove it, man. Fuckin' prove it!"

"Waddya wanna do?"

Madman waved his arm toward the river. "Fuckin' park's right over there, bro. Let's go raise some hell."

A few guys cackled and said it was a great idea. They joined Madman as he set out. Most of the others engaged in a collective shrug before following.

Benji and Howard lingered on the field.

"This will not end well," Benji said.

"Waddya gonna do?" Howard asked.

"Go home."

Benji headed toward Broadway, and a voice in Howard's head said that was the smart thing to do, but when he saw the group moving west, expanding as if it were a cancerous organism about to metastasize, he thought about the damage it could do unless someone controlled it.

* * *

"Can I call you Howard?"

The detective, name of Boyle, pulled a chair so tight they were sitting catty-corner. He put a Styrofoam cup on the table. Howard smelled burnt coffee.

The detective motioned to the container. "I'm on my fourth or fifth cup. I've been at this so long I've lost count."

I've got to explain, Howard said to himself. I've got to make him understand why I did what I did.

"I've looked over your background," Boyle said. "You're not the kinda guy we usually get in here."

"I'd like to talk to my mother," Howard said. "I'm gonna have a hard time telling her how I wound up in this situation."

"We'll let you talk to her. But there are some things I wanna ask you."

Howard had never been run in before, but he knew he should be careful around cops. "Like what?"

"Like why you were there."

This is my chance, Howard told himself. "Well, when I saw those guys heading for the park with that crazy kid leading them—I found out his name is Felipe—"

"Felipe Huerta. He's in custody. Was he the ringleader?"

"You could call him that. Yeah."

The detective nodded. "Felipe's been around the track a few times. Keep talking."

"When I saw them all going toward the park, I was afraid something bad was gonna happen, and I felt like I couldn't just let them go ahead, so I ran after them and joined up and tried to keep things from getting outta hand."

"But things did get outta hand, Howard."

"I know. And I'm sorry about that. I really am. But it woulda been worse if I hadn't been there. And this other kid, too—I think his name was Roberto..."

Maybe I can talk my way out of this, Howard said to himself. I might just get a slap on the wrist.

"Roberto Linares. We have him as well."

"We were kinda like the voices of reason. If we hadn't been there, Huerta was so crazy, he mighta killed someone."

"Well, Howard, that's just the problem." The detective's voice sounded sad, the way his mom's did a year ago when she told him that his grandmother had died.

"What're you talking about?" Howard asked.

"The girl," the detective said.

"What girl?"

"The girl you guys attacked. The one who's almost dead at Columbia-Presbyterian. They don't think she's gonna make it, Howard. It's amazing she's still alive."

"I have no idea what you're talking about."

The detective hung his head. He looked exhausted. Howard felt like telling him to take a nap. He'd done a study on this topic for one of his classes, and it confirmed his suspicion that people functioned badly when they lacked proper rest.

"You're a bright guy, Howard, and I'm surprised you're trying to bullshit me like this. We've got your pals singing like opera stars in the other rooms. A couple of them say you were the one who attacked her."

Howard felt himself getting indignant. "I've never attacked anyone in my life."

The door to the room banged open, and a second white man walked in. A gold shield was pinned to his ill-fitting sports jacket, and Howard figured he was another detective. This cop was all nervous tension, a guy who did not need caffeine to maintain wired-up energy, although he, too, was slurping from a Styrofoam cup.

The new detective glanced around the room before stopping beside Boyle and jerking his thumb at Howard.

"Four Eyes here say anything interesting?"

"Not yet," Boyle said.

Howard stared at the new guy's shield. His name was Haggerty, and he paraded around the table before parking his butt only inches from where Howard was sitting.

"You are in a shitload of trouble, my young friend," he said.

"I don't know anything about that girl," Howard said.

Haggerty smirked at Boyle. "I haven't said anything about a girl. Did you hear me say anything about a girl?"

"I told him about her," Boyle said.

Haggerty folded his arms across his chest. "Look at me."

Howard stared ahead but looked at nothing. Instead, he thought back to the park and his efforts to run when he heard the police sirens. But he was slow, and it was pitch dark, and when he came to a ten-foot-high chain-link fence, he knew there was no way he could climb it.

Haggerty leaned forward a bit, drew his arm back, and slapped Howard on the ear.

"I'm talking to you, kid. Look at me."

Howard thought of telling the detective that his career was over. But then he realized it would be his word against two cops, and there was no question about whom jurors and prosecutors would believe.

Howard looked.

"I've got a woman in the hospital who's gonna die any minute," Haggerty said. "I've got a bunch of canaries scattered all over this station house, chirping their heads off. It's amazing, my young friend—everyone admits he was there, but no one actually says he did anything to her. It's always somebody else. A couple of them even say it was you."

Christ, Howard said to himself, maybe I didn't notice a couple of guys breaking away from the group. I thought we all stayed together, but things got wild for a time, and it was hard to keep track of everybody.

"I never touched her," Howard told the detective.

"I dunno—" Haggerty glanced at the notes Boyle had been writing "—Howard. That's your name? Howard?"

"Uh-huh."

"I take one look at you, Howard, and I'll be frank—I see a young man who hasn't had his first taste of pussy. But you're curious. You're seventeen. Who isn't at that age?"

Howard shifted in his seat. He'd never had much success with girls. Their thoughts and desires were life's most impenetrable mystery.

"So here's what I think happened," Haggerty said. "You and your friends are running amok and then you see this woman jogging along, she's alone, her running tights are clinging to her body. Your imagination gets fired up, and you tell yourself you're never gonna have an opportunity as good as this." The detective paused. "Tell me if I'm wrong."

Howard thought over Haggerty's scenario. "It didn't happen that way. Couldn't've happened that way."

"Then how did it happen?"

Howard Baines licked his lips. He suddenly realized his throat was parched. Words came out in croaks.

"Can I have a glass of water?"

"After you tell us what happened, Howard."

Howard leaned back in his chair. These men would never let him leave unless he told them something they wanted to hear, and he needed that glass of water.

"Musta been Huerta," he said.

Chapter Seventeen

Michael Devine

1

September 27, 2023

His iPhone lit up shortly after ten. Haggerty calling.

"Whazzup?"

"You sitting down?"

Michael was in the rear seat of a black car heading to an auditorium near the stock exchange for his speech to the Lower Manhattan Business Council. Beside him, Rachel reviewed the final draft on her MacBook.

"No match, huh?"

"You're psychic."

"If I were psychic," Michael said, "I wouldn't have agreed to the test."

He put his iPhone in his pocket before letting out a long sigh of disappointment.

During the Riverside Runner trial, when Michael first gained a measure of public attention, a writer for *The New Yorker* described him as imperturbable. He had never thought of himself that way, but he liked the image it conveyed and, from then on, always tried to maintain a calm façade in the face of disaster.

Right now, however, he felt perturbed.

Rachel looked at her Android. "Shit."

"What is it?"

"The news about Huerta is trending already on Twitter, or X, or whatever the hell Elon Musk is calling it these days. I bet it's all over Facebook, too."

Michael's daily events were posted on his campaign website, so everyone in the media knew where he was headed. He could duck in through a side entrance, but that would make it look as if he were trying to hide. In any event, New York One was going to film his speech, and then someone was going to ask him a question about what had just happened. Probably several questions.

"What're they saying on social media?" he asked.

"That you're in big trouble. But on social media, everybody is always in big trouble."

Michael eased back against the headrest. "Ortega's gonna file more motions. He has new grounds, and if Judge Khan sees things his way, this case will get a lot more complicated."

"There'll be a crowd in front of the building," Rachel said. "Some smartass reporter will try to ask a gotcha question."

"I'll respond, but I won't say anything."

"You sure you wanna do that? We haven't had a chance to think this through."

"I know what I'd like to say. Not that I can actually say it."

"What's that?"

"As many as two dozen kids were rampaging through the park that night. So, as many as two dozen kids coulda been involved in the attack on Marie Antolini. The cops apprehended five. We charged four. Odds are the bastard who raped her got away. That's certainly what the DNA indicates, and I am really, really sorry about that. But the guys we convicted—they were accessories, and they got what they deserved."

The car swung onto Liberty Street. One block ahead, Michael saw the cameras and microphones that indicated a media encampment.

The driver, a turbaned Sikh, pointed to the crowd. "You want to avoid them, Boss? I can go around the corner, let you and the lady off there."

Michael knew a little about Sikhs: Tough men, warriors both for and against the British, fighters who never shrank from an enemy. But even they feared the media.

"Stop here. We'll walk up to them. It'll make a good visual."

"Whatever you say, Boss." The driver motioned toward the reporters. "Those jerks—they just stir up trouble. They have no idea about the real world. There are bad people out there who do bad things, and they must be punished."

"You sound like a man who's seen a lotta the world," Michael said. "Where are you from?"

Always a good question to ask in New York. The answer could be anywhere from New Jersey to New Delhi.

"Punjab, Boss. But I love it here. I became a citizen last year."

"That's great. Congratulations."

Michael shook his hand, got out of the car, and held the door open for his wife. The sun had risen above the tops of the skyscrapers, and Michael thought about flipping on his shades, but his top media consultant had told him that a candidate who wore sunglasses came across as untrustworthy. Just look at the president's approval ratings.

Michael guided Rachel by her elbow. Confident, protective, loving—this will come across well, he said to himself.

"There they are."

Reporters and camera operators stirred like locusts, getting ready to descend upon a tasty piece of vegetation. Michael stopped just before colliding with a boom mic. Rachel stepped to his side and gazed at him with the adoring look of a loyal political spouse.

Shouts and questions mingled into one screeching noise as the media coagulated. Michael knew what they wanted. As he waited for quiet, he wondered if he was live on New York One.

"Like you," he said, "I've just heard the news about the DNA results on Felipe Huerta. My initial reaction is this: The men who were convicted in the Riverside Park case were all at the scene and were, at the very least, aiding and abetting a horrific crime. I'm deeply sorry we've never gotten a

DNA match. Perhaps someday we will, and then we can finally put to rest the few remaining questions about the terrible events of that night." He paused. It was always good to wait a few seconds before delivering the exit line. "In the meantime, this changes nothing about the case."

* * *

The audience was composed of business people who believed rampant street crime was the natural condition of New York City unless the lower classes were whipped like recalcitrant mules. Michael knew he could tack to the right with this crowd, so he did, but he also mentioned new approaches to law enforcement as well as respecting the rights and dignity of everyone in Manhattan. When he was done, he received the round of warm applause that members of the elite always give to a candidate they perceive as a winner.

He glanced to the wings. Rachel tapped her watch. His next meeting was at noon with the Women's Empowerment Association in Chelsea, where he would reveal his plans to strengthen the sex crimes unit. He wanted to be on time, and it was getting close to lunch hour, so he had to build in a fudge factor because of the traffic.

"I wanna ask a question."

A man rose near the back. Michael squinted through his reading glasses to get a good look. The man looked in his late sixties, with gray hair and a paunch. His suit was blue, his shirt white, and his tie flaming red. Even from a distance, Michael detected the American flag pin in his lapel.

I've met this guy, Michael said to himself. He does business with Jacob. Of course, a lot of people do business with Jacob.

Michael felt like saying he had to leave, but the men in this audience believed their questions had to be answered whenever they posed them.

"I have time for one question." Michael forced a smile. "So I guess you're it."

"I know your father-in-law. He's been a great businessman for a long time."

"He agrees with you." Michael congratulated himself for getting some laughs from a usually humorless group, then suddenly found the name he'd been looking for. "You're Mr. Kaminsky, right? Seymour Kaminsky?"

"I was at your wedding. I've finally gotten over the fact that you stole one of our best girls."

Michael glanced to the side again. Rachel cast her eyes to the ceiling, as if she wanted to float away.

"What's on your mind, Mr. Kaminsky?"

"I wanna talk about stop and frisk."

Uh-oh, Michael thought.

"You've lived in this city a long time, just like me," Kaminsky said. The man's foghorn voice did not need a microphone. "You remember what it was like in the Seventies and Eighties, even into the Nineties, when thugs ruled the streets. I was afraid to go to the theater with my wife because Times Square was a cesspool. But we cut the crime rate there, and in a lotta other places, because we were tough. We did a lotta things that weren't pretty, but they were necessary, and we all know the city got a helluva lot better."

Murmurs of assent around the room.

"But now we've got all this politically correct bullshit, and things are backsliding, and New York is on the verge of becoming a hellhole again."

He spat out his next words as if they were the vilest epithets in the English language: "Defund the police. Abolish prisons. Black Lives Matter."

Michael noticed spittle spewing from the corners of the man's mouth, which reminded him that some folks should wear masks all the time.

"The criminals are rampaging again, but the judges say the cops can't use stop and frisk anymore. Now my wife is scared to go out after dark, and I don't blame her. I wanna know what you're gonna do about it."

Michael took a long sip of water while waiting for the applause to stop.

"The district attorney's office has little to do with stop and frisk," Michael said. "That's a matter for the mayor and the police department."

Kaminsky's face reddened in the classic manner of a business executive getting ready to upbraid a subordinate.

"That's a dodge, Mike, and you know it."

"I'm not opposed to stop and frisk," Michael said. "But the appeals courts have problems with the way the policy was implemented. And when the appeals courts have problems, you have to address them. I'm certainly open to working with the mayor and the police department on new techniques that the judges will uphold."

"There was nothing wrong with the old policy," Kaminsky said. "The city was safer."

Seymour Kaminsky was one of those men who had risen high in the world because he refused to take No for an answer—a trait that was often praised, but which Michael detested.

"I've been dealing with these issues a long time," Michael said, "so there's one thing I know: When the courts say you have to change something, you have to change it. And that creates a challenge. How do we balance people's rights against their need for a safe city? That's a problem, but it's surmountable, and I look forward to tackling it."

His answer generated tepid applause.

"I know you're caught between a rock and a hard place on this," Kaminsky said.

Michael wanted to tell the man to sit down and shut up, but he remembered that Seymour Kaminsky had given his campaign the maximum amount of money allowed by law.

"We all follow the news," Kaminsky said. "We know the kind of crap Rolando Ortega is pulling on the Riverside Park case. You did great work back then, and everyone in New York owes you a debt. The whole thing should be dead and buried, but he's dragging it into the open just so he can shake down the city. People like him are friggin' disgusting."

Michael raised his hands in an attempt to quiet the vigorous round of clapping.

"Rolando Ortega is a good lawyer, and he's doing what good lawyers are supposed to do—zealously represent the interests of his client." Michael paused for effect. "It just so happens that his client is guilty."

This produced the loudest applause of anything Michael had said, and he hoped that he had at last mollified Seymour Kaminsky. But the color in the man's face deepened to crimson. Something had enraged him, and he was about to let everyone know exactly what it was.

"This goes back to my point," Kaminsky said. "Those—"

He stopped as he searched for the epithet he wanted, and Michael feared he was about to spew the worst one of all.

"—animals he's representing." The moisture cascading from his lips made his flag pin gleam under the auditorium lights. "They're savages, and they deserve to be locked up like wild beasts, and we should never hear from them ever again. And if the police had just stopped and frisked them before they went to that park, nothing woulda happened to that poor girl. But the cops couldn't do anything until it was too late because of all this namby-pamby, politically correct horseshit."

Michael waited a long minute for the applause to subside.

You know one thing and one thing only, he said silently to the man who had just addressed him. You know your business. You have no knowledge of anything outside it, but Americans have this weird belief that anyone who's made a lot of money is a seer about everything.

"With all due respect, Mr. Kaminsky, I prosecuted those young men, and it was one of the saddest duties of my career. They were not, are not, savages and animals. They made a horrible mistake, and they are paying for it, but we should never lose sight of anybody's humanity."

In front of a goo-goo group, this line would have received passionate applause, but the members of the Lower Manhattan Business Council were absolutely quiet.

To these people, Michael reminded himself, the world's teeming masses are extras in their movie of life.

"Yeah, yeah, yeah," Kaminsky said. "I know you've gotta say that baloney."

He was not giving up. Men like Seymour Kaminsky never gave up. Michael sensed his poll numbers dropping by the second.

"It's not baloney," Michael said. "I'm running to be the district attorney of everyone in Manhattan—not just one slice of the population."

"If you took a survey of everyone in Manhattan," Kaminsky said, "you'd find that most of them agree with me. And we should put Ortega in jail, too."

This prompted vigorous applause and even the stamping of some designer shoes. Kaminsky finally sat down. Michael sipped ice water until the room was quiet.

Time to get in the last word, he told himself.

"I understand that emotions are running high," he said. "The Riverside Park case is still a scar on this city, and we had a setback today. Despite that, I'm confident that this matter will be resolved quickly."

He paused, then raised his voice the way he sometimes did in front of jurors when he was afraid he was losing their attention.

"Everything we did was proper and legal and ethical. Everything. The correct verdicts were rendered. No matter what the professional second-guessers keep saying, those men were properly convicted, and they belong in prison."

Even Seymour Kaminsky rose to his feet as raucous applause filled the room. In the wings, Rachel pointed to her watch and motioned him to join her.

"New York One cut to you live," she said as they began walking down a corridor.

"How did I look?"

"Forceful but empathetic. It's a neat trick."

Twenty feet ahead, standing by a door that would get them out of the building, Michael saw Seamus O'Toole—Marie Antolini's former professor, now a free-floating media savant. He had advised winning political candidates in every English-speaking country, and at his father-in-law's insistence, Michael had brought him into his campaign as a consultant.

"I got here as soon as I heard about the DNA test," O'Toole said. "A shame you couldn't pin it on that creep."

"I got in front of the cameras because I didn't wanna look like I was hiding," Michael said.

"That was the right move."

"How do we play it from here?"

Before O'Toole could answer, Michael heard his wife utter two words with clarity and conviction: "That fucker."

Rachel stared at her Android as if it had turned radioactive.

"What now?" O'Toole asked.

"Rolando Ortega's on New York One," Rachel said. "He says the DNA result means the case should be reopened. Asserting the innocence of the men who were convicted and all that crap."

"He's focusing on the criminals," O'Toole said, "and forgetting about the victim."

"That's a good point," Michael said.

O'Toole looked straight at him. "That's the point you should be making."

Rachel squeezed her husband's wrist. "Like Daddy said—worth every penny."

"People need to remember that Marie is a real person," O'Toole said. "They should know what she was like before she was attacked—a truly remarkable talent. She was one of those people who really stood out. I'm sorry I lost contact with her."

"We're still in touch," Michael said. "Mostly by email."

"How's she doing?" O'Toole asked.

"As well as can be expected."

"The next time you write her, tell her I said hello."

2

June 1, 2012

"You sure about this?"

Brendan Haggerty's shoulder brushed against Michael's as they strode down the hospital hallway.

"I'm not sure about it at all," Michael said. "But you know how it goes. Excrement flows downhill, and we're at the bottom of Mount Everest."

Nurses, technicians, and doctors all nodded at Michael, but the nonwhite ones took a step back when they saw the badge pinned to Haggerty's jacket.

The prosecutor and the detective stopped a few feet from Marie Antolini's door. Voices came from her room.

"Who's in there?" Haggerty asked.

"She has visitors sometimes," Michael said. "Friends from school. Sometimes, one of her teachers. They're trying to help."

The doctors were saying she could go home in a week or two. Michael had doubts.

He leaned his head in and saw a single tube running into Marie's forearm. Rajeev Dalweet and Gloria Estevez stood by the bed. Haggerty followed Michael into the room, bringing tension with him. Michael made the introductions. Rajeev stood perfectly still, as if he were afraid any movement would provoke a beating, while Gloria eyed the cop as if she were certain he was about to plant evidence.

"I'd like to ask Ms. Antolini a few questions," Haggerty said.

"We'll be on our way," Rajeev said.

He was out of the room in a nanosecond. Gloria sauntered behind, glaring at the detective, who glared back.

Michael stopped by Marie's bed. Gauze still covered her nose, which plastic surgeons had reconstructed.

"Marie, do you remember Detective Haggerty?"

She squinted. "We've talked before?"

Haggerty stepped toward her. "Shortly after you got here, Ms. Antolini. It was a few weeks ago."

"I have trouble keeping my thoughts straight. Everything gets jumbled. Things come back to me, but then I lose them again."

Michael raised his eyebrows to Haggerty and silently said, *Good luck.*

Haggerty stooped. His face was close to hers. "Can I call you Marie?"

"That's my name. At least that's what they tell me."

Michael winced.

"I wanna talk to you about that night, Marie." Haggerty had shed the bad-cop toughness from his voice. Now, he was a father confessor. "The night you were attacked."

"I'm sorry, but I don't remember anything."

"Let's try something else, Marie," Haggerty said. "Can you recall any details about that day? The morning? The afternoon?"

She squinted. Thinking hard. "I was in a building at some point. A building with ivy on its sides."

"You were going to school," Haggerty said. "You were studying journalism."

"I was in front of a camera," she said. "I was sitting down. There were lights in my eyes. I was reading something."

For the first time, Michael felt encouraged about her memory. In the timeline of Marie Antolini's day that his office and the cops had assembled, he knew that she had spent an hour and a half in a television lab working on a practice broadcast. He had watched the tape himself several times. Although she was still a student, she'd delivered the news with professional poise.

"That's good, Marie," Haggerty said. "Real good. Because that happened in the afternoon. It was one of your classes. Do you remember what you did after that?"

She looked wide-eyed at Michael with a silent plea: *Tell me what to say.*

"I was in a room. A kitchen." She scrunched her face as much as her surgeries would allow. The effort of recall was all-consuming. "I was making something, then eating it. Lettuce, tomatoes, a little turkey thrown in..."

Michael nodded. This also gibed with the timeline. Several people saw her go back to her room. After the attack, when detectives checked out her apartment in Graduate Housing, they found a washed-out colander in the dish drainer.

"You're doing great, Marie," Haggerty said. "You had dinner after your class. Did you do anything after dinner? Did you work on your computer? Did you send any emails? Did you talk to anyone, either in person or on the phone?"

The subdued rush of air that came out of her reminded Michael of a deflating tire. "I believe I was on my computer awhile. I don't really remember what I did, though."

This was consistent with the timeline. At 8:23 p.m., Marie had sent an email to Seamus O'Toole about her end-of-semester assignment.

"You're remembering just fine, Marie," Haggerty said. "You sent one of your professors an email. After that, do you recall changing into tights and a T-shirt? Putting on your jogging shoes?"

Her email to O'Toole had said she was going for a run in Riverside Park. She hoped he would respond by the time she got back. Time was so short now, with the school year coming to an end.

Marie nodded a bit. "It was dark, I think. I didn't know the temperature, but it was cool that day. I believe I put on a jacket."

"You did, Marie. We found one only a few feet from where we found you."

"I had earbuds. I musta been carrying an iPod. I was listening to music and running."

"This is all great, Marie," Haggerty said. "You're doing really well. Do you remember what you were listening to on your iPod?"

"Matchbox Twenty. I like their singer. He's cute. I wish I could remember his name."

"Rob Thomas," Michael said.

Marie smiled. "Thank you, Michael."

Haggerty resumed his gentle but intense questioning. "Okay, Marie, you're doing fantastic. You're in the park. You're athletic, so you're running along and listening to Matchbox Twenty on your iPod. Is any of this helping you form a picture in your mind?"

She closed her eyes, and for a moment Michael feared the trauma that would overcome her if she suddenly remembered all the details of the attack.

I do not want her to go through that, he said to himself. I can't ask that of her.

"It was dark," she said, "but I could see bits of the river through the trees. Then I blacked out."

"What made you black out?" Haggerty asked.

"Something hit me from behind. I didn't see what it was."

That was consistent with her injuries. Blunt force trauma in the rear of her skull, the medical people said, probably caused by an object like a lead

126

pipe.

"Do you recall anything after being hit?" Haggerty asked.

"I'm trying to think. It's hard for me."

"I understand, Marie. Take your time."

They all remained frozen like Kabuki performers for several of the longest minutes Michael had ever endured. He heard gurneys being wheeled in the hallway and nurses asking each other when their next break was.

"It was like a dream," she said. "I don't even know if it was real or if I imagined it."

"Tell me what it was, Marie."

"I felt like I was floating over a bed of grass and mud. But somebody must've been dragging me."

"Did you see who was doing it?"

She gulped. "A dark form. Male. Glimpsed from behind. I heard a voice, or maybe voices, but I couldn't make out the words. That's all I remember."

She shook her head. A tear leaked from the corner of her eye.

"I don't even know if it's real. I'm so sorry."

Chapter Eighteen

Sheila Devine

1

September 28, 2023

"We will file a motion for a new trial," Rolando Ortega said. As Sheila mentally ran through all the footage she'd already shot, she doubted she could cram everything into two hours. Christ, she thought, I hadn't planned on making *The Sorrow and the Pity*.

"The DA will oppose it," Tamika Riley said.

"The authorities never admit error," Ortega said, "or even concede that a mistake is possible. It would destroy their conception of themselves."

The phones kept ringing. Dolores told the callers that Señor Ortega was in conference.

"What grounds do we cite for the new trial?" Tamika asked. "The professors always tell us that an appeals court will assume the judge and jury applied the facts and the law correctly. We hafta prove that an egregious mistake was made."

Ortega went into Socratic Method mode. "What egregious mistake did the prosecution and the police make?"

"Becoming prosecutors and police in the first place?" Tamika asked.

"Clever girl," Ortega said. "But that won't get the appeals court to see things our way."

Dolores ignored the ringing phones for a moment and said, "The request for a DNA test means the authorities still have doubts about their own case."

"There's a reason Dolores has worked with me so long," Ortega told Tamika. "But we won't use the word 'doubts.' It's too weak. Our position is that the request for a DNA test to link the crime to Felipe Huerta, and the subsequent failure of that test, undermine the entirety of the prosecution's case. The physical evidence places none of these men at the scene of the crime, so the only proper recourse is a new trial."

"I better get working on that motion," Tamika said. "Is there anything else you want me to do?"

Ortega nodded. "Find Felipe Huerta."

* * *

Joel Moscowitz nursed the ginormous latte permanently attached to his hand while he sat beside Sheila at the editing console in her home office.

"This is great stuff," he said as he watched the scene in Ortega's office.

Sheila tried to hide her surprise as she thanked him. Praise from Joel was as rare as a Happy Ramadan greeting from Tucker Carlson.

"This is going even better than I thought." Joel's free hand started jerking as he slugged down some of his latte—the telltale sign of a caffeine-induced brainstorm. "Everyone is talking about this case. It'd be great if we could post something while it's still hot."

"I'm not even sure what I have yet," Sheila said. "I have no idea where it's gonna end up."

"That's okay," Joel said. "Rough-cut some stuff right now, and post the best five minutes you have. We'll call it a work-in-progress. Put it on YouTube. If we promote it the right way, it'll go viral."

Sheila pushed herself away from the console. She'd been staring at the screen for hours, and everything in front of her was a blur.

"I hate to tip my hand," she said.

"What part of 'work-in-progress' don't you understand?"

Sheila tried to stretch. She felt tight all over and feared it was too late to schedule a yoga class.

"I'd like to talk to Felipe Huerta myself," she said. "Of course, if I do that, I better make sure my Mace still works."

"Keep in touch with Ortega's intern," Joel said. "See if she finds him."

"I wanna get to him before she does. If Ortega's people talk to him first, he'll start remembering events the way they want him to, instead of the way they actually occurred."

"You have any idea where to find him?"

Sheila told him about the emails she had exchanged with Bashir el-Hassan. Joel chugged his latte. He had another appointment, and he was always fifteen minutes late for everything.

"You didn't tell Ortega about this, did you?" he asked.

"Of course not."

Joel glanced at an image on the screen of Tamika Riley before pointing to Sheila. "Who's the clever girl?"

* * *

She booked the last spot in the five p.m. class at the Y, squeezed into her tights, and fetched her mat. As she headed for the door, she checked her iPhone for email. Most of it was spam, but there was a message from Bashir el-Hassan, and she opened it outside while she dodged pedestrians, dogs, and baby strollers.

Felipe Huerta, el-Hassan wrote, claimed to suffer from headaches that were chronic and debilitating. There was a chance, the reporter added, that Huerta was prone to migraines. It was also possible that Huerta had a serious but undiagnosed malady—brain tumors, for example. But, given the man's personal history, el-Hassan cautioned Sheila that everything the man had asserted about his health could be complete bullshit.

There was one more thing el-Hassan wanted her to know: He was reasonably certain he had seen Huerta in the neighborhood recently, pushing a shopping cart full of bottles and cans while shouting obscenities at the world in Spanglish. El-Hassan had no idea if Huerta recognized him, and the guy scared him so much he made no attempt to approach.

2

September 29, 2023

After making sure her Mace functioned properly, Sheila took the subway to Gowanus. The stench from the canal reminded her of Brooklyn's toxic past.

She began her search at the homeless shelter near the Fourth Street Basin.

"Waddya want?" asked the security guard, a scratchy-voiced Black man with graying hair and a potbelly.

"I'd like to talk to the director of this place," Sheila said.

He looked at Sheila as if she'd just beamed down from the mother ship. "Where you from?"

Sheila took her card from her bag and placed it in front of him. "I'm a filmmaker."

"Hollywood?"

"Documentaries."

"Oh."

Sheila went on: "I'm working on a project. Something I discovered led me here. I've got a few questions to ask."

"You can't film here," the guard said. His tag said Mandell, and Sheila wondered if that was his first or last name. His tone veered into the righteousness she associated with preachers. "We protect the residents' privacy jealously."

"I'm delighted to hear that," Sheila said. "I'm not here to film any of your residents. I just wanna ask your director a few questions. Shouldn't take more than five minutes."

Mandell gave her the hard stare she recognized from so many African Americans. Black people were convinced—with considerable justification, Sheila reminded herself—that white people were always trying to snow

131

them.

"Our director is a busy lady. I'll give her this—" Mandell held up Sheila's card as if it bore Covid "—but I have no idea when she'll be able to see you, or if she'll be able to see you at all."

"That's all I can ask." Sheila glanced around. There was no place to sit in the foyer. "It's a nice day. I'll wait outside."

She stood on the steps, took out her iPhone, and tried not to inhale too deeply as she went through her email. When she checked her news feed, she noticed that Nelson Hernandez, Michael's main opponent, had gained four points in the New York One tracking poll.

"Ms. Devine."

At the top of the concrete landing stood a well-coiffed Black woman with straight hair and carefully applied makeup right off the cover of *Ebony*. Sheila guessed that her dark blue dress, accessorized with a chiffon scarf, was from Bloomingdale's.

That is not a homeless person, Sheila thought.

"That's me. And you are?"

"Hortense LeBeau. I am the director of this facility. You said you had some questions you wanted to ask me."

I know what I wanna ask now, Sheila said to herself. How can you afford an outfit like that on a civil service salary?

"As my card says, I'm a filmmaker."

"I remember the movie you made about the soldiers with PTSD. That VA facility is run by a dear friend of mine. You showed a great deal of sensitivity."

Unprepared for recognition and praise, Sheila struggled to say something that possessed a smidgen of intelligence. "Thank you."

"Would you like to film me?"

Sheila did a double take. "You don't even know what I'm gonna ask."

"I'm not afraid of the media."

Sheila started recording with her iPhone. She described her project and said she was looking for a man named Felipe Huerta.

"When he was here, I recognized Mr. Huerta's name from the reports

132

about the Riverside Park case," Hortense LeBeau said. "I wondered if it was the same gentleman."

That's a word I've never heard anyone use to describe him, Sheila thought.

"He was…" Hortense LeBeau cast her eyes to the sky. Sheila noticed the use of the past tense. "Troubled."

"How so?"

"We have certain rules. Procedures and processes. He had difficulty following them." Hortense LeBeau paused. "All. Of. Them."

"Does that mean Mr. Huerta is no longer living here?"

"Correct."

I have to keep looking, Sheila said to herself.

"Are there any incidents involving Mr. Huerta that stand out in your mind?"

"We have families here," Hortense LeBeau said. "A lot of single mothers. So there are many children, especially little ones. You know how kids can be."

Sheila nodded. She did know.

Hortense LeBeau continued: "One night, this sweet young woman named Esmerelda was trying to calm her twins. They were about a year old, and they were fussing up a storm. Esmeralda was doing her best, but sometimes things don't go the way you want."

Sheila remembered one night when Dylan, then six months old, was especially inconsolable. At three in the morning, as she got out of bed for the sixth time in two hours, she yelled as loudly as she could, "What the fuck is your problem?" Down on the mattress, Wesley stirred, and she knew he wasn't resting either, and in the weariest tones she'd ever heard, he muttered, "Sometimes, they just like to cry."

"Mr. Huerta had obviously never spent much time around children," Hortense LeBeau said. "Instead of talking to a member of the staff about the matter and trying to resolve it that way, he decided to take things into his own hands."

"I'm willing to wager that it did not go well."

Felipe Huerta stormed into the tiny room Esmeralda shared with her niñas and threatened to bash the brats' heads against the goddamn walls if she didn't find a way to shut their fucking mouths. This prompted the other shelter residents, as well as the nighttime crew, to crowd into the space and the narrow hall outside it despite the distancing rules that were in place during the pandemic. The staff tried to separate Esmerelda and her children from Huerta, but by this time, everyone was screaming, and Huerta was the loudest one of all, referring to the young mother over and over as a puta and a cono.

"After that incident," Hortense LeBeau said, "it became impossible for Mr. Huerta to remain here."

"You kicked him out?"

"We told him his presence was disruptive, and he could no longer stay within the system."

"Did he abuse drugs and alcohol while he was here?"

"Of course. We spoke to him numerous times about the way he flouted our regulations. He'd be good for a day or two. Then he'd backslide."

Sheila told Hortense LeBeau about the article that had led her to the shelter, particularly Huerta's complaints that the authorities were giving him a hard time about the medicinal marijuana he needed.

"Mr. Huerta procured marijuana whenever he wanted to," the woman said.

"But then he had to pay market rates," Sheila said. "He use any other drugs?"

"Crack, I suspect. And opioids are everywhere."

Sheila winced. It was all too easy to imagine Felipe Huerta's behavior while he was drugged up or, even worse, looking for the money that would sate his addictions.

"Did you ever hear him talk about the Riverside Park case?" Sheila asked.

"Not specifically."

"That's an interesting choice of words."

Hortense LeBeau licked her lips. She was a composed woman who did not want to appear rattled when she was viewed by the audience at Sundance.

"The night I was telling you about," she said, "when he was threatening

Esmerelda and her kids, the staff and the residents separated them, and the guards took Mr. Huerta to my office. They called me, of course, and I got here quickly. I live in Bedford-Stuyvesant."

Probably in a really nice brownstone, Sheila thought.

"When I arrived, I was briefed on what had happened. Then I went in to see Mr. Huerta. He was belligerent—"

No surprise there, Sheila thought.

"—and by this point, I'd had enough of him. So I told him we'd have to remove him from the facility, and he started flailing about wildly. The guards restrained him. As it turned out, we needed all four of them—one on every limb. Mr. Huerta began screaming about the things he had done to the women who'd done him wrong, and they all had it coming, and he vowed that he was gonna come back here and do the same thing to me, and then he'd take care of Esmerelda and her children because they were the ones who were ruining his life." Hortense LeBeau paused. "I have never been so frightened, Ms. Devine."

"You could have had him arrested," Sheila said.

"I wanted him out of here. He was a threat to the people in this facility. Many of them are fragile."

"Weren't you concerned he'd make good on his threat? Come back after you and Esmerelda and her kids?"

"Of course I was. All the members of the security staff were put on alert about him, but he has never returned, and, fortunately, Esmerelda and her children have transitioned to a more traditional and stable housing arrangement."

"I don't know if I should tell you this…" Sheila's voice trailed off.

Hortense LeBeau gave her a look that said, *Out with it, white woman.*

"I've been in touch with a reporter for the Gowanus news site. He says he thought he saw Huerta in the neighborhood recently."

Hortense LeBeau looked like a sheriff in the Wild West who had just heard that the murderous outlaw she threw in prison was due back in town on the morning train.

"Back when the Riverside Park case was in the news," she said, "I figured those young men were railroaded—you know, browbeaten until they confessed to a crime they didn't commit. But now..." She shook her head. "Mr. Huerta is the type of man who is entirely capable of perpetrating an outrage like that."

"But the DNA didn't match."

"Maybe he did attack her. Maybe he beat her within an inch of her life, and somebody else committed the rape. How many young men were on that spree in the park that night?"

"As many as two dozen," Sheila said.

Hortense LeBeau shrugged. Sheila shrugged back. The possibilities of what had occurred in Riverside Park never seemed to narrow.

Chapter Nineteen

Michael Devine

1

June 8, 2012

For weeks, Michael had been dreading this moment: Pasquale and Regina Antolini flanking him as they walked through the hospital hallway. Normally, Michael registered the sights and sounds and smells of the place, but today, he focused only on what was about to happen, and on all the things that could go wrong.

The doctors and therapists and psychologists kept telling him it was time. He remained unconvinced, and he had stopped by her room the previous night. He sat beside her after pulling up a chair. All the tubes had been removed from her body. The scars and bruises had disappeared. Now, the damage was invisible.

Although they had spoken about it before, he reminded her that he would bring her parents to visit in the morning.

"Do you think it's best?" she asked.

He tried to smile. "I'm not sure it's the best. But the doctors do."

"What if I don't recognize them?"

I have no answer for that, he thought.

"I'm sure you'll be fine," he said.

"You'll be here?"

"Of course."

"That's good. I like talking to you."

Now, they were outside her room. The Antolinis were solid people, solidly built, solidly dressed. Mrs. Antolini held roses.

Michael tapped on the door. A nurse was taking Marie's pulse.

"I'm with Ms. Antolini's parents," he said.

The nurse beamed. "We've been expecting them. I'll let you visit, and I'll take those flowers. I'll put them in a vase."

Michael stepped aside as she left the room. The Antolinis walked in. The father spoke first.

"Hello, Marie."

He shifted from foot to foot. The mother blinked a few times. Marie looked at her parents as if she were running into two people at a party whom she had met before, but could not quite place.

"Hi," she said at last.

"We've been awfully worried about you," the father said.

"Thanks."

The father went on: "So many people have told us how concerned they are. The Battaglias, the Federicis, the Paladinos—they all wanted to make food to bring to you, but we told them we didn't think the hospital would allow it."

He's chattering, Michael said to himself. Usually, it's the woman who talks while the man stays silent, but Mrs. Antolini is on the verge of sobbing, and I understand why.

"That's very nice of all of them," Marie said. She sounded like a politician at a fundraiser, thanking some people she had encountered once in her life for contributing a few dollars to her campaign.

"And, of course, there's Aunt Donatella and Aunt Maria and Uncle Luigi." The father was still jabbering. "They all wanted to come, but we thought it might be too much."

"I appreciate that," Marie said.

"Your cousins, too. Anthony and Francesca and Vito and Rafaella and

Stefano and Arianna and…" His voice trailed off. Michael wondered how many cousins Marie had. Trying to think of them all made her father sound tired.

"We even talked to Rocco," Pasquale Antolini said.

"Who?" Marie kept her eyes shut.

"Rocco. Your old boyfriend. I know you two had some problems—"

The mother's foot swung out and whacked the father in the shin. He glared at her. She returned the hard look.

"He asked after you," the father said. His voice was barely audible. "He said he hoped you were doing well."

"That's quite kind of him," Marie said.

The mother swallowed hard. "I wanna ask you something, Marie."

"Go ahead." Now, she sounded like a job applicant trying to please the H.R. people during a hiring interview.

"Do you remember who we are? Do you remember anything at all about the neighborhood, and the family?"

Marie cast her eyes toward the ceiling. The scrambling of her memory, with so much of it lost, had robbed her of the ability to dissemble.

How is she gonna phrase this? Michael asked himself. How bad is it gonna be for all of us?

"I recall bits of things," she said. "I try to think back, and to remember my life, but it's like watching a television with really bad reception. I can see the outlines of objects and people, but not their features. Everything is blurry. It all jumbles together."

She leaned back on the pillow, closed her eyes, sighed loudly. Remembrance had made her weary, and she was more tired than sad. She nodded slightly at Michael, who knew what she wanted. Since he could always get away with playing the stressed-for-time prosecutor, he looked at his watch.

"I think we should go," he said. "Marie needs her rest, and I have a lotta work to do."

Marie's parents kissed her on the cheek, and she smiled weakly at them. Michael expected it was all over, but as they were leaving, she called out in a voice more forceful than he had ever heard from her: "Michael."

He turned. It was late in the morning. Sunlight slipped through the slats in the window. For a moment, Marie was wrapped in the expressive glow he associated with Turner's paintings.

"Can you stay?" she asked. "Just for a minute?"

"Of course."

He walked to her bed. Her eyes opened so wide he could see right into her.

"You did well," he said.

"Did I?"

"You didn't think so?"

She breathed deeply. "I was trying to remember who they were. I tried to summon pictures, memories…" She shook her head. "The best I could do was a foggy glob. Maybe they fit in, maybe they don't. I can't tell."

"It'll get better," Michael said. *It has to,* he thought.

She kept clenching and unclenching her right fist. "You're real. It's like you're my pipeline to the world. Everybody else seems…off, somehow. Like they're part of the picture, but not important to it."

The veins in her wrist throbbed as she worked an imaginary spaldeen. Michael rested his hand on hers, and she laced her fingers through his. Her grip was tight, and it made sense to Michael because everyone who knew Marie talked about her vigor and intensity. She ran ten miles a day and lifted weights three times a week at the gym. Her friends said she was thinking about a triathlon, but she wouldn't enter unless she was convinced she'd do well. Marie Antolini never did anything halfway.

And then, in an action so sudden it seemed spasmodic, she reached up, and her lips brushed his cheek, and her free hand pressed against his face, and he heard her say, "Michael, thank you, thank you so much, thank you for everything."

* * *

A few minutes later, he guided Marie's parents to the reception area, where Seamus O'Toole was talking to a physician's assistant. It took Michael a moment to process the scene, but then O'Toole approached him with the air of a man who was convinced he could get anybody to tell him exactly what he wanted to know.

"How are you doing, Counselor?"

They shook hands.

"I'm here with Marie's parents," Michael said. "We've just finished visiting her. It was pretty intense."

Michael made introductions. Nods were exchanged.

"I suppose Marie could use some downtime," O'Toole said.

"I think she could," Michael said.

"I understand." O'Toole's smile could not mask his disappointment. "I'll come back again. Maybe tomorrow. But I'd like to see her soon. I'm starting a freelance assignment in Europe in a week, and I'll be gone awhile."

Michael steered the group toward an elevator.

"That sounds awfully interesting," Mrs. Antolini said. "Traveling around the world to make a living."

"It never gets dull." O'Toole flashed a smile that exuded Irish charm. "I'm not sure if that's good or bad."

They crowded into the elevator. Michael hit the button for the lobby.

"We were so impressed when Marie told us you were one of her professors," Mr. Antolini said.

O'Toole thanked him.

"We remember watching you on CNN," Mrs. Antolini said. "Iraq. Afghanistan. Things like that."

O'Toole nodded in appreciation. Mrs. Antolini pointed to his neck.

"You used to wear a St. Christopher's medal," she said. "We noticed that because we have a saint in the yard ourselves."

"I don't have it anymore." He smiled again. "Nobody's shooting at me these days."

"I understood why Marie wanted that career," Mrs. Antolini said, "although I worried, too."

O'Toole nodded in the sagely avuncular manner that cable news anchors like to employ. "It's a mother's sad fate to worry about her children. But both of you should be proud. You raised a remarkable girl. She was my best student. I kept telling her, 'I'd rather have your future than my past.'"

2

September 29, 2023

"Shit," Rachel said as she frowned at her Android.

"What now?" Michael asked.

He brought the glass of cabernet he'd been fantasizing about for hours to his lips.

"The fucking *Times* just posted a fucking editorial saying you should debate Nelson Hernandez right away." She shook her head like an atheist hearing a believer talk about the Virgin Birth. "Where the fuck is that idiot getting his money? He has ads all over the place."

"I can't figure out why anyone would contribute to his campaign," Michael said, "but I do know I fired him because he isn't fit to run the Traffic Violations Bureau, much less the entire office."

Rachel slid her phone in front of him. "Read this."

The editorial had the innocuous headline "A Necessary Discussion," but in a few short paragraphs, it said that Rolando Ortega was raising unsettling questions about the handling of the Riverside Park case. The public interest required a full, robust, and immediate vetting of the matter.

"They're grandstanding," Michael said as he pushed her phone back. "I have to debate him, and they know it. The public financing laws require it."

Rachel reminded him that they had yet to set a date. Michael said he hoped to do it the Sunday before the election, when everyone was watching football.

After dinner, he headed for his desktop and placed the remnants of his wine as far away as his arm could stretch. He opened his Gmail, which he used only for personal matters. Twenty-two unread messages. They could wait. He had put this one off long enough.

He clicked Compose and began typing in her name. Although they hadn't communicated for six months, it filled out instantly.

She lived about ninety minutes outside Philadelphia, near Hershey. She once told Michael that when the weather was nice, she liked to go to the theme park and watch the grownups get on rides with their kids. For reasons she couldn't explain, it made her feel good inside.

My Dearest Marie:

Just get started, he said to himself. *The words will come.*

> *I've been remiss, and I apologize. My only excuse is this: With my new responsibilities, and with the demands of my campaign, I've fallen out of contact with far too many people.*

He finished the wine and hoped for inspiration.

> *A situation has developed that you should be aware of, if you haven't heard about it already.*

Situation, he thought. *That's a lawyer's euphemism. It's a goddamn debacle.*

> *A prominent attorney here is trying to reopen your case. He represents one of the men who attacked you, and he'll probably end up representing all of them. He argues that new evidence has arisen that casts doubt on their guilt. Our position is simple: What he's saying is nonsense. Rest assured that we are fighting him every step of the way.*

Michael told her that he did not believe the legal maneuverings would require her to testify again, but she should prepare herself because judges' rulings are unpredictable. He asked how she was doing and hoped she was faring well. He said one of his kids was in college, and the other was in law school, and he was confident of winning the election and that he thought of her often.

He heard the door rattle. After nearly a quarter century of marriage, he knew when Rachel wanted to see him.

"Come on in, Hon."

He kept his eyes on the screen as the doorknob turned. He finished the email with a postscript: one of the media consultants on his campaign was Seamus O'Toole, her former professor, and he sent his regards.

It really is a small world, Michael wrote.

He hit Send and turned to his wife, who bore the look of a woman who had just learned that her financial adviser had embezzled all of her retirement money.

"Have things gone from bad to worse?" Michael asked.

"They've gone from horrible to catastrophic."

Chapter Twenty

Sheila Devine

September 29, 2023

S he left at five in the morning after filling her thermos with Wesley's best coffee. She had hoped the long drive would turn pretty once she left the city, but the sky clouded, and a cold rain fell sporadically. When she picked up a Buffalo radio station, the DJ said sleet was likely overnight.

The riot that had made the place famous occurred before she was born, but its name was always uttered as if it were the worst hellhole in New York. She had tried to avoid making a trip here, but another Riverside defendant had indicated he was ready to sign up with Rolando Ortega, and this was where he was.

Ulysses Watkins had been incarcerated behind Attica's barbed wire and concrete walls for more than a decade.

When she saw him, he was sitting behind a heavy glass partition and wearing the obligatory orange jumpsuit. His arms were thick. So was the rest of him. Sheila thought he resembled a tree trunk that had absorbed too much rain.

When she picked up the phone that would let her communicate, she wondered if anyone was listening in.

"You the film lady?" he asked.

"That's me."

"Rolando says I should talk to you."

Ulysses Watkins had played football. Ortega's lawsuit was the equivalent of a Hail Mary.

"I've talked to the other defendants," she said. "I have a good idea of what happened in the park that night."

"We didn't attack no lady," Ulysses said. "I never raped nobody. I never did that shit."

"When the police brought you in—"

Ulysses held up his hand like a running back fending off a would-be tackler. Sheila wondered if he had CTE and was glad she had never given Dylan permission to play football, although her son's lack of athletic ability meant he would have been cut after the first tryout.

"I'm tryin' to remember," he said. "It's hard sometimes."

If this guy has brain damage, Sheila thought, he could be suing people for the rest of his life.

"They told me to sign some shit. They said if I did that, I could go home. So I signed."

"But they didn't let you leave."

"They lied to me. People lied to me all my life."

"Why did you go to the park that night?"

"To keep hangin' with the guys."

"After the soccer game."

"That's right."

"Why were you playing soccer? It wasn't your game. You were a football player, right?"

"I was chillin' on a stoop with a friend of mine, and some dude I knew from school walked by and said they was playin' a soccer game on the field about a block away. I said I wasn't interested, but my buddy was. So I went."

"Who was your buddy?"

"Felipe. I called him Fills."

Sheila wanted to make sure she had heard him correctly: "Are you talking about Felipe Huerta?"

"Yeah. We hung out all the time."

Felipe Huerta's presence at the soccer game had always seemed inexplicable. Nobody claimed to know him. He had just shown up, like a specter, to turn a friendly game between guys from the neighborhood into a night that resembled the most harrowing parts of *Lord of the Flies*.

Now, here was Ulysses Watkins, one of the four men convicted in the assault on the Riverside Runner, casually admitting that he and the evil spirit were buddies.

"How long had you known Felipe?" Sheila asked.

"Couple years."

"And you guys hung out together?"

"Got high a lot. Drank beer and shit."

"Anything else?"

"Waddya mean?"

"Felipe had a rap sheet. At the age of nineteen, he looked like an aspiring career criminal. You ever help him out with any of the stuff he pulled?"

"Oh, yeah. Breaking and entering. We stole some cars, too. Did a carjacking once." He chuckled. "That was fun. Some white dude in a Mercedes with Jersey plates. There were four, five of us, all bros, surrounding his ass, and his eyes bugged out to the Palisades. We got his butt outta the car and kicked him around a little, but we didn't hurt him much. He was a stockbroker and shit. Had a lotta cash on him. Probably lookin' to buy dope on the street. So we took the car to a place Fills knew, and they were impressed it was a Mercedes, but we didn't say nothin' 'bout the cash. Just kept that to ourselves and split it up even. Fills was always fair that way."

"A regular Robin Hood," Sheila said.

"Yeah. He liked to rob people."

Sheila realized that the man she was interviewing had lived his entire life in an irony-free zone.

"Why did Felipe wanna play in the soccer game?"

"That's what I asked when we were walking there. I told him soccer was a sissy game, and he said we'd play a while, but there'd be a whole bunch of guys there, so when it was over, we could go to the park and raise some hell."

Holy crap, Sheila thought. Huerta had the whole thing in mind from the moment he went there. The night went exactly the way he wanted.

"Okay," Sheila said. "You guys went to the park. You say you raised hell. I say you committed assault and battery. But did you ever see the runner that night?"

"No." He sounded emphatic.

"Were you with Felipe while all the guys were in the park?"

"Part of the time. But when we heard the cops comin' we split up."

"Could Felipe have attacked the runner?"

"Doubt it."

"Why?"

"Fills came to visit me once, a few years after I got here. He told me some stuff."

This is really good, Sheila said to herself. But he might clam up if you tell him how good it is. Keep your voice calm and neutral and matter-of-fact.

"What did he tell you?"

Chapter Twenty-One

Ulysses Watkins

September 12, 2018

Ulysses Watkins' days were repetitive. He liked it that way because he never had to think about what to do.

Wake up.

Breakfast.

Work assignment No. 1.

Cell.

Lunch.

Gym. (Weights, mostly.)

Work assignment No. 2.

Cell.

Exercise yard.

Dinner.

Sleep.

He had no visitors, but there was no one he wanted to see. He'd always figured he'd wind up in prison, and now that he was here, he was determined to get through it like a man. That meant not complaining, standing up for yourself, and being as tough as possible.

He was in his bunk, staring at a corner in the ceiling as a spider wove a web. Spiders were patient. A man could learn a lot watching a spider.

A guard rattled the bars.

"What you want?" Ulysses asked.

"Somebody's here to see you."

It sounded like a joke. Ulysses hated jokes.

"You shittin' me?"

"Do I look like I'm shitting you?"

The guard swung the cell door open. The guard was a fat white guy. All the guards were fat white guys. No one Black or thin lived north of the Bronx.

The guard cuffed him. Ulysses hated being cuffed. Hated being seen that way. Another reason he was glad nobody came to see him. A second guard fell in behind. Ulysses walked between them.

"Who wants to see me?" Ulysses asked.

"Beyoncé," the jailer said.

This seemed unlikely. "If you dunno," Ulysses said, "just tell me you dunno."

"Nobody told us nothin'," the guard said, "'cept that somebody wanted to see you."

The visitors' area was a place without shadows. The guard pointed to a chair. A glass partition separated prisoners from visitors. Ulysses would have to pick up a phone to talk to the person on the other side.

When Ulysses sat down, he looked through the glass at Felipe Huerta. He was surprised to see Fills, but he would've been surprised to see anyone. The dude looked older, but that's what happened. Everyone got older. Felipe's eyes were wide and unblinking, and his cheeks had hollowed out, and Ulysses wondered if he was using junk even more frequently than he had before.

Ulysses wrapped his hand around the phone. His palm was wet.

"Hey," he said.

"Hey."

"Wazzup?"

"Cops sent me up for some bullshit. I just got out."

"Waddya gonna do now?"

"I had time to think, U." Fills had always called him U. "That's one thing about prison. Gives a man time to think."

"What're you thinkin'?"

"Way we lived before, U, it was bullshit. We gotta put something together. Something where we can make real money."

Ulysses found himself nodding. Fills went on:

"I wanna stop hustlin' all day for penny-ante shit. I wanna put together an organization. I know people. I got intel on all the shit comin' into the 'hood. I can get a hand in that shit. I just need some cash to set me up."

"I ain't got no money," Ulysses said.

"I did some time with this white dude who worked on Wall Street. He told me about this shit called venture capital. That's what I need. Venture capital."

Ulysses had no idea what Fills was talking about. "How you gonna get that?"

"I need some guys who'll make all the other dudes know I'm serious about doing business. Guys who'll help me get that venture capital."

Ulysses tried to figure out what Fills wanted. "How do I fit in?"

"I'm gonna be meetin' people. You come with me when I do that. Just stand there and look pissed off. You don't hafta say nothin'."

"I can do that."

Fills fingered a piece of junk hanging around his neck. He seemed to like the thing. "When you gettin' out?"

"Dunno, man. Long time."

"How long?"

Ulysses shrugged. He might get part of his sentence knocked off for good behavior, but in a high-profile case like his, any sign of mercy would provoke a media shitstorm.

"Ten years," he said. "Maybe more."

Fills slammed a closed fist on the counter beneath him. "Fuck, man. I could use a guy like you. They fucked us over but good."

"Tell me about it."

"Thing is, we didn't even do the worst shit they said we did."

"I know that. You know that. Nobody wants to listen."

Fills leaned close to the glass and dropped his voice so low Ulysses could barely hear.

"I'm gonna tell you somethin' ' bout that night. Somethin' I never told nobody."

"All right."

"Remember when all the sirens started, and we all went runnin' and shit?"

"Yeah."

"You and me ran a bit. Then that girl cop stopped us, and we split up."

"I remember."

"So it's dark and shit, and I can't see too good. But I know the park, and I'm startin' to feel better 'cause the sirens are gettin' quiet, and then I hear some weird noises."

"Like what?"

"Rustling. Grunting. Panting. Like some guy's whackin' off or somethin'. So I get closer to look."

"Makes sense."

"And then I see some dude in a sweat jacket. He's on top of this girl, and he's goin' at it and she ain't sayin' nothin' so I figure maybe she's passed out drunk and shit. His pants are halfway down his butt, and I'm thinkin' of sayin' somethin', but then I hear those fuckin' sirens again, and the white guy musta heard 'em too 'cause he just gets off the chick and pulls up his shit and runs away. That's what I'm gonna do, too, but then I see somethin' shiny on the ground next to her, and it might be worth money and shit, so I snatch it and get outta there. But, fuck it, U, all of that stuff messed up my...waddya call it?"

"Concentration?"

"That's it. Anyway, cops got me. But I'd been in before. I knew you didn't tell them nothin' 'til you talked to a mouthpiece."

"Wish I had a chance to talk to you. I told them what they told me to say. I thought they'd let me go home."

"Cops don't work like that, U. Never have. Never will."

"You never told them what you saw?"

Fills shook his head. "You tell cops somethin' they don't wanna hear, they stomp all over you 'til you shut up."

"You get a look at that white dude's face?"

Fills shook his head again before letting out the loudest laugh Ulysses had ever heard from him.

"Might recognize his white ass, though."

Chapter Twenty-Two

Sheila Devine

September 29, 2023

S he sat in her Toyota, furiously typing what she remembered into her laptop. When she finished, she checked her news feed for the first time all day. She had a tough drive back to Brooklyn and the interview had lasted longer than expected. Now, she feared she'd hit rush hour when she got to the city.

She wanted to see if there was anything she needed to know, but it was just the usual:

Violence around the Persian Gulf.

Huge price swings on Wall Street.

Wildfires in California.

A deadly new virus in a country she'd barely heard of.

Toward the end of the scroll, a story got her attention—a white cop had fatally shot a Black motorist, sparking protests and backlash. The incident occurred in Philadelphia. Although Sheila's plate was full, this might be something she could dive into once her current project was over.

Three paragraphs in, her jaw swung open so wide it almost hit her knees.

* * *

She drove like Danica Patrick but instead of heading home she put the car in a garage a block from Ortega's office. As she ran along the sidewalk clutching her camera, she drew strange looks from passersby, wondering what the deal was with the white chick in skinny jeans trying to channel Flo-Jo.

At the office, Dolores and Tamika were talking into constantly ringing phones while surfing through computers. The famously composed Rolando Ortega had loosened his tie. Sheila began recording the scene with her handheld.

"I have reached out to the attorney representing the patrolman," Ortega said.

"Any luck?" Sheila asked.

Ortega shook his head. "I expect no luck, but I must make the effort."

"Who's representing him?"

"A lawyer for the police union in Philadelphia, who has sensibly advised his client to keep quiet. Whenever they get into legal trouble, police officers immediately invoke the constitutional rights they usually disparage."

During a seemingly routine traffic stop in a godawful part of North Philadelphia, Police Officer Rocco Cantone had shot and killed Luttrell Aldridge, a thirty-two-year-old African American who was driving a 2009 Ford Taurus with a broken taillight. A surveillance camera at a nearby 7-Eleven recorded the encounter, which was brief. Officer Cantone approached the car, bent down by the driver's side window, and then, a second later, drew his service weapon and fired three times.

The mayor appealed for calm.

The district attorney said a full and impartial investigation was underway.

Local activists said this was the type of brutality that Black people regularly encountered at the hands of the police.

To Sheila's eyes, it was impossible to tell from the footage exactly what Luttrell Aldridge had done in the moments before he was shot. The recording's ambiguity, she assured herself, would not stop everyone from reaching the conclusions they preferred.

"What do you do if Officer Cantone's lawyer never responds to you?"

Sheila asked.

Tamika Riley piped up while keeping her gaze fixed on the screen in front of her. "We file a motion."

"Concurrent to our request to reopen the case," Ortega said, "we believe we can ask the court to compel Officer Cantone to testify about what he did the night Ms. Antolini was attacked. He has never done that under oath."

Detective Haggerty had told Sheila that Rocco Cantone, recently split from Marie Antolini, stayed home in Philadelphia that day, eating dinner with his family and watching *Law & Order* on TV. In Haggerty's view, the lameness of the alibi contributed to its validity.

"You're making a face, Ms. Devine," Ortega said.

"If you bring Rocco Cantone into this," Sheila said, "it's only a matter of time before the victim gets dragged back in, too."

"As you may recall," Ortega said, "Ms. Antolini wrote a book about her experiences, particularly her recovery. I've read it."

"I have, too."

"It's quite moving."

"It is."

"She put her name on the book, Ms. Devine. So the anonymity normally given to victims of sexual assault no longer applies in this case."

Marie Antolini's book, *A Victim No Longer*, was written with the assistance of a staff writer at New York magazine, which excerpted portions of it. The book sold well, and Marie even appeared on an Oprah Winfrey special before moving back to Pennsylvania, where, for the past several years, she had lived out of the public eye.

"You will need to talk to her for your film," Ortega said.

Sheila had been procrastinating. It was the interview she least wanted to do.

"I'm not sure she'll talk."

"You must make the effort," Ortega said.

* * *

She brought home Thai food. Wesley dug into a cupboard that sheltered a bottle of Shiraz from the Hunter Valley. Sheila took a few swigs and dug into the massaman curry and began to feel human for the first time all day.

"Philadelphia," Dylan said.

There goes my good mood, she thought.

"What about it?" Wesley asked.

"Don't you think we should talk about it?" Dylan asked.

"It's all over my feed," Bethany said. "So I linked to an article on philly.com. Already, I've got one hundred thirty-six likes and twenty-seven shares. I'm trending."

Sheila reached for the pad thai. "Waddya think?" she asked her kids.

"It don't look good for that cop," Dylan said.

"Doesn't look good."

"Whatever."

"No, whatever," Sheila said. "Your father and I keep making this point— good grammar is important. Otherwise, you sound like an idiot."

Dylan glared a second and seemed about to say something sharp, but he had an instinct for when his mother needed little excuse to bite off his head. He once accused her of being a praying mantis in another life; she replied that in her current incarnation, she was even meaner than that.

"That cop just shot the guy," Dylan said. "Bam! No due process or nothin'. Anything."

Sheila silently accepted the grammatical apology. "Could you see what happened in the car?" she asked.

Dylan worked his food a bit. "No."

"Maybe the cop had a reason to shoot."

"That cop didn't have no reason to shoot."

"How in the world did you pass your English classes?" Wesley asked.

Sheila smiled for the first time all day. Two against one always worked best.

"Any reason," Dylan said. Sheila recognized that her son would continue to make his point with the earnestness of a youthful idealist who believed that fairness was the most important virtue. She pitied him for what he would have to learn.

"They didn't find a gun on the driver," Dylan said.

"Not on his person," Sheila said. "But there was one in the glove compartment. Maybe he was reaching for it. We can't tell from the video."

"The cop coulda planted the gun in the glove compartment," Dylan said. "It wasn't registered to nobody. Anybody."

"Well," Sheila said, "he couldn't have done that when he walked up to the car and fired those shots, because he didn't have the time. So he would've had to find an unregistered gun somewhere nearby, open the passenger door, and stick the gun in the glove compartment before any of the other cops arrived. If he'd done that, the surveillance camera woulda picked it up, and it'd be all over YouTube by now."

Dylan wiped his mouth. Sheila could tell he was stalling as he tried to come up with a response.

"But cops pull that kinda stuff all the time," Dylan said. "You know that. I don't like criminals any more than you do, but the police are always jumping to conclusions, and sometimes they're wrong, and people like me suffer the consequences."

Sheila gulped some Shiraz. As the daughter of one of the most dishonest officers in the long history of an ethically challenged department, she was in no position to launch a philosophical defense of the way the police operate.

"The guy had priors," Sheila said.

"The cop couldn't have known that," Dylan said.

Sheila had no comeback and felt grateful when Wesley spoke up.

"What do we do," he asked, "when we are stopped by a police officer?"

Dylan looked sullen. "We cooperate."

"How do we cooperate?" Wesley asked.

"We are polite," Dylan said. "We look him or her in the eye. We refer to him or her as 'Sir' or 'Ma'am.'"

"What else?"

"We do everything the police officer tells us to do. Above all else, we don't make no sudden movements."

"'Any' sudden movements," Sheila said.

Dylan winked at his mother. "Them, too."

* * *

As Sheila put her iPhone on the nightstand, she asked her husband how many times he had given The Talk to Dylan.

Wesley drew the covers over his shoulders. He looked as tired as she felt.

"We are well into double figures by now," he mumbled.

"Does it do any good?"

"It never hurts to go over the rules."

Sheila stretched out beside Wesley. "He never tells me anything. How many times has he been stopped by the police?"

"We are well into double figures by now."

Dylan was a big, caramel-colored kid with the largest 'fro this side of Questlove. Every cop in New York was convinced he was a gangbanger.

"How many times have you been stopped by the police?" Sheila asked.

"I lost count. That's why I asked for that get-out-of-jail-free card."

Wesley had grown weary of being halted by law enforcement as he drove and walked to his coffeehouses around Brooklyn. It ate into his time, and eating into his time damaged his business. So, on the advice of his brother-in-law, the prosecutor, one day Wesley made an appointment with the commander of the Fort Greene precinct. He described what kept happening to him and then asked the man if he could write a letter, on official NYPD stationery, testifying that Wesley McBride was a law-abiding business owner who had good relations with the NYPD and he should be allowed to go about his affairs unmolested. Wesley had brought plenty of coffee and pastries to the meeting, and he left with the letter he wanted.

"I withheld some information from Dylan," Sheila said. "I feel bad about that. But I didn't know how he'd handle it."

"What was the information?" Wesley asked.

"It's about the cop who shot the motorist."

"What about him?"

"You notice his name?"

"Italian name. There are a lot of Italians in Philadelphia."

"The cop's name is Rocco Cantone."

"Should I know who he is?"

"He was once the boyfriend of Marie Antolini. The Riverside Runner. She had an order of protection from him."

Wesley opened his eyes wide and propped himself up against the headboard.

I may have blundered, Sheila said to herself. I really don't feel like having a conversation.

"That sounds important," he said.

Sheila sat straight up as she flicked on the light. She felt like Suzanne Pleshette in *The Bob Newhart Show*.

"They had a big argument about a week before she was attacked," Sheila said. "The police came and escorted Rocco outta there. She made a point of saying she never wanted to see him again."

"And the cops just ignored this after she was attacked?" Even for a man who believed the police were often bigoted and incompetent, Wesley sounded incredulous.

"They knew all about it. They went to Philadelphia and checked out his alibi. He said he was home that night with his parents. They ate dinner, watched *Law & Order* and went to bed."

"Coulda happened that way, I guess."

"Coulda."

"But in an incident like that, isn't the significant other the one you suspect first?"

"It is." Sheila reached for her iPhone and held it like a talisman. "I've been trying to reach Michael all day. Texting. Email. Phone." She paused. "He's ghosting me."

"This musta hit him like a punch in the gut," Wesley said.

"The fact that Rocco Cantone was once Marie's boyfriend is not yet part of the story coming outta that shooting. But it will be." Sheila closed her eyes and shook her head. "I shoulda known."

"Known what?"

"That sooner or later Marie Antolini would move to the front and center of this thing, no matter what I or anyone else did."

Chapter Twenty-Three

Michael Devine

1

September 30, 2023

Dearest *Michael,* the email began.

> She always started her emails to him with "Dearest," and he always wondered if he was the only one she addressed that way.

Many thanks for your note. I hadn't heard from you in a while, and I was beginning to fear you had forgotten me.

Never gonna happen, he silently told her.

We get the news, even out here in horse-and-buggy America—

She lived near Amish country. She liked the slow pace and simple style.

—and I'm aware, at least broadly, of what's going on in the case.

Michael chastised himself: I shoulda been in touch with her earlier. I shoulda been the first one to tell her about this.

Obviously, the incident (as I call it) is a painful episode I've tried to get past. Just as obviously, it keeps coming up and may never be fully put to rest. I'm all right with that.

The incident had robbed her of many things, but not of her will.

I've carved out a life for myself that I am content with, and I have no desire to return to the public eye. I never wanted to be identified as only a victim, and I refuse to define myself that way. But if events force me to speak out again, I will do so—and I hope, with every fiber of my being, that you will be with me if I have to do it.

What choice do I have? Michael asked the screen.

As the saying goes, 'Whatever doesn't kill you makes you stronger.' I think that was written by Nietzsche, although I once heard Serena Williams attribute it to Kelly Clarkson.

She added a smile emoji. For the first time in days, Michael found himself amused by something.

The email went on to describe what was going on in her life. She liked her job at Hershey Medical Center, where she worked in both physical and mental therapy with people who were recovering from trauma. She spent most weekends in Philadelphia with her parents, who were now retired. They still lived in the same rowhouse where she grew up. Her father talked about moving to Florida, but her mother wouldn't hear of it, and she suspected they'd compromise by eventually becoming snowbirds. She went to the gym five days a week, and nowadays she did her cardio work on ellipticals because they were easy on her knees. Pounding her legs on treadmills had led to tendinitis, and she had not run outdoors since the incident.

She wished him luck in his campaign. She knew he was an excellent district attorney.

He heard the door behind him swing open. He knew who it was.

"You look engrossed," Rachel said.

"An email from Marie."

"How's she doing?"

"She sounds all right." Michael looked up at his wife. "You'll never believe who called me."

Rachel shrugged.

"Jamie Quinn," Michael said. "He talks to my sister sometimes, but I haven't heard from him in years."

"What did you say to him?"

"Nothing. I was so surprised when his name popped up, I let it go to voicemail."

"What did he say?"

Michael adopted a gravelly outer-borough accent that had been honed in Fiorello LaGuardia's New York. "'That cop in Philadelphia. I remember that name. I dunno if anyone else does. Nobody remembers a friggin' thing anymore. Gimme a call. I got somethin' goin' on. I'm not dead. I still know people at the *News*. If that don't work, I'll do a whatchamacallit. Blog.'"

"He's on the cutting edge of the internet, circa 2003."

"I have to talk to him, but I don't want to."

"Why's that?"

"Because Jamie Quinn's greatest cause—first, last and always—is Jamie Quinn."

* * *

After telling Rachel he'd be off the grid awhile, Michael took a cab to Quinn's building in Tribeca. The place had been redesigned by Robert A.M. Stern, and Michael reminded himself that few occupations were more lucrative than being a man of the people.

He expected a home health aide to open the door and usher him in, so he was surprised when Quinn, hunched over his walker, did it himself.

"You got my message," the old newshound growled.

As Michael's eyes ran over the exposed brick walls, he wondered if they were original to the building. It was entirely possible that Quinn's second wife had ordered something new that looked Nineteenth Century.

The aging man pushed his walker toward the living area and said, "The full extent of Rocco Cantone's shit has yet to hit the fan."

Michael appreciated the lack of pleasantries.

Quinn went on. "But it will. It's the weekend, so everyone's moving slow. By Monday, it'll be everywhere."

"The recent incident in Philadelphia has nothing to do with the Riverside Park case," Michael said.

Quinn plunked himself in a high-backed chair by the window and motioned for Michael to take the seat closest to him.

"Maybe you're right, Counselor, but even if you are, it's not gonna help you much."

"There's no reason to drag the victim's name out in public again."

"Marie Antolini wrote a book. You can find it on Amazon."

Pleading with Quinn was useless. "If you're looking for a comment, I just gave you one."

Quinn leaned forward. He was breathing hard. His heyday had ended long ago, and whenever people spoke about him now, it was usually to note how shocked they were that he was still alive.

"Here's the thing, Counselor. People like to make connections. They like to believe that one thing is related to another thing, even if they're not. Especially if they're not. Because otherwise, you start thinking that life is just a series of random events that make no sense whatsoever, and if people believed that, they'd be terrified all the time." He shrugged. "Most people are terrified all the time anyway."

"As a prosecutor," Michael said, "you learn that random events play a big part in life. Sometimes people are just in the wrong place at the wrong time."

"You had a good line of attack at the trial," Quinn said. "The victim was white, and she was assaulted by these rampaging Black and Latin kids—"

Michael cut him off. "It wasn't about race."

"You're the only one who believes that."

Michael bolted to his feet and paced around. Like many onetime athletes, he was prone to restlessness.

"Those guys were in the park that night," he said. "Maybe they just wanted to raise some hell. I dunno. I wasn't with them, and frankly, I never cared about their motivation. I didn't think the guys we indicted were bad kids, but they were weak. Anyway, things got outta hand, and they wound up assaulting Marie within an inch of her life. I woulda gone after them if they were white or yellow or pink or polka dot."

"A lotta guys on that rampage got away. At least ten. Maybe more."

"That still pisses me off."

"So it's entirely possible that the actual rapist ran off into the dark and was never apprehended."

"The guys we got were aiding and abetting. They were just as guilty."

"Judge Khan made that point in her instructions. She told the jurors that all you had to establish was that the defendants were at the scene of the attack, and the lack of physical evidence in and of itself didn't prove or disprove anything. In the old days, Counselor, that was called a hanging charge, and it worked out well for you."

Michael glared at Quinn. This hack used my father as a source before crucifying him in print, he said to himself. Now the old bastard's performing the same dance with me.

Quinn motioned to the chair Michael had just vacated. "Siddown. You're making me nervous. At my age, if I get nervous, I might have a heart attack."

Don't tempt me, Michael thought.

"Lemme give you another theory about what mighta happened that night," Quinn said.

Michael sat down. Quinn wheezed and coughed, then resumed talking once the phlegm subsided.

"Marie Antolini was being stalked. Some creep kept tracking her movements and knew she was gonna go for a run in the park that night. That was her routine, wasn't it?"

Michael nodded. Her friends kept telling her she was crazy, but Marie liked to run along the river at night after she completed her coursework. She told everyone it helped her unwind, and it was a lot healthier than drinking.

Quinn went on: "So he waits in the park for her, and when she runs by, he overtakes her from behind. Since she never saw him, she can't make an ID. As it turns out, he beats her so bad her brain is scrambled forever. To be honest about it, I don't think he meant for that to happen. I think he meant to rape her and then kill her."

"So this stalker was lying in ambush in the park at the same time those kids were running amok." Michael shook his head. "It's an enormous stretch, and I've never believed in coincidences."

"I'm not claiming my theory is perfect, but it solves your DNA problem." Quinn reached to a side table and held up a small digital audio recorder. "I'm gonna put you on the record now, Counselor. I've got enough to write this thing up. You can leave if you want."

Michael adopted his speaking-to-the-public voice. "Go ahead, Mr. Quinn. I've been expecting this."

"Waddya gonna do when Rolando Ortega demands a DNA sample from Officer Cantone?"

"Officer Cantone's lawyer will respond, so I'm not gonna do anything. But I figure he or she will fight it because Ortega's grasping at straws."

"After the attack, during the investigation, did Rocco Cantone's name come up?"

"It did."

"Did you know Marie Antolini had an order of protection against him?"

"I did."

"Was he ever a serious suspect in the case?"

"No."

"Why not?"

"We checked him out."

"Tell me about it."

2

May 29, 2012

"You wanted to see me."

Haggerty looked haggard. Michael tossed him a copy of the *Amsterdam News*.

"You see this?"

Haggerty picked up the paper like a lab worker poking at a sponge covered with dangerous microbes. After a few seconds, his face turned an angry shade of red.

"Those assholes." Spittle flew from the corner of his mouth. "Those cocksucking motherfuckers."

Not for the first time, Michael was struck by the different ways in which whites and Blacks regarded the m/f-word.

The front page of the *Amsterdam News* was dominated by an article that said the victim of the Riverside Park attack had obtained an order of protection against her former boyfriend, a white man who had never been investigated for involvement in the crime because the police and prosecutors were pursuing the classic racist agenda of blaming a horrific act of violence on young men of color.

The third paragraph of the story mentioned the name of the ex: Rocco Cantone.

The fourth paragraph gave the name of the victim: Marie Antolini, right there in print for the world to read. It was the first time any media outlet had identified her.

"I can't believe they did this." Haggerty's spittle continued to fly around the room. "Those shitheads printed her name. I'm gonna arrest those assholes right now."

"It's not illegal to publish a rape victim's name," Michael said.

Haggerty blinked a few times. "It isn't?"

"It's contrary to the conventions the media usually follow," Michael said. "Actually, it's just about the only time they show good judgment."

Haggerty threw the paper onto Michael's desk. "Fuck 'em. I bet if I got a warrant to search their newsroom, I'd find something to send 'em all to jail for a long time."

Michael picked up the paper and made a show of looking at the article. He hoped the detective was just venting.

"The story is almost all hyperbole and horseshit, but it contains a kernel of relevance." Michael paused. "Have we looked closely enough at young Mr. Cantone?"

"I went to Philadelphia and checked him out." The flow of Haggerty's spittle slowed to a trickle. "The night of the attack, he ate spaghetti and meatballs with his parents. They also had salad and garlic bread. For dessert, they drank decaf espresso and shared some biscotti in the living room while they watched *Law & Order*. Then they all went to bed. Young Mr. Cantone has a job at a local deli, and he had to be there at six in the morning. Which he was."

Michael looked hard at the detective, whose nose was flaring as if he were a horse resisting the bit and bridle.

"I believe," Michael said in a thinking-out-loud voice, "that I'd like to go to Philadelphia and talk to young Mr. Cantone myself."

Haggerty blinked a few times, as if a flashbulb had gone off right in front of his eyes.

"You're kidding, right?"

"It'll be on the Q.T.," Michael said. "You and me. We slip down to Philly, we talk to Cantone, we come back here. We don't tell anyone."

"Why do you wanna do this?"

"Because I don't want anyone saying I overlooked something important or obvious, or swept it under the rug."

* * *

The next morning they left early to beat the traffic on the Jersey Turnpike, so they reached Philly in ninety minutes. Haggerty was surprised Michael didn't ask for receipts, and Michael kept saying, "That's because we're not really doing this."

Michael wore a polo shirt and dad jeans and skipped his morning shave. Although he had encouraged Haggerty to dress casually, the man still looked like a cop—pressed white shirt, dark pants, shades, fierce demeanor.

At eight-thirty, they walked into Giuseppe's Salumeria on South Broad Street. Michael was pleased to see that the place was empty except for three old men sitting in a corner, sipping cappuccinos and speaking Italian.

"Where's Cantone?" Michael's question to Haggerty was barely audible.

The detective looked past the long glass counter filled with meats and cheeses and pointed toward an open door that led into a storeroom. "Looks like him in back."

Michael saw a form in a white apron that covered Levis and a cream-colored T-shirt. As they got closer, Michael could make out the definition in the guy's arms, and he wondered if Cantone went to the gym for hours a day, or just popped 'roids. The guy had dark hair, chiseled jaw, pouty lips—matinee-idol looks, but no inclination to cash in on them.

Michael and Haggerty stopped outside the storeroom. The cop coughed. Cantone turned around, blinked a few times, and shook his head vigorously, as if he hoped his action would make an unwelcome sight disappear.

"Waddya doin' here?"

Haggerty said he was on an unofficial visit, then introduced Michael Devine to Rocco Cantone.

"Waddya need to talk to me for?" Cantone motioned to Haggerty. "I already talked to him."

"Because the defense lawyers, if they have any brains at all, are gonna mention that order of protection Marie had against you. I wanna convince the judge to keep that outta the trial. If I can't do that, then I'll hafta show the jury that what happened between you and Marie had no bearing on what occurred in the park that night."

"What if I tell you I don't wanna talk? What if I say I wanna speak to a lawyer?"

Michael tried to keep a poker face. The typical trusting, guiltless American civilian had no idea what his rights were and almost always told the authorities way more than they wanted to hear, but Rocco Cantone sounded like a man who was acquainted with his legal protections.

"You can call a lawyer if you want," Michael said. "But then Detective Haggerty and I will go back home, and I'll issue a subpoena to make you appear before the grand jury. You'll hafta come to New York, and you'll hafta explain to everyone here why you're going there, and once you're in the big bad city, I'll make sure the whole thing becomes a media circus."

Cantone hefted a box of cut-from-the-top sausage rolls and headed deep into the storeroom. "I got work to do. Come with me."

"Why'd she get an order of protection from you, Rocco?" Michael asked.

"Why don't you ask her?" Cantone said.

"She can't remember a thing because of what happened in the park, Asshole."

Cantone stopped and turned. Michael noticed a silver crucifix around his neck but doubted this guy had ever taken Christianity seriously.

"I feel real bad about what happened to Marie," he said. "I hope you put those shitheads in jail for the rest of their lives. It's what they deserve. They're animals."

No, they're not, Michael thought. They're human beings who did something reprehensible. Sometimes, people rise to the occasion; much more often, they fall.

"Then I need your help," Michael told Cantone. "You better tell me about the order of protection."

Cantone puffed up his cheeks before blowing air out of them. He reminded Michael of a balloon-making machine at a kids' party.

"We got into an argument," he said. "I guess it was loud."

"What were you arguing about?" Michael asked.

"It was personal."

"A lot of people heard you two arguing. Somebody called the police. Once the officers arrived, it stopped being personal."

Cantone picked up the box again and zigzagged Michael and Haggerty farther into the storeroom, as if he was hoping they'd get lost.

"I didn't understand what she was tryin' to do," Cantone said. "Livin' in

New York. Workin' in TV. Like she was gonna be Katie Couric or somethin'."

"What did you want her to do?" Michael asked.

"Stay here. We coulda gotten married. I could provide."

Stacking shelves in the salumeria, Michael thought. That's a promising career path.

"We coulda had kids. She coulda cooked and kept house. It woulda been great."

"What did she think of that idea?" Michael asked.

Cantone put the box on the floor and began putting the rolls on metal trays that were stacked on a pushcart.

"She said the TV thing was gonna work out great," he said. "She said one of her professors kept telling her she had a lotta talent and she'd wind up being an anchor on CNN or some shit like that."

"You sound skeptical."

"Pipe dreams. You gotta stay grounded."

Michael looked around the storeroom and thought, *It doesn't get more grounded than this.*

"From what I heard," he said, "she accused you of lacking ambition."

"I like it here just fine. I don't see no point in goin' nowhere else."

"What did you say to her?"

"I told her it was time to come home. We could figure out if it was gonna work out between us. Actually, I wanted to ask her to marry me. But I didn't wanna do it there. I had the spot all planned out. The steps that Stallone ran up in the movie. I was gonna get a ring and everything. It woulda been nice."

Chapter Twenty-Four

Rocco Cantone

1

April 7, 2012

S he loved the life she thought she was going to lead. Right now, she bunked alone in a cubicle with the bathroom down the hall, but she'd always believed in herself, and now she was babbling about how she was gonna get a job on-air at a TV station, and then she'd become an anchor, or maybe she'd travel around the world like Christiane Amanpour. There was always a crisis somewhere. It was all so exciting.

He knew he'd hate to be around when it all turned to shit, as it inevitably would.

"D'ya hear me, Rocco?" Her voice wasn't loud, but it was hard and feisty. He had never admitted this to anyone, especially to her, but whenever she behaved this way, he got turned on. "It's finally over. At long last. We've been dancing around this for years, but I can't go on with you. You're like a goddamn chain that keeps me tied down."

He should have left right then, just walked out the door without saying a word so he could take the next bus to Philly. Then he'd give her the silent treatment for a while. It had always worked before. They always reconnected, and the makeup sex was great.

But he stayed there. It felt like she was challenging him. As if she thought all the problems in her life were his fault.

"I'm draggin' you down?" He bit the words. "That's the most ridiculous thing you've ever said—and that's sayin' a lot."

"You have no ambition, Rocco. None."

"That's not true."

"Then waddya wanna do with your life?"

"I dunno."

She threw up her arms like a ref signaling a touchdown. "You just proved my point."

"I wanna work. I wanna a job and I wanna a house and I want us to have kids."

"That is not within miles of being good enough. I'm not gonna live in a fucking rowhouse in South Philly the rest of my life."

Rocco was growing angry and horny. "Leaving Philly was the worst thing that ever happened to you. You believe the bullshit they're tellin' you here?"

"Leaving was the best thing that ever happened to me. I got away from you and that goddamn neighborhood and those small-minded people, and now I have a chance to go places I've only dreamed about. And you wanna drag me back there? Jesus Christ, Rocco, get a clue."

She'd let something slip. He knew she wouldn't think he'd pick up on it, but he had.

"Waddya mean you're gonna go places?" he asked.

"Waddya think it means?" She looked away from him. She'd never been good at lying. "It means I'm gonna go places."

"With who?" he asked. Keep your voice as quiet as possible, he told himself. It's much more effective that way.

"That's none of your business."

"We've been together a long time. It is my business."

"I meet people, Rocco. Okay? I've met people here who travel around the world, and now I've got a chance to do it, and that's what I'm gonna do."

She'd dodged his question, so he rephrased it: "Who are you goin' with?"

"I don't have to tell you that."

"It's some guy, ain't it? Some rich fuck. He's gonna pay your way while you sleep with him, right? Nice deal you've worked out for yourself."

"Get outta here, Rocco." She was screaming at him as loudly as she ever had, and that was saying something. "I don't ever wanna see you again."

He had never hit her. He knew plenty of guys who smacked their women around, but he didn't think it was right, especially since he was much bigger than she was. And over the years, they had broken up so many times that, of course, they wound up seeing other people while they were split.

But this was different. Right now, they were a couple, and she was sneaking around.

She yanked open the door.

"Leave. Forever. I mean it."

The room was so small it took him only two strides to reach her. He grabbed the door and slammed it shut.

"I'm not goin' anywhere. Not 'til you tell me what's goin' on."

"I'll call the cops."

"You're gonna travel around the world on some guy's dime? You're just a high-class whore."

"I've had it with you, Rocco. Get outta here!"

She reached for the door, but he grabbed her arm before she could put her hand on the knob. Her size was deceptive because she was strong and athletic, and he could feel her muscles twitching as she writhed from him. He really was getting aroused by all this, and he wondered if she was, too.

"Don't touch me!"

Her voice was usually layered with an erotic toughness, but now she was shrieking. He'd never heard her like that—high-pitched words that sounded as if they'd scraped against sandpaper before escaping her mouth. The nerve-racking noise ran up his spine as she squirmed in his hands, and he kept thinking, over and over: *She has to listen to me. Why won't she listen?*

"Marie. Please."

"Stop touching me!"

"Marie."

As she struggled, he wrapped his arms tighter around her, and the whole

175

thing resembled an awkward dance as they bumped and crashed into the furniture, the books and the computer, and he was aware that things were toppling to the floor, and she just kept screeching.

He repeated, like a mantra, "Listen to me, calm down, listen to me." She was the one who was hysterical.

They ended up on the bed. He was on top. She wriggled underneath like a fish that had just been hooked, and he pinned both her wrists against the mattress. He tried to tell her she couldn't do this to him, couldn't leave him this way, they could talk things over, and make everything all right, but for God's sake she had to shut up for a minute.

The funniest thing was this: He had never wanted her so badly.

That was when the cops came. The door started shaking, and he thought it was an earthquake or something, but then he heard a masculine bass full of command telling them to open up for the NYPD.

He was impressed that somebody could swoop in from outside and take control of a situation. Later on, whenever he thought about that night, he realized that this was the moment he began to consider becoming a police officer.

He let her up. Welts covered her wrists and forearms and he noticed scratches on her cheeks. His neck hurt, and he realized she must have grabbed at his crucifix while they were tussling.

As she approached the door she smoothed her clothes and hair. Always preparing for that TV career. He thought she'd tell them to go away. Marie and Rocco were adults and this was a domestic situation and they could resolve it themselves.

Two uniformed officers stood in the hall. The guy with the voice was Black, six-foot-two and more than two hundred pounds. His partner was smaller and Asian, a wiry type who looked like he did martial arts in his spare time. Both of them exuded a do-not-mess-with-us vibe, which Rocco eventually respected.

"You live here?"

It was the Black cop. Probably the senior guy, which meant he'd do the talking.

"I do," Marie said.

"Who's this?"

She waved her arm in Rocco's direction as if she were shooing away a fly. "My ex-boyfriend."

He wanted to explain the situation. He wanted to tell them he'd been dating Marie since high school. He'd even taken the day off from work to visit because she said she was so busy at school she couldn't come home for Easter.

The cops stepped inside without being asked. Half of Marie's possessions were on the floor.

"Did he assault you, Miss?"

Rocco wanted to shout that the question was bogus, but the cops' faces were masks, and he had no idea how they'd react.

"I'd prefer not to get into that, Officer." Marie's voice was strong and clear. I guess they work on that at this bullshit school, Rocco thought. "I'd just like to get him outta here."

The Black cop looked at Rocco as if he were a small and annoying dog that had yet to be house-trained. "You heard the lady. Let's go."

"No."

Rocco was surprised at what he was saying. He had never talked back to a policeman, and, in the back of his head, he wondered if it was because the guy was Black, and then he thought: *No, that's not it, I'm not like that.*

The Asian cop wrapped his hand around Rocco's bicep. "C'mon, fella. Time to leave."

Rocco tried to pull away, but the cop's grip was too strong. "You don't understand. I need to talk to her."

"Ma'am?" the Black cop asked Marie.

"Officer," she said.

That's a smart move, Rocco told himself. Show the Black guy some respect.

Marie adopted a newscaster's voice, and Rocco said to himself: Maybe she is good at it.

"I don't ever want to talk to this man, or see him, for the rest of my life."

At that moment, she looked beautiful and tough and sexy and fit and intelligent, and he suddenly realized he might have been too headstrong because he'd never find another woman like this and would it be too bad to follow her and support her in what she was trying to do and besides New York wasn't that far from Philly and he could go back whenever he wanted.

He tried to break free. "C'mon, Marie, we gotta talk."

She narrowed her eyes. The lines on her forehead furrowed like canals, and she started hissing like the world's most venomous viper: "We have nothing to talk about. Leave. Me. Alone."

"You heard her." It was the Black cop again, sounding like a dean of discipline who was running out of patience with the most rambunctious kid in the class. "Let's go, pal."

Rocco reached out for just one more touch of her smooth, tight skin. But she jumped back and hollered as if he were an enormous cockroach that had just crawled into view, and now both cops had their arms wrapped around him, and he was twisting around as if he were in a straitjacket and they were telling him to go, Goddammit, and she was yelling that she wanted him out of her life forever and he couldn't help it, his voice was rising, he wanted everyone to know what he was ready to do: "This ain't over, Marie. Not by a long shot. I'll be back here. This ain't finished yet."

Straining against the cops was like trying to fight the current on a slide at a water park. He found himself in the hall, and his arms were wedged behind his back before he felt hard and cold metal snap over his wrists as the officers cuffed him. Doors up and down the hall opened a bit. Free entertainment for everyone. Marie stood a few feet away.

"You wanna press charges, ma'am?" the Black cop asked.

Her face scrunched in thought. They must teach her to do that in those horseshit classes, Rocco thought.

"I'd hafta see him in court, wouldn't I?" she asked.

"Probably," the cop said.

She shook her head. "I don't wanna press charges. I just want him to go away. Forever."

"That ain't gonna happen, Marie!"

The Black cop glared at Rocco and said, "I strongly advise you to keep your mouth shut."

Rocco blinked a few times. An African American had never talked to him like that before.

The Asian cop stepped between Marie and Rocco, who didn't like the way he was looking at her. Rocco could always tell when a man was interested in his girlfriend.

"If I can suggest something, Ms. Antolini," he said.

"Call me Marie," she replied in her most alluring voice, and suddenly Rocco was overcome with the feeling of rage that must have surged over O.J. when he saw that waiter walking up to his wife's home. Rocco never condoned what O.J. did, of course, but he understood.

"Well, Marie, my partner and I, we see a lotta incidents like this. And a lotta times, when a man is saying the kinds of things your ex-boyfriend is saying—well, he's telling the truth. It isn't over."

"So you're telling me I should press charges?" She sounded as if she was inviting him in for a glass of wine.

"We'd hate to come back here," the Black cop said.

"There is something else you can do," the Asian cop said.

"What is it?" Marie asked. Her voice was seductive. Rocco wanted to tear off her clothes. Go at it right there, and they'd already had sex that day right after he got off the bus from Philly. God, he loved this woman, and he loved his desire for her.

"You can obtain an order of protection," the Asian cop said.

"Will that do any good?"

"Hard to say. But if you have one, and we come back here because he's bothering you, we can arrest him right away. We'd swear out the warrant and tell the judge what happened, you wouldn't need to testify, and he'd spend a few weeks in Rikers thinking things over."

She squinted to look at the cop's nametag. "That's good advice, Officer Fung. Where'd you learn that?"

"I go to law school in my spare time. I wanna join the DA's office someday."

Marie smiled at him as wide as she could, and Rocco thought, Why don't you just sink to your knees and give him a blowjob?

"A man with ambition," she said. "I like that."

2

April 13, 2012

He got home, hungry and bone-tired, a little before seven after pulling a double at Giuseppe's. Ma's gravy simmered in the kitchen, and he felt grateful dinner would soon be on the table.

He collapsed on the recliner in the living room, reached for the remote, clicked on the TV.

Is this all there is? he asked himself. *Wake up, go to work, come home, eat, fall asleep? Day after fucking day? Shit, there's gotta be more to life than this.*

He once had more. He once had Marie. No other girl was like her.

The news was on. National stuff. They were still going on about that case in New York where the jogger got attacked.

"Didja hear?"

It was Ma's voice, somewhere behind him.

"Hear what, Ma?"

What he really wanted was a beer. He wondered if he should ask her for one.

She motioned toward the TV. "That thing. They call her the Riverside Runner."

"It's been all over the news for days, Ma."

"It was Marie."

He muted the TV and swiveled his head even though it took all his energy. Ma stood in the doorway. Her face was ashen, and she rubbed her hands as if she were fingering rosary beads.

"Waddya mean?" he asked.

"I heard it at Santucci's. I was shopping for tomatoes for the gravy, getting some oregano and garlic, too. Roseann Gambino was there, and Francine Paladino. We were talking at the vegetable stand."

"With all due respect, Ma, what the hell are you saying?"

"Well, you know that Francine is good friends with Regina Antolini."

Rocco was unaware of the friendship, but he nodded anyway.

"Well, Francine has been at Regina's for days. Regina's been crying her eyes out. Those savages left Marie for dead in the park, but she survived, thank God—" Ma made the Sign of the Cross "—but now her doctors are afraid she's gonna be a vegetable, like the zucchini we were looking at."

Rocco tried to make sense of what Ma had just said. Her line of conversation usually zigzagged like a riderless horse. He once asked Pa how he coped with it, and the man just waved his hand and said, "We've been married a long time. I know what she means."

Rocco pointed to the TV. "You telling me they know that Marie was the girl who was attacked in the park?"

"She was an athletic girl," Ma said. "You know how she was always running and working out and stuff."

"I know, Ma. We ran together sometimes."

Rocco preferred weights at the gym. Cardio was a chore. But Marie liked to run, and whenever they jogged along the Schuylkill, it would turn into a race, and she always beat him. She'd laugh as he came across the imaginary finish line, puffing and sweating and feeling his heart trying to crash through his chest wall. He'd put on a good act, but he hated losing to a girl. Most times, she made it up to him later with a furious bout of lovemaking.

God, he missed her.

"Are you listening to me, Rocco?" Ma asked.

"Sorry. My mind was wandering."

Ma began talking real fast. "Anyway, Marie was runnin' through that park at night, and she had on headphones or somethin', and the police say she couldn'ta heard nothin', and those creatures mauled her like they were a buncha wild bears. People like that are why we need the electric chair. Let 'em fry, I say."

Rocco looked at the TV. The news had moved on. Some terrorists had done something somewhere.

181

"There's one thing I gotta ask you about," Ma said.

"Go ahead."

"That paper you got. The order of rejection."

A marshal had come to the house. The document, which looked official, was signed by a judge. Ma and Pa were there when it happened, and Rocco wanted to crawl inside a closet and never come out, but instead, he took the paper and mumbled that he accepted it.

"They're gonna come around and ask about that and everything you've been doing, aren't they?" Ma said.

Rocco slid down in the chair. He didn't feel like thinking, but all sorts of crap was likely to happen, and he tried to consider the possibilities.

"I guess they will, Ma."

"What are we gonna tell 'em?"

Rocco pointed at *Wheel of Fortune* on the flickering screen. A contestant had just bought a vowel.

"We tell 'em I was home. Watchin' TV."

Chapter Twenty-Five

Michael Devine

1

May 30, 2012

Rocco Cantone delivered his story about his final argument with Marie Antolini in a way that struck Michael as almost practiced. He had dealt with witnesses like this, people who spent hours rehearsing in front of a mirror. Eventually, they convinced themselves that everything they said was true.

"When was the last time you were in New York?" Michael asked.

"What kind of bullshit question is that?" Rocco asked.

Michael's stock answer was ready: "The kind of bullshit question the lead prosecutor in a case like this gets to ask."

Rocco shrugged. "The last time I was there was the night Marie and me had that fight. The only reason I ever went to that city was to see her."

"And you never tried to make contact with her after that?"

"She had an order of protection. What was I supposed to do?"

"Here's the thing, Rocco," Michael said. "A lotta times, when a woman gets an order of protection, the guy thinks: 'She doesn't mean it. She's overreacting. Typical hysterical female. If I can just see her and talk to her, she'll come to her senses, and everything'll be fine.'"

"I understand that," Rocco said.

Michael resisted the urge to grab this guy by his apron strings and shake a smidgen of sense into him. "But here's what happens in real life: The woman sees the guy and freaks out, then he freaks out, then things get outta control, and then people like Detective Haggerty and myself wind up getting involved. If we're lucky, nobody's dead. You follow what I'm saying?"

"Not really."

Michael adopted his cross-examining-a-perp voice. "After you received the lawful order forbidding you from making contact with Marie Antolini, or coming anywhere near her, did you try to call her, or see her, or do anything at all that could be regarded as a violation?"

Rocco looked straight at the prosecutor.

He's not intimidated, Michael thought. I'm not sure if that's a good sign or a bad one.

Rocco drew himself up to his full height. He was a tall and handsome young man.

Marie was right, Michael thought. You really can do something with your life if you show even a bit of drive.

"Despite what you might think, Counselor, I can read. I know what that order said and what it meant. So, no, I did not violate it. I've never broken the law in my life." He shrugged. "Well, there was that one drunk and disorderly charge. But the judge dismissed it because my record was clean. He just told me to stay outta trouble."

Haggerty folded his arms across his chest and leaned his back against a floor-to-ceiling stack of boxes. "I've got a question for you, Rocco."

"Will you guys ever leave me alone?"

"We will if you tell us the truth," Michael said.

Rocco rolled his eyes.

"When you two had that big fight in her room," Haggerty said, "she told you she was going somewhere, probably overseas, with a guy."

"Not in so many words—but I could figure it out."

"You have any idea who this guy was? Or is?"

Rocco shook his head, and Michael tried hard to avoid looking at Haggerty, but he was sure they were both thinking the same thing: If Marie Antolini had entered a relationship with a man who was promising to take her abroad, they'd better find out who he was and ask him some questions before a defense attorney unearthed his existence.

"Let's get back to the night Marie was attacked," Michael said. "What did you do?"

Rocco pointed to Haggerty. "I already told him."

"Tell me."

"I got home from work. I ate dinner with Ma and Pa. Spaghetti. Meatballs. Gravy. Salad. Bread. Then we watched TV. *Law & Order*. Then I went to bed. Ma and Pa stayed up to watch the eleven o'clock news, but I hafta get up early for work. I was here at six in the morning."

Haggerty nodded. "I checked that out, Counselor. Owner says he was here at six."

"Tell me about the episode you watched," Michael said.

"Huh?" Rocco asked.

"You watched *Law & Order* with your parents," Michael said. "What was the episode about?"

Rocco scratched his chiseled chin. "Geez, y'know, a lotta those shows are the same. Somebody commits a crime, the cops investigate it, they charge somebody, the DA takes over, and it goes to trial..."

"Welcome to my world," Michael said.

"You expect me to remember the details?"

"A few of them."

Rocco put his hand to his chin. That's what a dumb person does when he's trying to imitate a smart one, Michael thought.

"Lemme think..."

You do that, Michael said to himself.

"It was about a guy who was in jail for rape," Rocco said. "He said he didn't do it. Claimed his confession was—whatchamacallit, it starts with 'co'..."

"Coerced?" Michael said.

"That's it."

Michael told himself not to look at Haggerty. He kept his gaze locked on the deep brown eyes of Marie Antolini's ex-boyfriend.

"Anyway, the guy asked for a DNA test. And guess what?"

Rocco Cantone returned Michael's hard stare.

"He didn't do it. They put the wrong man in prison."

2

September 30, 2023

Michael had stayed with Jamie Quinn far longer than he intended. The slanting afternoon shadows on the loft's walls and floors reminded him of the crazy camera angles the directors used on the old *Batman* TV show.

"All of that is extremely interesting," Quinn said with a wheezy neutrality.

"It all checked," Michael said. "That's what the episode was about. I talked to his parents. They said Rocco was home that night, and they all watched *Law & Order* together. There's no record the guy was anywhere else on the day Marie was attacked. Certainly nothing that puts him in New York."

"You talk to his parents about Marie?" Quinn asked.

"Of course."

"What did they say?"

"They liked Marie, but they never thought it was a good match. The mother told me she thought Marie was headstrong—not a good fit for Rocco."

"You ask them about the order of protection?"

"Of course."

"What did they say?"

"The mother said the order was actually a blessing in disguise. It meant the relationship was definitely over, and Rocco could start looking at other girls, which was what she wanted all along."

"The father say anything?"

"Not really. You know how it is. Fathers always think their kids' lives will work out somehow, while mothers are convinced their children are constantly on the verge of catastrophe."

"And what did you think of all this, Counselor?"

"Are we still on the record, Mr. Quinn?"

"You bet."

Michael cleared his throat. "After talking to Rocco Cantone and his parents, I was convinced that we had apprehended the correct perpetrators. I saw no reason to question him further, and I was determined to keep any mention of him or the order of protection out of the trial. It was irrelevant. Judge Khan saw it the same way. At trial, the defense wasn't allowed to mention the relationship between Cantone and Marie because they couldn't establish a connection between him and the attack."

Under his bushy eyebrows, Quinn's glare was fierce. "I've been around the track more times than you've had cold beers. I know what you're doing."

"What am I doing, Mr. Quinn?"

"Dodging my question." The old reporter snapped off the tape recorder. "Let's go off the record, Counselor. You spent close to a day in Philadelphia talking to Rocco Cantone and his parents. What did you really think of them and what they were telling you?"

Michael took a deep breath. He knew what he thought, but he had never articulated it—even to Rachel, and he told her almost everything.

"There was something off about what Rocco and his parents said to me. To this day, I dunno if they lied, but I'm convinced they didn't tell me everything."

"Then why didn't you question him under oath, Counselor?"

"Because he didn't attack Marie Antolini. Whatever he was trying to hide was his own goddamn business. I was convinced then, and I am convinced today, that the guys we put away were involved in the assault." He thought of Felipe Huerta, but decided to avoid mentioning him. "We didn't get all of them. I acknowledge that. But sometimes, a partial victory is the only kind you can get."

Chapter Twenty-Six

Sheila Devine

October 2, 2023

She took the G to 9th Street and looked over the scene from the elevated station. Sleek glass condos brushed against fading brick warehouses that lined a canal that was purple and putrid. Developers called the neighborhood authentic; Sheila suspected they were running out of places to build high-end apartments.

From her perch, she spied them—dingy humans (maybe male, maybe female) in clothes the color of muck peering into Dumpsters, trash cans, and recycling bins.

There's a movie here, she said to herself, but I don't have the gumption to make it.

As she walked down the steps, she shoved her iPhone in her pocket so she could whip it out to either record the scene or call for help. On the street, industrial-size weeds rose to her eyeballs. A person on hands and knees foraged the curbside. A bent and withered hand wearing torn gloves picked up a can of Diet Coke and held it the way Indiana Jones displayed a relic.

Sheila called out. "Excuse me."

The person turned. Frightened eyes peered through a dirt-encrusted face, and Sheila reminded herself that the hardcore homeless had two modes of behavior: scared and aggressive.

The eyes blinked. The person straightened and moved away.

"I wanna talk to you," Sheila said.

The person backed up. Sheila thought of the animals she had seen on National Geographic documentaries who were trying to avoid predators.

"Policía?" the person asked.

The voice was high-pitched. Sheila figured she was talking to a woman.

"No soy la policía."

"Eres un trabajador social?"

"No. Soy un cineaste."

"Como Hollywood?"

"Hago documentales."

"Oh."

Great, Sheila thought. I can crush people's hopes in two languages.

"Estoy buscando un hombre llamado Felipe Huerta," Sheila said. "Lo conoces?"

The woman shuddered, and a torrent of words flooded out, and Sheila felt like telling her to speak way more slowly, but she concentrated as intensely as she could and felt she understood at least a bit of it:

Felipe Huerta was a bad and dangerous man who consumed all kinds of powerful drugs and nobody wanted anything to do with him and if Sheila had any sense at all she would stay away from the guy because he was as loco as anybody in la historia del mundo.

"No tengo otra opción," Sheila said.

The woman clasped her hands as if she were praying. In a low and halting voice that Sheila strained to hear, she said that, as far as she knew, el hombre loco had been exiled to an embankment underneath the expressway. Nobody else ever went there.

Sheila reached into her bag and took out a twenty-dollar bill. The woman's mouth gaped as Sheila extended the money.

"Gracias, Señora. Muchas, muchas gracias."

"De nada," Sheila said.

The woman made the bill disappear into one of the many folds in her tattered clothing. "Vaya con Dios," she said.

If He exists, Sheila told herself, I will need His help.

* * *

As sludge oozed around her ankles, she regretted her decision to wear sneakers instead of workboots. Stagnant water exuded a stench that combined chemicals with garbage while highway traffic throbbed overhead. The road's pillars shook whenever an 18-wheeler rumbled by.

Sheila's mind shifted from heaven to the underworld. If there is a hell, she thought, it looks like this.

Up ahead, she noticed a concrete slab that had once been a piece of the expressway. Beside the slab was a lump of fabric that looked as if something might be underneath. As she moved toward it, the muck surged to her shins, and when she got close, she saw that the thing was a piece of drapery with a rose pattern, probably discarded when a nouveau-riche hedge funder renovated a Carroll Gardens brownstone.

She bent over. Traffic din pounded her ears. She touched the Mace in her bag, just to make sure, before peeling away the fabric.

In the filth, she saw a figure that looked more like a skeleton than a man. Withered skin stretched over protruding bones. A muck-covered pendant lay against his chest. No sounds of breath. She pulled the fabric all the way off. No movement. She reached down to feel his pulse and figured her next move was a call to 911.

And then the thing on the ground hissed and sprang to its feet, and she found herself shrieking before landing on her ass, and the creature loomed overhead, arms flailing and teeth bared, emitting sounds she'd never heard from a human. Her bag had fallen a few feet away, so she rolled over and crawled toward it, but in her peripheral vision, she sensed that he was trying to reach it, too. He was used to the sludge and the noise, and she knew if he grabbed her stuff, she'd never get it back.

She swung her arm at his ankles and hit bone. The creature pitched face-first into the goop. As she reached for her bag, she heard words:

"Perra loca! Puta! Ramera!"

She took out the Mace. As the creature rose from the slime, he spread his hands and howled. When he lunged at her, she aimed a long spray at his eyes.

At first, he kept coming, as if he were an otherworldly force that could not be halted by anything on Earth. But after a few seconds, the neurons and synapses finally registered what was happening, and he screamed with pain as he covered his eyes and rolled in the mire as if it would somehow cure him.

Sheila wobbled to her feet.

Everything, she thought. I'll hafta throw out everything I'm wearing, and I'm never gonna get all this crap outta my hair.

"Are you Felipe Huerta?" she asked.

"Fuck you," he said.

"You don't have enough money to fuck me."

He raised his scum-covered hands to his eyes in an effort to rub away the gunk and the Mace, but succeeded only in moving the crud around.

"I think I like you," he said.

"Are you Felipe Huerta?"

"You from Social Services?"

I am a shit-covered Ninja, she thought. Do I look like I'm from freakin' Social Services?

"I'm a filmmaker."

"Hollywood?"

"Documentaries."

"Oh."

"I'm working on a movie about that night, Felipe."

"What fucking night you fucking talking about?"

"The night in the park. The runner. You wound up skating on the charges, but your pals are still in prison."

"I got no fuckin' pals. What the fuck you talkin' about?"

"Ulysses Watkins, for starters. He's in Attica. You talked to him a few years ago about venture capital."

Huerta blinked. Despite the drugs and the booze and the meds and the rage, he tried to connect his mind.

"U," he said. "Big Black dude. Haven't thought about him in a long time."

Don't give it away, Sheila thought. Don't tell him what Ulysses told you.

"He thought you were a friend," Sheila said.

"Never had no friends," Huerta said. "Don't believe in 'em."

"You invited him to play in that soccer game," Sheila said.

Huerta brought his knees up under his chin. He looked perfectly at home in the toxic stew.

"Didn't wanna play no fuckin' pansy soccer game," he said. "Wanted to go to the park and raise some hell. Knew U would be good at that."

Sheila's voice went into blue-font mode. "You succeeded. Congratulations."

Huerta tried to smile. Most of his teeth were missing. "Thanks."

Sheila took out her iPhone and engaged the video.

"Tell me about the park, Felipe. Tell me what happened with the runner."

Chapter Twenty-Seven

Felipe Huerta

April 11, 2012

H e loved the dark. The darker, the better. No lights. No moon. The world had abandoned him the moment he was born, and now he was gonna wreck it. He had waited forever for an opportunity like this, and these maricóns would do whatever he said to prove their manhood. Together, they'd destroy everything they touched.

He had no mama.

No papa.

No familia at all.

Foster homes. Crap schools. Fights with everyone. Life was an exercise in cruelty, so he was crueler than anyone. Didn't give a fuck what people thought. Fucking idiots didn't know what it took. He did.

In the park now. Minions around him—an army of pussies, but they'd try to show him they were as tough as he was.

Smelly old guy reeking of Ripple on the bench. His crap all around. They dumped every piece on the ground. Threw some of it in the river. Felipe wielded broken glass. Wanted to drag it across the bastard's throat. Blood spurting from an open wound was the most glorious sight on Earth.

"No, man."

A maricón piping up. What the fuck?

"Don't do it, man."

The guy who was talking wore glasses thicker than a window in a skyscraper.

"Why not?" Felipe shouted. He felt his power surging. "Why the fuck shouldn't I waste this fuckin' piece of shit right now?"

Four Eyes tried to sound reasonable. Fuck that. "What he do to you, man?"

For a moment, Felipe wanted to go after the nerd. Just stab him with the shard right through his fucking geek shield. The maricóns looked at Felipe, and he knew they were wondering what he was gonna do.

"Fuck it. Let's beat this fuckin' worthless mierda."

When they were done, the creature moaned on the ground. Coughed. Puked up blood.

Moving through the park. The gang was a living organism. Breathing. Swelling. Pulsating. It could sweep away everything in its path.

Old woman in rags asleep on a bench. They pushed her Pathmark cart down a ravine. She bellowed at them, and he told the senile bitch to shut up, shut up, shut up, but she just kept yelling, so he finally slapped her across her withered cheeks twenty or thirty times until she stopped.

Asshole on a bicycle. Felipe hurled a rock at him. Smashed his head. The rider wobbled and fell, and the whole thing was so goddamn funny. The shithead looked around and started swearing, but when the gang ran at him, his eyes got white and buggy, and he just got back on that bike and pedaled away as fast as he could even though he was bleeding from his nose and ears.

A guy and his girlfriend walking along. Arms around each other. Kissing. Lovey-dovey shit. Felipe couldn't stand it. The group swarmed, and the girl ran away screaming that they were animals, and Felipe felt like saying, Yes, you are prey, and we are predators who will seize whatever we want. They surrounded lover boy and beat him so good he wouldn't do the nasty for a long, long time.

Sirens.

Cops were easy to handle. You just had to keep quiet. They'd lose their cool and scream at you, and then you'd just tell them you wanted a lawyer, and they'd keep screaming at you, but all you had to say, over and over, was that you weren't gonna tell them nothin' 'til you talked to a mouthpiece.

Nobody should ever say a word to a cop.

But Felipe had been dead right about one thing: The guys with him were maricóns. When they heard the police coming, their eyes went wide like they were little babies, and they scattered like dry leaves blown by the wind. Felipe shouted that they should stick together. They could take on the cops. If they started a fight with those pigs, the people would join them.

A vision: Manhattan engulfed in battle, the city destroyed, bodies filling the street and flames all around and Felipe standing atop a pile of wreckage proclaiming himself emperor of everything he could see.

Instead it was just him and U. He'd known the guy a while. Big Black dude wasn't afraid of the cops, either.

"What the fuck, man?" U asked.

"Guess we gotta get out, bro."

"Shit." He dragged out the word into four syllables.

"I know whatcha mean. It's been fun."

They knew the park, so they cut through some trees and bushes, and the sirens grew softer, and the two of them started laughing about the shit they'd pulled, and U said they should do it again sometime, and Felipe agreed, but they'd hafta go somewhere different because the cops would be all over this park for a while. Idiota policia would wanna show the place was safe and all that crap.

U told Felipe he was smart. He hadn't thought of it that way.

"Police! Halt!"

It was a female voice, and Felipe felt like running right at her. How can a man be afraid of a woman?

But then U spoke softly: "Shit, man, bitch has a gun."

The Black dude ran north. Felipe figured he was heading home. Savvy move. U could get back to his apartment and lock the door. Fucking cops would have to get a warrant and shit.

Felipe slipped and slid toward the river. On TV, the police were always firing at fleeing suspects, but that was Hollywood bullshit. Cops had procedures, and he was young and quick and familiar with the terrain, and nobody was gonna catch him.

In a thicket. Heart racing. He'd been running. Told himself to inhale deeply but quietly. He needed to be silent. His feet crunched twigs and leaves, and he told himself to slow down and take it easy and, above all else, be careful.

Noise.

He stopped. Stayed still. It sounded like grunting, and he wondered what it meant. He hushed himself as he crept toward whatever it was.

Clothes on the ground: exercise gear and shit. Shredded tights in the dirt and headphones draped over a bush beside a bra that had been ripped in half, and when he heard a man moaning, *Oh God, Oh God, Oh God,* Felipe understood exactly what he had stumbled upon.

The girl was flat on the ground. Legs spread. Eyes closed. She wasn't moving or talking and Felipe thought she might be drunk or stoned. Chicks high on junk did wild stuff all the time.

She was white. Looked kinda small. Not his taste. Felipe liked a woman with meat on her bones.

The dude on top of her was maybe a foot bigger than she was, but his dark clothing and hoodie hid almost all his features. Felipe noticed one thing—the guy's pants were bunched around his shins, and he definitely had a white ass. His voice was weird, too. Some kinda accent. Probably from a foreign country, like Nebraska or something. Definitely not the 'hood.

Felipe considered joining. He liked the nasty as much as anyone. He wasn't queer or nothin', though it was getting cold, and he realized the guy he was watching must really want that woman if he was willing to do it outside, with the weather so bad.

He heard sirens again, and the guy musta heard them too because he sprang up like ash coming out of a volcano before hitching his pants and running away real fast. Felipe knew he had to get outta there as well, but something shiny was on the ground next to the girl. It might be gold or silver, so he grabbed it and bolted. Maybe he'd sell it, though the thing looked nice, so it could be a keeper.

But now his focus was messed up. He tried to orient himself, but he didn't recognize the surroundings. He tried to spot the moon or the stars or even goddamn New Jersey, but it was cloudy and foggy, so nothing worked.

Fuck, he thought. Where the fuck am I?

Wandering now. One way, then the other. Sirens in the distance. Chain-link fence before him. Felipe looked left and right to see if he could get around it, but the thing stretched as far as he could see. Ten feet high. He wondered what the fuck it was doing there and then laughed because probably it'd been put there by one of those do-good dirtbags in an effort to keep men like Felipe Huerta from having fun.

He climbed. The metal was wet, and his fingers and feet kept losing their grip, but he stayed at it and was almost to the top. He figured he'd swing his butt over and drop to the ground and resume running. He wished he knew where he was.

And then light beamed straight into his eyes while a bull-horned voice broke through his eardrums and remained inside his head forever:

"Stay right there, Asshole."

Chapter Twenty-Eight

Michael Devine

October 2, 2023

H e picked up the intercom when it buzzed from the lobby.
"Mr. Devine?"
The concierge sounded concerned.
"What is it?"

"There are demonstrators outside the building, sir."

The concierge, Eduardo, had worked there for years. His smooth voice had a slight Latin accent. If Michael remembered correctly, he had fled El Salvador in the Eighties.

"They're holding placards, sir. With your name on them. We can keep them a few feet away, but there are TV cameras and photographers around, so we don't want to create a scene."

"I understand. Thanks for the heads-up."

"You can leave through the back way, sir. We can send the service elevator up for you."

Michael thought this over. "I appreciate the offer, Eduardo, but I'll head for work the way I usually do."

He knew why the protesters were there. Citing a blog post by the former *Daily News* columnist Jamie Quinn, the *Times* had splashed a story about Rocco Cantone all over its front page and website. Links to social media meant it was trending like crazy. The article focused on Mr. Cantone's fatal encounter with Luttrell Aldridge, the unarmed African-American motorist in Philadelphia, but about halfway through the reporters brought up the police officer's one-time romantic relationship with Marie Antolini, the victim in the Riverside Runner case. The news organization of record noted that police and prosecutors in New York had determined at the time of the attack that Mr. Cantone had no involvement in the brutal assault.

"Lemme guess," Rachel said as she thumbed a text. "The jackals are outside."

"Apparently, they're baying quite loudly."

"I'll wear a power outfit."

* * *

Out the revolving door. A nod to the doorman. Rachel's arm entwined with his. Once he was on the sidewalk, the noise from the crowd morphed from chants to screams to din.

He glanced at the professionally made signs. The placard that caught his attention said MICHAEL DEVINE ENSLAVES PEOPLE OF COLOR.

By now, cops had arrived. Barricades along the street had pushed the demonstration to the side because regular people needed access to the building.

He recognized a few reporters whose shouted questions were swallowed by the cacophony. An Uber waited by the curb.

Rachel leaned into his ear. The act looked chaste yet intimate. He hoped this visual made the news.

"Waddya gonna do?" she asked.

"Talk to them," he replied. "It'll look bad if we just duck into the car."

He reminded himself not to smile as he approached the crew from New York One. This was a serious development in a serious story, and he was a serious public servant.

The reporter thrust her microphone at him and asked, "Do you have any comment about what happened in Philadelphia?"

Michael regarded the question the way a running back reacts to a wide-open hole in the defensive line. He had to restrain himself from speaking too quickly:

"The events in Philadelphia are a tragedy for everybody concerned. I know the district attorney there and the office he runs, and I'm sure a full and fair investigation is already underway and will result in a just outcome."

Rachel squeezed his elbow.

"What kind of an effect will this have on the district attorney's race?"

The reporter kept her microphone in his face. Her name was Zhen Xiang and Michael silently congratulated the assigning editor who'd had the savvy to send an Asian-American to cover the story.

"We will continue to conduct the campaign on the issues we've been talking about," Michael said. "We want a safe city where everyone is equal in the eyes of the law."

That's pretty good, he thought. On my better days, I even believe it myself.

"You have nothing but contempt for the people."

The words were clear and crisp and had undoubtedly been picked up by the cameras and smartphones recording the scene. Michael looked in the direction of the voice and saw the crowd parting, Cecil B. DeMille fashion, to allow a woman of color to walk to the front. After a second he recognized LaToya Crawford, mother of Roberto Linares, and he feared this ferocious lady was going to dog him the rest of his life.

She was coiffed and made up and wearing a sophisticated but understated ensemble. Michael guessed she'd had her work done at Saks and wondered who was bankrolling her.

Rolando Ortega, he said to himself. That cabrón is one slick motherfucker.

LaToya Crawford was just getting started.

"You persecuted my son because he is Black and Latin," she said.

"Ma'am—"

"Don't 'ma'am' me. You put him in prison because of the color of his skin. There were people you could have prosecuted, but you didn't because they were white."

"Ms. Crawford—"

"Don't think you can get away with this phony show of respect."

Spitting her words. Eyes wide and bulging. Despite the makeover, she came across as the world's angriest parent, and he knew how bad she'd look on TV and the internet.

Marshall McLuhan still reigns, he said to himself. It's a cool medium. You can't act hot.

"You have this police officer in Philadelphia. We all know his name. We all saw what he did the other night. We all know what he's capable of."

Shouts of "Amen" and "Tell it."

"He dated that poor girl who was raped and beaten in the park. He's mean, he's vicious, and she finally got wise to him."

Shouts of "Speak the truth."

"She got an order of protection 'gainst him, but it didn't do no good 'cause he came back here and tried to kill her, and now he killed a brother in Philadelphia, and it's all your fault 'cause you let him get away with it!"

LaToya Crawford was screeching with the pain of the aggrieved.

"There is blood on your hands, Mr. Prosecutor. Blood all over your body, and there is no way you'll ever wash it off!"

The crowd roared in righteous approval as the woman sagged like a marathoner who had just crossed the finish line. Michael reminded himself to straighten his back. Rachel pressed closer.

"After the crime occurred, Ms. Crawford, my office investigated the man you are alluding to."

What he wanted to say was: I went down to goddamn Philadelphia and talked to that schmuck myself.

"We knew all about his relationship with the victim. And we investigated his whereabouts on the day of the incident."

Pause. Michael felt as if he were back in the courtroom. It was dead quiet, and the jurors were soaking in every word he uttered.

"We found no evidence he was in New York that day."

Unlike your son, he felt like adding. We have plenty of evidence about that.

* * *

During the day, he addressed business roundtables and civic groups in between signing off on some high-profile plea deals. His pollster told him he'd lost two percentage points to undecided, but his lead was still outside the margin of error.

"Shit."

Rachel sat beside him in the backseat as they headed home. Michael could have sworn he'd once seen the driver in *Cats*.

"Another disaster?" Michael asked.

"Emails from Seamus O'Toole. He says Rolando Ortega has a press availability tomorrow morning during which he is going to pull a very large rabbit out of a very small hat."

She handed her phone to Michael, who read the message and wondered if this was something he should worry about, or if O'Toole was engaged in a typical media overreaction.

Don't kid yourself, Michael thought. If Ortega's holding a news scrum, he thinks he has something good.

Michael took out his iPhone and pressed O'Toole's number.

"I'm still a reporter at heart," O'Toole said. "I ask questions. I hear things. Sometimes, I even discover information before it gets on the internet."

"Go ahead," Michael said. "What is it?"

Long sigh. "You won't like this one bit, Counselor. I don't, either."

Chapter Twenty-Nine

Sheila Devine

October 3, 2023

T he conference room was packed, and she was glad Ortega had let her in early. She decided to use the Sony handheld rather than her phone because she wanted the footage to look official, not jumpy. She still did not know the purpose of this free-for-all, but she was sitting only six feet from the microphones that Ortega's office had set up. Doughnuts were spread beside a huge coffee urn on a table near the door.

Ortega entered shortly after nine, trailed by Dolores, Tamika, and a Black man Sheila did not recognize. The lawyer sat behind one microphone. The Black guy took another. He was middle-aged and paunchy. A bushy mustache flecked with gray curled around his mouth.

Sheila wondered if this was going out live on the cable networks. If Michael was watching.

Ortega began: "Ladies and gentlemen, I want to thank you for coming on such short notice."

Michael had once asked Sheila why Rolando Ortega always received such glowing treatment from the news media. Sheila thought it over before replying that he did something she had never observed from any other public figure: He was always courteous to reporters, even when he was telling them to buzz off.

"The man beside me is DeMarcus Daniels. For the last twenty years, Mr. Daniels has been a driver for the MaxiBus company, which operates throughout the Northeast. Mr. Daniels is based in Philadelphia, where he has lived his entire life. He has a statement to read, after which we will take a few questions."

Sheila zoomed in on the driver. Sweat beaded on his temples. When he started to speak in a high-pitched voice, he read the words reallyreallyfast, as if he just wanted to get this thing over with, but Sheila kept reminding herself to focus on what he was saying, instead of how he said it, because his assertions bordered on earth-shaking:

DeMarcus Daniels was willing to testify, under oath, so help him God, that on April 11, 2012, on his regular route between Philadelphia and New York, when he dropped off his passengers at Chatham Square, shortly before five p.m. just as the schedule said, one of the people who exited was Rocco Cantone, former boyfriend of Marie Antolini, the Riverside Runner.

As the man spoke, she panned the increasingly tense crowd and was surprised to see Rajeev Dalweet, current CNN anchor and former J-school friend of Marie's, parked near the doughnuts.

I hafta talk to him when this is over, she said to herself. This story is going national. Maybe even global.

As soon as DeMarcus Daniels finished, the reporters exploded with shouts and roars. Ortega raised his hands in an attempt to quell the din.

"Before we get to your questions," he said in his most soothing voice, "I want to add a comment that all of you may find useful.

"Mr. Daniels contacted my office early yesterday morning to tell us what he just told you. We have checked out his story, and we have also given this courageous gentleman a lie detector examination. As you all know, such tests are inadmissible in a court of law. However, I will tell you right now, unequivocally, that Mr. Daniels passed it with flying colors."

The reporters all looked wide-eyed. Every member of the media Sheila had ever talked to regarded lie detectors as infallible.

"After all this time—"

She swung her camera around. Rajeev Dalweet was speaking.

"—how can you be sure it was Mr. Cantone who rode your bus?"

"Well," Daniels said, "I just remember that he was a very, very unusual passenger."

"Why was that?"

"He was white."

The reporters tittered, but Dalweet kept his voice clear and even and uninflected. He made anchor's money for a reason.

"I'm not sure I follow you, Mr. Daniels."

The bus driver licked his lips. Sheila sensed he was thirsty. As if some kind of telepathy were at work, Tamika slipped a bottle of Poland Spring in front of him.

Daniels sucked on the water a few seconds before answering.

"MaxiBus caters to members of the Asian community. Our hubs are in all the Chinatowns along the East Coast—D.C., Baltimore, Philly, New York, Boston. We do have a few brothers and sisters riding us, too, 'cause the prices are good, but I hardly ever see any white people on my bus, so they tend to stand out."

"But after all these years—"

Skepticism from Dalweet. Sheila shared it.

"—how can you be sure the white man you saw on your bus was Rocco Cantone?"

Daniels slugged more water. "Well, sir, I got a good look at him on the ride 'cause he was sitting in the front row, right behind me. I examined his features even though he was wearing a hoodie. It was like he didn't want nobody to recognize him even though he was a good-looking man." Daniels shrugged. "People who act like that always stand out."

"What did he do when he got off the bus?"

"Got right out and walked away double-time. Didn't have no luggage. Looked like he had a hot date or somethin'."

"There's no record that Rocco Cantone traveled to New York that day."

Daniels shrugged again. "Mighta paid cash. That's not my concern. I just took his ticket. He was first in line."

An Android-gazing reporter beside Sheila muttered that in 2012 a round-trip ticket between New York and Philadelphia on MaxiBus cost twenty dollars.

"How can you be sure it was that day?" Dalweet asked.

"April Eleventh is a special day in my family. It's my wife's birthday. When I got back to Philly that night, we went out to dinner, and I told her about the passenger. We both agreed it was very, very unusual."

"Why didn't you say anything until now?"

"I never made no connection before," Daniels said. "But then there were all these reports about the police officer who murdered that brother—"

Sheila expected Ortega to wince, but he remained serene and unflappable, like a poker player who's confident he has the best hand even if all his money is in the pot.

"—and when I saw his picture, he looked familiar, so I did some Google searching on my device when I was laid over in D.C. the other day."

Daniels displayed his iPhone.

Thanks to Steve Jobs, Sheila said to herself, everybody can be an investigative journalist.

Ortega nodded at Daniels in what looked like a prearranged signal. The bus driver leaned away from his mic while the lawyer spoke up.

"We are going to amend our filing with the courts as we seek to remedy the injustice that has been done to my clients."

Sheila noticed the use of the plural. All four of them must have signed up with him by now, she said to herself. That's what I'd do.

"We will provide Mr. Daniels' statement, although, obviously, we cannot include the results of the lie detector."

But everyone sure as shit knows about it, Sheila thought.

"We firmly believe this new piece of information, coupled with the lack of proof from the examination of the DNA found at the scene, establishes ample reasons to vacate the convictions of my clients and grant our request for a new trial."

Reporters lunged for the remaining doughnuts as Ortega and his entourage left the room. Sheila squirmed toward Rajeev Dalweet, who was talking just outside the door with his camera operator, a heavyset Latina with tricolored hair.

He doesn't have to shoot his own footage, Sheila said to herself. He really is a star.

"I'll do a standup on the street," Dalweet was saying. "Pedestrians moving around. A real New York scene."

The camera operator said she'd see him outside the building in a few minutes. First, she had to pee. He told her to be quick and to make sure she washed her hands.

Sheila introduced herself. Dalweet nodded.

"I saw the film about your father," he said. "Terrific stuff."

"Thank you."

"The Oscars screwed you over."

"Don't get me started."

"I've heard you were working on a documentary about this case."

"You heard right."

"How does your brother feel about that?"

"He hasn't spoken to me on the record yet."

"Dredging up all of this can't be good for his campaign."

"He's still gonna win."

"In 2016, everybody thought Hillary was gonna win."

Touché, Sheila said to herself. "Why are you here? I thought you were an anchor."

"Sometimes I like to get out of the office."

"And you knew Marie."

"That's right."

Sheila wondered if CNN was planning an instadoc. Would be just like those pricks to steal my thunder, she thought. Well, screw them. I have access to Ortega, and they don't.

"Have you been in touch with her since all this began?" Sheila asked.

"I haven't talked to her in a long time. The attack—" Dalweet pointed to his head "—scrambled her brain. I visited her in the hospital a few times while she was recovering and talked to her at the trial. She barely remembered who I was."

Sheila wanted to keep going, but Dalweet looked at his iPhone.

"I gotta finish my segment," he said. "And I have a dozen texts to reply to. Christ, I haven't even checked my email for an hour."

"I wanna talk to you about Marie," Sheila said.

As Dalweet walked away, she thought she heard him say, "Maybe."

* * *

She trailed Dalweet to the Time Warner Center on Columbus Circle, then camped out in CNN's lobby until he agreed to see her. When she reached his office, he pointed her to a chair whose metal arms needed polishing. The narrow room had a sweeping view of Central Park, where the trees were beginning to turn.

"How well did you know Marie Antolini?" she asked.

"The three of us were kind of a team."

"Three of you?"

"Marie and myself and Gloria Estevez. We worked on projects together and fantasized that at some point, we'd all be on the same morning show." He smiled, displaying anchor teeth. "You know what it's like when you're a kid. You think limits are for other people."

"What happened to Gloria Estevez?" Sheila asked. "I'm not familiar with that name."

"She went back to Texas. We lost touch. I think she worked for a cable station there."

"What was grad school like?"

"Intense. You ever do grad work?"

Sheila shook her head.

"It's not like being an undergrad," he said. "No time for partying. You work all the time."

"I heard Marie was regarded as a real talent."

"Our adviser thought she had the best future of all of us."

"Who was your adviser?"

"Seamus O'Toole."

Sheila remembered seeing O'Toole on CNN in the Nineties and Aughts, standing amid rubble in whatever part of the world was blowing itself up that week. On location, he was noted for wearing a St. Christopher's medal, and Sheila understood why. Now, he was consulting Michael's campaign. Star reporters always price themselves out of the market, but Seamus O'Toole had managed a second act.

"What did he think of you?" she asked Dalweet.

"He's surprised I wound up here."

Dalweet swept his arm in a gesture intended to take in all of New York and, perhaps, the world. Sunlight glinted off a silver bracelet with beads and a cameo of an elephant trunk. Sheila had looked into his background: A Jersey kid whose parents emigrated from Bangalore, he bussed tables at their restaurant on Route 17 all through high school and college (Rutgers, Class of '09).

"Sounds like Marie was the teacher's pet," Sheila said.

"That's fair to say," Dalweet replied.

"Today, that has creepy connotations."

"As far as I know, nothing of that nature occurred."

"Would she have told you?"

"I'd like to think so."

"Would she have told Gloria?"

"If you can find her, you can ask."

"Did Marie ever talk about Rocco Cantone?"

The question produced a chuckle. "Oh, yeah."

"What did she say?"

"She complained about her boyfriend back home, who had no ambition whatsoever. I finally asked why she stayed with him, and that stopped her short. After a minute, she laughed and said, 'Inertia.'"

"You ever meet him?"

"Once. He didn't say much. But he was a handsome guy. Gloria took me aside and said, 'Now I get it.'"

"Did you have any romantic feelings toward Marie?"

Dalweet blinked a few times. "Say that again."

"You're an intelligent man. You know what I'm getting at."

Dalweet looked at the ceiling, and Sheila suddenly wished she was filming. Interviewees acting uncomfortable always made good footage.

"I liked Marie very much," he said. "But if I brought home a woman who wasn't from the subcontinent, my parents would have disowned me."

"Tell me about that night. Tell me what you did. Tell me how you reacted when you heard the news." Sheila reached into her bag and took out her Sony. "You know what this is. Can we go on the record?"

It took Dalweet a few long seconds, but eventually he nodded.

"April Eleventh, Two Thousand Twelve," Sheila said. "What do you remember?"

"I was in the editing lab. I knocked off pretty late—close to midnight, I think. I went back to my room in grad school housing. While I was walking there, I heard lots of sirens. Police and ambulance. You get used to those sounds in New York, but there were more than usual. Now that I look back at it, as an aspiring journalist, I should have investigated. But I was bone-tired and needed some sleep."

"When did you find out about Marie?"

"The next day, she wasn't around. Not in class. Not responding to calls or texts, or emails. Gloria and I went to her room. Not there. We became concerned. Marie was super-responsible, super-ambitious, and it was totally unlike her to just blow off everything and disappear.

"Around lunchtime, we went to Professor O'Toole's office. He was white as a sheet. That's when we realized something awful had happened."

He stopped. Sheila told him to keep going.

"He asked if we'd heard about the attack in Riverside Park the previous night. We had. It was all over the news. He took a really deep breath, and he was barely able to get the words out, but he said, 'The victim was Marie.'"

This is really good, Sheila thought as she looked at him through the viewfinder. "How did you react?"

"I went numb. Gloria started crying. She kept saying, 'Oh my God, oh my God,' and she couldn't believe it had happened. Professor O'Toole said it was all too true and told us to keep the information to ourselves. Obviously, her name wouldn't be released to the public. At that point, only a few people at the school knew she was the victim."

"What did you do next?"

"Went to the hospital. The scene was chaotic, but Professor O'Toole got us in through a side entrance. At the information desk, we said we were friends of Marie's, and the nurse looked at us really sharply and asked how we knew that she was the victim because the hospital wasn't giving that information out to the public. O'Toole said he had been a reporter, and now he was a professor at Columbia. Marie was one of his students, and it was his job to find out things like that. Then the nurse looked at him more closely and said she remembered seeing him on CNN. She eased up a bit after that."

"Did you get to see Marie?"

"Not that day. Everybody thought she was gonna die. A priest gave her the last rites. But she was resilient. The doctors, the nurses—they all said they'd never seen someone survive after losing so much blood. But she was in a coma for days. Whenever we got to the hospital, Professor O'Toole did most of the talking. He always asked if she'd regained consciousness and if she was saying anything. He always sounded so worried about her."

"But she came out of it," Sheila said.

"The doctors said they didn't like to use words like 'miracle,' but one of the nurses told me that's exactly what it was. Professor O'Toole asked if she could remember anything about that night, or anything at all, and one of the doctors shook his head and said she barely had any memory left at all about anything."

"You visited her anyway," Sheila said.

"It was painful. She put on a façade, but we could tell she barely knew who we were."

That's why she latched onto Michael, Sheila thought. Like a newborn attaching herself to her caregiver.

"That's when you met my brother," Sheila said.

"He's a stone-cold bastard." Dalweet smiled a bit. "I mean that in a good way."

"He acts that way on the job. He's warmer in private."

"And then there was his investigator. Detective Haggerty. He kept looking at me like he thought I did it. He looked at Professor O'Toole the same way. Gloria, too."

"Cops think everybody is guilty of something."

"I know what you're trying to do."

Sheila had no idea what she was trying to do. "Please enlighten me."

"Poke holes in my story. See if there are any inconsistencies. Maybe I was obsessed with Marie. Maybe I stalked her. Maybe I attacked her in the park and was more than pleased those guys took the rap for what happened."

Keep going, Sheila said silently. Maybe you'll talk yourself into jail.

"Detective Haggerty checked my whereabouts that night. People told him they saw me in the editing lab. My logout time was noted, and a surveillance camera recorded me entering my building ten minutes after that and never leaving until the following morning."

His story was plausible, although Sheila found herself thinking about the color of his butt.

Chapter Thirty

Michael Devine

1

October 4, 2023

War council at campaign headquarters. Top people sitting around a small rectangular table. Rachel at his right. Her father beside her. The pollster fiddled with his MacBook. Assistants flanked him.

Time for the PowerPoint. "Here's the trend," the pollster said.

The line representing Michael's support sloped downward on a trajectory that was gradual but noticeable.

"I can't see so good," Jacob Meyer said. "What's his percentage?"

"The three-day rolling average is fifty-two."

"That's still more than half," Meyer said.

"His support was close to sixty-three weeks ago. It's been eroding, but those numbers moved into undecided. Until—"

One of the assistants clicked on a new window. A red line depicted the level of support for Nelson Hernandez. That line was flat as a calm sea until the last week.

"In our last three-day rolling average, the opposition has gained five percentage points. The election is a month away. He has plenty of time to gain ground, and the direction is worrying."

The pollster pushed his glasses back onto the bridge of his nose. He wore a shirt buttoned all the way to the collar, but no tie. He was thirty-three but looked like he barely shaved. His name was Warren Petersen, and he came from one of the big flat states. Jacob Meyer had insisted on hiring him because in 2016, as a young statistics geek, he was the only pollster who predicted that Trump would sweep the Midwest.

"The decline in your support has coincided with the re-emergence of the Riverside Runner case," Petersen said. "You still have a healthy lead, but we can't be sure it'll hold up unless this issue is laid to rest."

"You see the latest development?" Michael asked.

"I was up all night crunching the numbers. I haven't even looked at my Twitter feed this morning." Petersen looked like he wanted to flagellate himself for such an egregious oversight before adding: "I shouldn't call it Twitter anymore, but it's hard to change."

"After that news conference yesterday," Michael said, "Rolando Ortega filed a motion asking for a test to match Rocco Cantone's DNA with the semen that was found at the crime scene."

Jacob Meyer spoke up: "If those savages who attacked that poor girl had just gotten the death penalty like I wanted, we wouldn't be going through this bullshit."

Petersen's assistants were both mixed race, gender fluid, and a decade younger than he was. As their faces darkened, they bit their lower lips. Michael figured they had heard plenty of horror stories about old and powerful white guys, but had never spent a lot of time with one.

"If you'll permit me to interject."

Heads turned toward the end of the table, where Seamus O'Toole perched on the edge of a chair.

"You'll be debating your opponent tomorrow night," O'Toole said. "Whether we like it or not, this case will dominate the event."

"The debate's on a Thursday night," Meyer said. "You're going up against the NFL and the baseball playoffs."

"Part of our plan," Rachel said. "We're hoping nobody will watch."

"Good luck with that," O'Toole said.

"Why does Michael even have to debate at all?" Meyer asked.

"Campaign finance law," Rachel said.

"Stupidest thing they ever passed," Meyer said.

O'Toole went on. "We need a gotcha moment that will show the voters you're qualified to be the DA, and your opponent is a blundering gasbag who's trying to exploit a tragedy."

Rachel turned to the pollster. "What do voters say about Hernandez? Give us the negative stuff."

Petersen looked at his MacBook. "Inexperienced. Shallow. Two-faced. Ready to say anything to anybody."

"Michael takes on the tough cases," Rachel said. "Makes the tough decisions. When I was a kid, I loved Mr. Rogers, but you don't want him as your district attorney."

"Mr. Rogers was a wimp," Jacob Meyer said. "I can't believe I let you watch that crap."

2

October 5, 2023

The debate was sponsored by the League of Women Voters and New York One. Both organizations had commandeered the Times Center, which was packed with people who'd been shut out at the TKTS booth.

Outside the building, protesters waved placards and chanted through bullhorns. Michael had gotten used to them, but his father-in-law wondered why the NYPD couldn't just firehose those useless agitators the way the cops did in Alabama back in the Sixties. Sometimes, Michael wondered if the man meant what he said, or if his political expressions were a form of performance art.

A helmet-haired TV blonde moderated the panel. To her right was a stubbly Latino from the *Times* and to her left a Black blogger from a website in Washington Heights. The camera lights were harsh and unforgiving.

Michael reminded himself not to squint. He and Hernandez both wore power suits with white shirts. It looked as if they'd gone shopping together at Brooks Brothers. Michael had chosen a striped tie, while his opponent had opted for politician red.

They shook hands. Polite applause from the crowd. The candidates went behind their respective lecterns like boxers returning to their corners before the opening bell. Michael was glad to see a tall glass of water within easy reach. He always got thirsty during these things.

The moderator said the candidates had drawn lots. The challenger, Nelson Hernandez, would make his statement first.

"I want to talk about the elephant in the room," he said.

Michael had to show his opponent respect he did not feel, so he reminded himself to retain a neutral expression. Nelson Hernandez was bilingual, had a silvery voice, and looked good on camera—one of those dangerous men who possessed far more ambition than intelligence.

"The Riverside Park case is threatening to tear our city apart again," Hernandez said.

It could tear us apart again because of demagogues like you, Michael thought.

"And the reason this is happening is because of the stonewalling and the incompetence of the current district attorney's office."

Michael wished he was back on the pitcher's mound, and Hernandez was at the plate, so he could tuck a fastball right under the bastard's chin.

"The new evidence that continues to be uncovered raises significant questions," Hernandez said. "And all we get from the district attorney's office is more of the same: 'The case is settled. There's nothing to see here. Move along.' I submit there is something to see, and I am not going to move along. So, I am prepared to make this pledge:

"After I am sworn in as your district attorney, my first official action will be to undertake a top-to-bottom review of the Riverside Park case, with a fresh set of eyes and no preconceptions. We will subject this case to the type of rigorous analysis the current DA seems allergic to, and we will base our conclusions on a dispassionate examination of all the evidence."

Sustained applause. The moderator asked the audience to please refrain from making any kind of noise until the conclusion of the debate. Michael heard whoops and cheers coming from the demonstrators on West 41st Street, who were reacting to what they'd just seen on their smartphones.

"Mr. Devine?" the moderator said.

If Michael had opened the debate, he would have stressed his record, especially his office's high rate of convictions because of the professionalism of the people who worked for him. He would also have noted that the number of violent crimes was beginning to come down, after that troubling spike during the pandemic.

"Don't forget about community outreach," Seamus O'Toole had said.

"And what, exactly, is community outreach?" Michael had asked.

"Damned if I know, but it sounds good."

Michael glanced at Hernandez, who was half-heartedly suppressing a shit-eating grin.

This is why it's always best to win the coin toss, Michael thought. Go first so you can set the tempo and agenda. Now I have to react to this incompetent sonuvabitch.

"The attack on the Riverside Park runner was one of the most heinous crimes I've ever dealt with," Michael said. "From beginning to end, the case was handled with thoroughness and respect by everyone involved—police, judges, jurors, and, most especially, the attorneys under my supervision. We examined all the evidence, and we went where it took us. I took no pleasure in prosecuting the case, but justice had to be done.

"There have been reports in the media of new evidence in the case. Believe me, my office has looked very closely at this so-called new evidence. It is, in our view, a rehash of old claims that have never withstood the test of truth. Nothing has happened to change our belief that the jury rendered the correct verdict—a verdict that has been upheld numerous times over the years.

"Now I want to focus your attention on something my opponent said in his opening remarks—or, more precisely, something he did not say."

Michael paused. It was like being in the courtroom—everyone hanging on his words. He was again thankful that he had done theater in high school, even if his mother considered it a waste of time.

"My opponent said he would conduct a review of the case. Here's a news flash—we review cases all the time. We have certainly reviewed the Riverside Park case over the past few weeks. My opponent did not say he would reopen the case or agree to the proposals that it be retried. And there's a reason for that—the case was decided correctly. I submit that in this matter, as in many others, my opponent offers soundbites." Dramatic pause. "Soundbites are no substitute for good policy and efficient administration."

A few boos floated into the auditorium from outside. The moderator turned to the *Times* reporter. The *Times* always went first.

"Mr. Devine," he said, "the Riverside Park case resonates with people of color throughout this city."

It resonates with everyone, Michael felt like saying. But he stayed quiet.

"Many of them believe your refusal to reopen the case is just another example of a power structure that disdains and discounts people who are not white. What would you say to them?"

"I have the same message to everyone in Manhattan—my office is fair and impartial. We will always give a hearing to the residents of this borough, and we are dedicated to reaching out to every member of the community.

"But I have to add this: While everybody is entitled to a hearing, nobody is entitled to the answer they want. In this job, you have to make tough decisions. This is something my opponent doesn't understand. Once you're sworn in as district attorney, you can't go around pandering to people."

Nelson Hernandez responded that this was the type of arrogant and out-of-touch answer that showed why a change of leadership was so desperately needed at One Hogan Place. New York's new realities demanded new solutions.

Michael resisted the urge to sigh in despair the way Al Gore did when he was debating George W. Bush before the election in 2000. Gore had been absolutely right, but everyone talked about how rude he'd been.

I fired you, Michael felt like saying to Hernandez. *You were the head of the Public Corruption Unit, but you never uncovered any corruption.*

The moderator turned to the blogger, who had kinky hair dyed four different colors as well as studs in her earlobes and nostrils.

"I don't think you understand something, Mr. District Attorney," she said.

I already know I don't like you, Michael said to himself.

"You fail to comprehend just how fed up the people are. We are constantly mistreated by so-called law enforcement, and when we have legitimate issues, they are dismissed as if our grievances don't matter. We are tired of this, and a day of reckoning is coming."

The spectators stirred. Michael sensed they wanted to applaud, but the moderator glared at them the way the nuns used to stare down an unruly class back when he went to Catholic school.

He expected the blogger to continue. Instead, she sat back and nodded in self-satisfaction.

Michael bent toward the mic. He possessed a particular disdain for journalists who preferred pontificating to asking questions. If you want to make speeches, he felt like saying, run for office.

"What's your question?" he asked.

Brown eyes flashed with anger. The blogger leaned forward and came close to wrapping her lips around her mic.

"My question?" Her voice rose with the passion of indignation. "People of color deal with all kinds of disrespect from entitled white men, and your office treats us like we're three-year-olds. Serious issues have arisen in the Riverside Park case, and you're trying to sweep them under the rug. Mr. Hernandez has said he will bring a fresh set of eyes to this matter, and he has pledged to re-examine it."

The blogger smiled mirthlessly. She had talked her way into a question.

"So I want to ask you this, Mr. District Attorney: What assurance do we have that you will ever, under any circumstances, reopen a case that many of us regard as a miscarriage of justice?"

They are guilty, Michael felt like saying. They are guilty beyond a reasonable doubt, and I want to stop fighting about this case because there are so many other, more important things I want to do to make this city better.

Why can't I make you see that?

* * *

Warren Petersen ran his index finger over the screen of his tablet as he searched for the data he wanted.

"You lost one and a half points during the debate," he told Michael.

"Fucking pansies," Jacob Meyer said.

"How can you be so precise?" Rachel asked.

"The metrics we've developed allow us to track changes in sentiment in real time," Petersen said. "The trend is showing an acceleration of the erosion, if you get what I mean."

"I'm afraid I do," Rachel said.

O'Toole looked over Petersen's shoulder. "The erosion could become a freefall."

"Precisely," Petersen said.

Michael sat slumped in a hard wooden chair in the conference room at campaign headquarters. Jacket off. Sleeves rolled up. Tie loose. For the first time in years, he wanted to get rip-roaring drunk.

"We could try to touch base with Marie," O'Toole said. "See if she's willing to say anything that would—"

"No."

Michael was surprised at how quickly that word came out.

O'Toole went on, quietly. "Given everything that's occurred, a statement from her could be powerful."

"Goddamn good point," Meyer said.

Not for the first time, Michael wondered if his father-in-law would ever utter a sentence that lacked profanity.

"Marie has been through way too much," Michael said. "I can't ask her to do that."

"Maybe somebody else can," O'Toole said. "If someone from the campaign reaches out to her and requests—"

Michael interrupted. "If anybody from the campaign contacts Marie

Antolini, it'll be me. Understood?"

Silence and, finally, nods. Rachel stood behind her husband and kneaded the tight-as-a-drum muscles in his upper back.

"What's next?" she asked.

Loose ends, Michael thought. Even after all these years, loose ends are still flapping all over the place.

"Let's go home," he said to Rachel. "We can split a bottle of wine and get some sleep."

"After that?"

He knew the answer, but he had learned one important lesson in his rise from dingy low-rent apartments in Freehold Township: the bigger the decision, the better it is to keep your own counsel. On this one, he would confide in nobody. Not even his wife.

Chapter Thirty-One

Sheila Devine

October 7, 2023

She had not intended to spend her weekend stalking the spots in and around Philadelphia where Rocco Cantone could be hiding, but the list of media people who wanted to talk to him was long, and she was determined to be the first to question him before he had time to hone his answers.

She asked around as a professional filmmaker.

Nothing.

Next, she adopted the pose of a pleasantly attractive female posing perky inquiries. Think Mary Tyler Moore in the Seventies.

Dead ends.

Finally, she forked over some money.

A Latino at a hoagie shop in Cantone's neighborhood looked at the twenty she had given him before rubbing his fingers together. She handed him twenty more and hoped she could write it off as a business expense.

"He likes to hang at a place a couple blocks from here." The hombre had tattoos on his knuckles. Possible gangbanger. "I see him there all the time when I deliver sandwiches."

"I need a name and address," Sheila said.

* * *

The Santa Maria Hunt & Fish Club was on a side street two blocks off Broad. A Google search revealed the place was a gathering spot for Mob members and their hangers-on.

In addition to everything else, Sheila told herself, Rocco Cantone is a cop who likes to knock back beers with wise guys.

The Santa Maria Hunt & Fish Club did not have a website, of course, but after a few clicks she ascertained that the place was males-only, of course.

Forget Title IX, she thought. In neighborhoods like this, the men are still pissed about the Nineteenth Amendment.

She found an Italian bakery catty-corner from the club, ordered a cappuccino, and kept watch on the place, a boxlike structure with a metal door and one tiny window shielded by iron bars. She opened her laptop and glanced around. As far as she could tell, this was a media-free zone. If her quarry appeared, either entering the place or departing it, she was prepared to leap onto the street with no advance notice.

She accessed YouTube and clicked on the video of the encounter between Rocco Cantone and Luttrell Aldridge. It already had more than five million views. Sheila broke it down frame by frame, as if she were a conspiracy theorist examining the Zapruder film. Officer Cantone had approached the vehicle, then drew his gun and fired only seconds after reaching the driver's side window. There was a heated online debate about whether he had employed proper police procedure. The motorist had reached for something in the front of the car. Law enforcement types said the officer justifiably feared that the man was trying to grab the gun in the glove compartment. Defund-the-police advocates said he was undoubtedly attempting to fetch paperwork wedged into a beverage container.

Nobody knew what Officer Cantone had been thinking during the encounter because, so far, he'd said nothing publicly. Sheila ran the scene repeatedly and felt like a replay official at the Super Bowl who couldn't tell if the receiver had landed inbounds.

She looked up from the screen and sipped the cappuccino. The taste was good, but she enjoyed the buzz even more. Her brain made connections. Sheila had been asking herself if Rocco Cantone was capable of the type of violence that had been visited upon Marie Antolini, and she realized: He joined the police department…every cop in the world is willing to use force…yes, he's capable of it.

The door to the social club jarred open. Two men stepped out. Except for their sunglasses, they made no effort to disguise themselves. Sheila sat bolt upright and asked herself if she was imagining things. For a moment, she just stayed where she was, her mouth widening, until the men began striding down the street. Sheila scooped up her laptop and cappuccino and ran after them as they approached a sedan halfway down the block. One of the men raised his keys and pointed. She heard a blip, noticed the New York plates, and told herself: Of course. Unmarked NYPD car. I shoulda noticed that right away.

The men got into the vehicle. Sheila sprinted. Breaths came hard and fast. Her workouts needed more cardio. The car started, but it was wedged in tight, so the driver had to do a few back-and-forth maneuvers before he was ready to pull into traffic.

Sheila got right in front of the sedan and held up her hands. The tinted windows disappointed her because she really wanted to see the men's reaction to her presence.

She walked around to the passenger side and rapped on the window. After a moment, it rolled down. The expression on her brother's face was a combination of totally angry and completely stunned.

She leaned down until her mouth was only inches from his ear.

"As Ricky Ricardo used to say to Lucy," she told him, "you've got some 'splainin' to do."

*　*　*

"So, he's in there?"

Michael and Haggerty sat poker-faced in the front seat while she peppered them with questions. She'd been at it for ten minutes, and they'd still admitted nothing, although Haggerty had turned off the ignition after putting the car all the way back in its parking spot.

She kept turning her head. She was still ready to sprint after Cantone if he came out of the club.

"C'mon," Sheila said in the I'm-reaching-the-end-of-my-rope voice she sometimes employed with her kids. "You came down here for the same reason I did."

Michael replied thirty seconds later. "We need something from you."

"Like what?"

"Information."

"What kind of information?"

"Who have you talked to?"

Time to drop the bomb, Sheila said to herself.

"I found Felipe Huerta."

Michael and Haggerty exchanged glances in the rearview.

"I'm surprised he's alive," Michael said.

"He had some things to say," Sheila said.

Long silence.

"Mind sharing with the class?" Michael asked.

Sheila took out her iPhone, found the footage, and handed the device to her brother.

"Scariest interview I ever conducted," she said.

Michael propped up the phone so both he and Haggerty could watch. "I could delete this," the detective said.

"With my son's help," Sheila said, "I stashed copies all over the cloud."

Haggerty and Michael watched the interview in silence. When it was over, Michael returned her iPhone.

"You think that would stand up in court?" he asked.

"I'm not conducting a trial," Sheila said. "I'm making a movie."

She also knew that a competent attorney would destroy Huerta on the stand, and Michael was way better than competent.

"We could demand that you turn that over to us," Haggerty said. "Evidence and shit."

"I haven't told Ortega about this yet," Sheila said, "but if you file a motion, he'll find out about it. Discovery and shit."

Haggerty drummed his fingers on the dash.

"My turn," Sheila said. "Is Rocco Cantone in there?"

Michael scrunched his face, and his lips disappeared. Sheila recognized the look from his baseball days when he was running on fumes but still needed to strike out the other team's best hitter.

"He's in there," Michael said.

"What did he say to you?" Sheila asked.

Michael and Haggerty exchanged sideways glances.

"Not much," Haggerty said.

"Care to elaborate?" Sheila asked.

A deep and loud silence. For the first time in her life, Sheila wished she was the Laurence Olivier character in *Marathon Man*, extracting teeth and facts from a hapless Dustin Hoffman.

Michael began to speak slowly, like a kindergarten teacher telling the kids how to cut with scissors.

"We asked him about what the bus driver said. Officer Cantone informed us, politely but firmly, that he had no response at all to the driver's comments. We asked him why, and he said his attorneys had told him to say nothing about any judicial matters unless he was under oath and being advised by counsel."

Sheila was unsurprised. Nobody lawyers up more quickly than a cop in legal trouble.

"So then," Michael continued, "I asked him point-blank if he'd been in New York that day. And he shook his head and smiled a bit and said: 'Sorry, Counselor, I can't say anything at all about that. But I'd be happy to talk about the Phillies.'"

"That's a total non-denial," Sheila said.

"I can't dispute that."

"Is that all you asked him?"

Michael looked puzzled. "Waddya mean?"

"There's one big question that you two gentlemen, with the full weight and majesty of the law behind you, should have asked Rocco Cantone."

Haggerty let his sarcasm drip over the words as he said, "Please enlighten us."

Sheila ignored his tone. "'Did you attack Marie Antolini?'"

The men looked at each other in the rearview, and then at Sheila, and then back at each other, as if they were shy adolescents at a high school dance who were afraid to talk to the girls.

"No," Michael said. "We didn't ask him that."

"Why not?"

"Because he didn't do it, that's why," Haggerty said.

Sheila's voice rose. "How can you be so sure?"

The detective's face flushed, and Sheila expected him to shout at her, but Michael punched his arm. Instead, Haggerty looked again in the rearview, and his eyebrows rose a centimeter.

"That's him," he said.

Sheila twisted one-eighty. A man in a hoodie, accompanied by two elderly gentlemen in fedoras, stepped out of the club.

"Cantone?" she asked.

Haggerty nodded. "The guys he's with used to run with Nicky Scarfo."

Sheila bolted from the car. The sun was high and strong, and she wished she'd had time to throw on her Ray-Bans. Up ahead, the three men strolled down the street with the air of paisans who knew nothing bad would happen to them as long as they stayed in South Philly.

They must have heard her because they slowed, stopped, and turned. Sheila was dressed in Brooklyn black—leather jacket and skinny jeans—and the men looked intrigued as she gasped to a halt.

"Officer Cantone?" she asked.

The cop straightened. Even behind his shades and underneath his hoodie, she could see his chiseled features, wavy hair, and pouty lips, and she said to herself: I can see why the girls were attracted. Probably still are.

"What's it to ya?" growled the guy on Cantone's right.

Sheila was facing men from the old school, in the worst sense of the term.

"My name is Sheila Devine. I'm a filmmaker."

"Hollywood?"

"Documentaries."

"Oh."

The other old-timer narrowed his face. "We just talked to some goombah named Devine."

"My brother."

The second old-timer turned to the first one. "Her brother's the fuckin' DA."

"Fuck."

Sheila sensed an opening. "My brother and his detective friend forgot to ask Officer Cantone an important question. So I'm gonna do it."

"What the fuck?" the growler asked.

Sheila looked straight at Cantone, but his sunglasses were impenetrable. He fingered a silver crucifix at the base of his neck as if it were a talisman.

"On the night of April Eleventh, Two Thousand Twelve, did you attack Marie Antolini?"

Cantone rose onto the balls of his feet, as if he'd just received an electric shock to his spine, before spinning as quickly as he could and walking toward Broad Street.

* * *

She rode in the quiet car on the train back to New York. She liked the silence because it let her focus on the notes she was typing about her visit to Philly. When she was done with them, she looked over the background of the Riverside Runner case for the umpteenth time before putting on headphones to watch and listen to her interview with Felipe Huerta. It still creeped her out, but the man was emphatic:

He saw the attacker's white ass. And the attacker wore a hoodie.

Sheila noted that Rocco Cantone liked to wear hoodies. Then she shook her head.

That's not enough to go on, she said to herself.

She had created separate files for the drama's actors and by now almost all of them had extensive entries—interviews, biographies, pictures from then and now. As she toggled over the names, she asked herself what she was missing. Dogs that don't bark always reveal the most.

She realized she had almost nothing on Gloria Estevez, Marie Antolini's one-time BFF.

Sheila Googled combinations of "Gloria Estevez," and "Columbia Journalism School," and "Texas television stations," but the trail always petered out in 2016. The woman had returned to her native state and joined an all-news cable channel in San Antonio, but that lasted only a couple of years, and then...nothing.

People just don't disappear, Sheila said to herself. At least not anymore. Everyone is on the grid all the time.

Finally, in an act that bordered on desperation, Sheila typed in "Gloria Estevez" and "Riverside Runner" and waited to see if something popped up.

At the top was a column from the *Daily News* dated April 30, 2012. As she read through the overwrought and sentimental prose that was now familiar to her, she told herself:

Of course, he talked to her. During his career, he talked to everybody. And if anyone knows where she is, he does.

* * *

"People are gonna think there's something going on between us," Jamie Quinn said as soon as he picked up his phone.

"I've got a name for you," Sheila said. "Gloria Estevez. Friend of Marie Antolini's. I'm trying to find her."

"She was an attractive woman. Coulda stood to lose a few pounds. Am I allowed to say those things these days?"

"No. You have any idea where she is?"

"I think she wound up in Vegas. I'll hafta double-check."

"How long will that take?"

"Ten minutes. Come on over here. You're at Penn Station, right?"

"How'd you know that?"

"I can hear boarding announcements in the background. Plus, it sounds really crowded. Lotsa ambient noise. Plus, you sound outta breath, like you're running for a cab. I bet you just got back from Philly."

This was getting spooky. "I did."

"Everybody in the business wants to talk to Rocco Cantone. I bet you found him."

"He hangs out with mobsters."

"The Mafia's still strong down there. That town's always been thirty years behind the times."

The taxi line was a block long, so she Ubered. Quinn greeted her at the door and used his walker to ease back to his favorite chair. Sheila saw a sheaf of papers piled on a raised table within his reach. Beside the papers was a tumbler with brown liquid in it. He pointed to the glass.

"Scotch. You want some?"

"I hardly ever drink hard liquor." She thought a few seconds. "Okay, margaritas. If I'm eating Mexican."

He plopped into his chair and motioned toward a fifth of Johnny Walker Black on the counter that divided the loft's living area from its kitchen. "It's over there if you want any."

Sheila gazed at the sleek and classic bottle, then marched over and poured herself a shot while Quinn looked over the papers.

"I thought I knew what happened to Gloria Estevez," he said, "but I wanted to refresh my memory."

Sheila sat on the smooth but uncomfortable sofa opposite him and perched on the edge.

"I keep everything over there." Quinn waved his arm at a row of *Mad Men*-era metal filing cabinets in the corner. "I've got a system."

Sheila's eyes bugged out when she sipped the Scotch. "Holy crap, what's in this?"

"Alcohol."

She sipped again. The booze headed directly to her brain.

"America was a happier place when everybody went to bars instead of gyms," Quinn said.

Less yoga and more Johnny Walker; as the Scotch settled in, Sheila thought it could be a positive lifestyle change.

"Let's talk about Gloria Estevez," she said.

Quinn rustled the papers in his hand. Black-rimmed spectacles perched halfway down his nose. "You read my column about her?"

"I did."

"Good stuff, huh?"

Sheila raised her glass. "Salud."

"Like I said in the column, Gloria was traumatized by what happened. You woulda thought she was the one who'd been attacked. I talked to her about it, and she shifted between being glassy-eyed and weeping."

"Survivor's guilt?"

"Coulda been. The angle I took was that the runner wasn't the only victim. Look what happened to her best friend. But I got the feeling…" His voice trailed off.

"Got the feeling…what?"

"That she wasn't telling me everything. Like she was hiding something."

"What could she have been hiding?"

"That is one of the many Sixty-Four-Million-Dollar Questions surrounding this case. Maybe something was going on at school. Maybe she and Marie were actually…what do the kids call it now…frenemies."

Sheila swirled her Scotch. "You were one of the original skeptics about whether the guys in the park actually attacked the runner."

"Thanks for remembering."

"What if Gloria knew who did it? Or at least had an inkling?"

"Why wouldn't she have told anyone? Like your brother, for instance?"

"She was young, from outta town, didn't really know anyone, didn't know how things work here…" Sheila sipped her drink. Sometimes, booze was even more clarifying than caffeine. "Imagine what woulda happened if she doubted the official story. That's what you did, and everyone pissed all over you. And you were a goddamn icon."

"I'm still a goddamn icon." Quinn looked at the moldings as if they were about to reveal something. "Your point is plausible. I'm not sure it's accurate, but it's plausible. You'd have to track down Gloria and ask her."

"Which brings us back to what happened to her. Waddya got?"

Quinn looked over his papers. "She went back to Texas shortly after the attack. San Antonio. Ever been there?"

"Hot, dry, dusty. I didn't get it."

"It was home for her. She got a job on a local cable channel. General assignment reporter. I thought that'd be her first step. Attractive woman like her, a Latin, if she lost some weight, I figured she'd be on a fast track to a network job."

"Given the way the networks operate, I can't challenge your bigoted assumptions. Why didn't it work out for her in San Antonio?"

"She didn't get along with the news manager. She wanted better assignments, more hard news, but he kept giving her fluff. When she complained, he told her to—and this is a direct quote, at least according to a letter Gloria sent me—'stop worrying your pretty little head.'"

"Oh, Jesus."

"He also kept denigrating her work, sometimes in front of the entire newsroom. When you're young, and your confidence gets shredded like that..."

Sheila remembered some of her film school classmates, talented kids who were going to upend the cinematic world, landing their first job and getting their insides eviscerated like a trout that had been landed by a sadistic angler. For that reason and others, Sheila had always preferred working for herself.

Quinn kept talking. "So she decided, the hell with it, she was gonna make some money. She went to Vegas and took the courses you need and went to work in the casino at the Bellagio. Blackjack. Once again, she had problems with her supervisor. Not earning enough. Needed to turn the table quicker. That sorta thing."

"Was her supervisor male?"

"Yeah."

"Was she harassed?"

Quinn shrugged. "It's possible, but she never told me in so many words. We used to correspond every few months by snail mail. I like getting letters.

There's something permanent about them. You think a publisher's ever gonna print a collection of somebody's emails?"

Sheila nodded. The old man had a point, and she was enjoying the Scotch.

"Anyway, two years ago, I sent her a Christmas card with a long message on it. I always did. I like to send Christmas cards, too. And it came back from North Las Vegas, Nevada, with the notation 'Addressee Unknown.' I haven't heard from her since. So I Googled. Yeah, I know how to do that." He shook his head. "Nothing current."

Sheila had to try, so she sighed and said, "Give me that address anyway."

Chapter Thirty-Two

Michael Devine

October 7, 2023

"Take me to Thirtieth Street Station."

Haggerty looked at Michael as if a demon had suddenly taken possession of the DA's soul. "What the hell?"

"I gotta go somewhere."

"I thought we were heading back to New York."

"You go back to New York. There's something I hafta check out. By myself."

Haggerty stared at Michael for what seemed like hours.

"If you were any other guy," the detective said, "I'd think you had a woman on the side."

It's not like that, Michael responded silently. At least, I don't think it is.

* * *

Beyond the Philly exurbs, the train rolled past towns on life support. The gloom made him further depressed, so he thought about her and wondered how she was, if she'd be surprised to see him, and how both of them would react. They hadn't talked to each other face to face for several years.

At the Lancaster station, he used an old-school car service instead of

Ubering. The driver took him to Hershey Medical Center. Michael kept quiet and paid cash.

He knew she'd be there, although it was a Saturday. She had once emailed him that she liked working weekends because fewer people were around, the place was quieter, and the atmosphere let her focus on what she needed to do. After all this time, she still had trouble concentrating when stuff was going on around her.

Michael told a receptionist he was looking for Marie Antolini. The receptionist was a plain woman, somewhere between thirty and fifty, with a plain face and plain clothes and plain hair. Michael figured she was a member of one of those old-fashioned religious sects that proliferated in Middle American places that clung to the Eisenhower era.

"May I ask who wants to see her?" the receptionist asked in a plain voice.

"Michael Devine."

Back home, the receptionist would have either praised or berated him, but this woman had no reaction to his name, and he was glad.

"Please have a seat, Mr. Devine. I'll let her know you're here."

She did not ask to see ID, and no one had patted or wanded him, and he felt he had been transported to a strange parallel universe where nobody expected bad things to happen.

He resisted the urge to fiddle with his phone. He wanted to leave no trace of his visit. So he sat in a hard plastic chair, and although it was uncomfortable, he realized how tired he was, and as his lids drooped, he assured himself he was only resting his eyes.

"Hi there."

He bolted upright and wondered how long he'd been out.

"Didn't mean to wake you."

Her voice had always reassured him. Michael stood to take her in and surrendered to his impulse to smile as broadly as he could, but he was suddenly paralyzed because he couldn't figure out what he should do next. He wanted to hug her, but he was unsure if it was the right thing to do, considering #MeToo and the pandemic, so he stood there a second and felt like a schlump and was relieved when she put her arms around him and

235

leaned her head against his shoulder and said she was glad to see him. He returned her embrace, then stepped back. He kept forgetting that he was nearly a foot taller than she was.

"You look great," he said.

"You look like hell," she replied.

He laughed.

"We can talk in my office," she said.

* * *

They spent a few minutes discussing his kids and her job. She felt an enormous amount of satisfaction improving the lives of people who'd been traumatized.

"But that's not why you're here," she said.

She grinned. Her smile was a bit crooked, and it had been that way as long as he'd known her, and he wondered if that was a lingering effect of the incident.

"It isn't," he said.

"Your campaign?"

"Partly."

"I have an idea of what's going on in New York," she said. "We get the internet out here in the sticks, even if the service is lousy and only a few people know how to use it."

"The—"

Michael stopped. Whenever he talked to Marie, he never knew how to describe the callous creatures that had left her for dead.

"Some of the men who attacked you have taken on a new lawyer. His name's Rolando Ortega. He's the best private attorney in the city. He's throwing out all kinds of red herrings, and, yes, he's causing me a lotta problems."

She blinked a few times. Her eyes were wide and brown and guileless, and he sometimes considered the possibility that the incident had robbed her of the ability to lie.

"I thought you handled the case brilliantly," she said. "I wrote that in my book. If you want, I'll issue a statement to that effect. I'll appear with you in public. I'll talk to the media. I'll do anything to help you. You know that."

Michael silently mouthed a "thank you."

"But there's something else on your mind, Counselor," she said.

"It's my sister," he said.

Marie thought a few seconds, as if she were having trouble summoning a fact that should have been easy to remember.

"Sheila," she said.

"That's right."

"She makes documentaries."

"Right again."

Marie nodded as her mind sorted out the relevant details.

"I've tried to watch them, because I know you two are related. But the subject matter—they're tough to take. I never made it all the way through any of them. Except..."

"Except what?"

"The one about your father. I had no idea. You never told me."

"I didn't see the need."

"But growing up like that. He took bribes from everybody. He deserved to go to prison, but he was convicted of a murder he didn't commit. All of that must've been awful for you and your sister and your mother. When I watched it, I understood why you were so kind to me. So helpful. You understand people who've been damaged."

Michael squirmed. He had done dozens of sitdowns with journalists, but this was the first time an interviewer—however gentle and empathetic— fully grasped the events and forces that had molded him.

She woulda been really good at it, Michael said to himself. What a goddamn shame.

"Life damages everybody," he said. "Some more than others. From the time my father went away, I told myself I just had to get over it somehow. But my mother couldn't do that. She was bitter and resentful, and it ate away at her from the inside. It was a metaphorical cancer. That and the real cancer killed her early."

Marie gazed at him with eyes that said: Keep talking.

"My sister and I have different personalities, but we've always been close. It was us against the world, and I was determined to protect her."

"That doesn't surprise me," Marie said. "You're the protective type."

"Anyway, Rolando Ortega has recruited my sister to do a documentary about the case. He's giving her almost unlimited access. She's talked to the men he's representing, and she'll try to talk to you." Michael forced a smile. "When it comes to her work, my sister is nothing if not thorough."

"Should I talk to her?" Marie asked.

"That's up to you."

"What's your advice, Counselor?"

Michael sighed. "My sister is not easily discouraged. We're alike in that regard. She'll keep coming at you from different directions, at different times, and with different reasons. My advice is to rebuff her on the first few occasions."

"And then?"

"Agree to talk. Informally. On background only. No filming allowed. She'll bring her iPhone, and after a while, when she feels you've let your guard down, she'll ask if it's okay to record what you're saying."

"Will it be okay?"

"That's your call."

"Have you talked to her about the case?"

"Not on the record."

"What are you waiting for?"

Michael thought a few seconds. "Contrary to what the agitators and the media and my opponent think, we are taking another look at what happened. We need to, because we hafta be ready for the bullshit Rolando Ortega is gonna throw at us." He paused. "Excuse my language."

"I've heard the word before, Michael."

He smiled. "There's a chance you'll hafta testify again about all this. I want you to be ready. And I wanna talk to you about a few things, so I'll know how to proceed."

"Okay."

"I wanna do this informally. Just between us. At least for now."

"That's fine, Michael. I'd trust you with my life." The crooked smile again. "I already have."

He resisted the urge to sigh. So help me God, he thought, I wish you were just another victim.

"The other day, Ortega produced a bus driver who said Rocco Cantone rode from Philadelphia to New York on the day of the incident. Are you aware of that?"

Marie shook her head. "I've been busy."

"What do you remember about Rocco?" Michael asked.

"Bits and fragments. Like most of my life before the incident. A good-looking guy. I went to the movies with him, although I can't remember any of them." She laughed. "Eating. A lot of eating. Going to restaurants or just sitting in somebody's house. Sometimes, I'd cook. And then I recall running along the river with a guy beside me. We'd start racing. I usually won. That would upset him."

"How badly?"

"He didn't like losing to a girl. He'd sulk and mope. I think he wanted me to let him win. I used to say he needed to get in better shape. You can't expect to pick up running one day and win the Boston Marathon the next, although he believed he could."

"Did you have arguments with him? Bad ones?"

She scrunched her face. "I suppose. I've heard stories, but nothing comes to mind."

"You had an order of protection against him."

"That's what people have told me, but I don't recall getting it. I don't remember what led me to do it."

"Did you ever see Rocco after the incident?"

"No. But I did get…"

Her voice trailed off.

"What did you get?" Michael asked.

"I got a card and flowers from him after I went back home. Red roses.

The card said, 'I wish you the best, and I'm praying for you. Love, Rocco.' I asked my mother who Rocco was, and she started to cry."

"You two were together a long time," Michael said. "On again, off again."

She shook her head but held his gaze. "I couldn't write a coherent narrative about it. I just have pieces. Shards. Like broken glass lying on the floor that's impossible to glue together."

Michael paused and licked his lips. Marie looked at him like a dancer waiting for her partner to lead.

"You probably know where I'm going with this," he said. "You can tell me to stop right now if you want."

"I'll let you know if it's too much."

Michael took a breath. "On the night of the incident, we know that you were in your room until at least eight thirty-nine p.m., because that's when you sent an email to your professor. Seamus O'Toole. Do you remember him?"

"A little. He was nice to me. He encouraged me when I was in school."

"You sent him an email saying you were almost done with a project. You wrote that you were going for a run, but you wanted to talk to him about the assignment when you got back."

"For the life of me, Michael, I don't remember sending that email, and I have no idea what the project was about."

"He sent you a reply just before nine, saying you could reach out to him anytime. But you never replied to that, so we figure you left your room roughly five minutes before nine to go for your run. There was also a surveillance camera that recorded someone leaving your building at that time. We're not one hundred percent sure it was you, but it looked like a woman who matched your physical description."

"It all makes sense so far."

"We also looked through your email history. You almost always responded quickly to your professors when they sent you messages."

"I still do that when people email me." The crooked smile again. "No sense keeping folks waiting."

"So you went for a run," Michael said. "The night was cool. Damp. But it wasn't raining. Is any of that coming back to you?"

She looked straight at him, and he knew what she was thinking: I do not want to relive this, and I wouldn't even try to resurrect any memories of that night for anyone but you.

"I can remember some details about that night because of that detective—Haggerty, was that his name?"

"Yeah."

"He kept asking me about it. So there's stuff I recall. I had an iPod. Earbuds. I liked to listen to music while I ran. I'd zone out."

"Matchbox Twenty?" Michael asked.

Marie nodded. "Rob Thomas. I'm a fangirl. I met him once after a concert. He was sweet."

"You were running," Michael said. "You were listening to music. Do you remember anything else?"

"I had on a nylon shell," she said. "Kind of a light jacket. I didn't like wearing stuff like that. It felt inhibiting. But the night was...icky."

"Did the shell have a hood?"

"Yeah. I had it on. So, I was looking right ahead. Like a horse with blinders."

Michael ran a mental checklist: nighttime, music blocking out all other sounds, no peripheral vision; no wonder she didn't see or hear anything.

"Can you remember anything about the run itself?" Michael asked.

"I was going at a nice clip," she said. "I was feeling good. The endorphins must've kicked in. And then..."

"And then what?"

"Blackout."

"You don't remember anything until you were in the hospital?"

"I just recall..."

"Recall what?"

She bit hard into her lower lip. Michael hated himself for doing this to her.

"Being dragged along the ground. Feeling grass and mud on my back. I was looking at the sky, but it was totally dark. No stars or anything. I felt woozy, like my thoughts were outside my body. I must've passed out. Because the next thing I remember was the hospital. And, seeing you there. You were so kind."

"I have to ask you this, Marie, even though I don't want to."

Steel in her voice. "Go ahead."

"Did you see Rocco Cantone during the incident, or at any time that day?" She shook her head.

"Do you remember if he made any attempt to contact you that day?"

Michael had been involved in dozens of cases like this, ex-lovers refusing to release the objects of their obsession.

"As far as I know," Marie said, "he did not."

"Was he aware that you liked to run in the park at night?"

Marie took a long, long pause as she scoured the edges of her fragmented memory.

"He might have been."

Chapter Thirty-Three

Sheila Devine

October 8, 2023

G oogle Maps led Sheila on a virtual tour of North Las Vegas. She zeroed in on a rundown row of apartments, two stories high, beside a six-lane road lined with strip malls. She called the manager's office. It was Sunday, so she figured she'd get a recording, but a gruff voice that sounded male, middle-aged and Caucasian said, "Yeah?"

Sheila said she was looking for a woman who seemed to have fallen off the face of the Earth.

"After they leave here," the guy said, "that's what happens to them."

His accent screamed Jersey, so Sheila let her words come fast and natural.

"Her name is Gloria Estevez. She used to—"

Before Sheila could finish, Jersey Guy let out a loud and long "Jeeeeeessss suuuuuuuussssssssss."

Sometimes, Sheila said to herself, there really is no substitute for making a phone call.

"Sounds like you know her."

"What a pain in the ass," Jersey Guy said. Although it was a typical description for an unlikable person in the Garden State, it sounded as if he truly meant it.

"Why do you say that?"

Sheila's question produced a litany of complaints: She never paid her rent on time, her apartment was filthy, she sat on her ass all day watching cable news REALLY REALLY LOUD, so the neighbors complained, and she always bitched about the state of the complex—the air-conditioning, the plumbing, the water, the paint, and on and on and on and on.

Jersey Guy had worked himself into a state of righteous venting. "Look, I'm not gonna tell you everything's perfect here. We got problems. Every place does. But we do our best. You know what I mean?"

"I think I do."

"We're not the Ritz, but we don't advertise ourselves that way."

"Of course not."

"This is a clean and respectable establishment. I mean, what the hell did she want for six hundred dollars a month?"

Six hundred dollars?!?!?!? Sheila thought. Holy crap, sign me up.

"Lemme tell you why I'm calling, Mister—?"

"Leave my name out of it. I figure she owes you money. She owes everybody money."

"Actually, I'm doing a project, and her name has come up. I wanna get in touch with her and talk."

"What kinda project?"

"I'm a filmmaker."

"Hollywood?"

"Documentaries."

"Oh."

Sheila plowed on. "It's interesting you said she sat around all day watching cable news. She once worked in TV. Did you know that?"

"She told me that, but I figured it was bullshit. The broad needed to lose a few pounds to go on television, you know what I mean?"

Sheila told herself to ignore the sexism and weightism. "I'm interested in an incident that occurred while she was in grad school at Columbia. I wanna ask her about it, and I was wondering if you had any idea where I could find her."

That does not entail me flying out to North Las Vegas, Nevada, Sheila said silently.

"She left here about two years ago," Jersey Guy told her. "Skipped out. Owed six months' rent. I don't put up with crap like that. So I asked around, but nobody knew nothin'. I'm afraid I'm out the money, but then one of my tenants tells me he'd been at an air show way out in the desert, and he coulda sworn he'd seen her there. To make a long story short—"

Please do, Sheila thought.

"—I tracked her down to this shithole called Indian Springs. It's about an hour from here, and it's near an Air Force base. She's living in a trailer park. Figures, right?"

"Keep going," Sheila said.

"So I go to the trailer park, and I find out which tin can she's holed up in, and I knock on her door, and, geez, was she surprised to see me."

"What did you do?"

"Demanded the money she owed."

"What did she say?"

"Started swearing at me in Spanish. I know a little español and, lemme tell you, that chiquita has quite a mouth on her. She wouldn't pay, so I told her I'd file a motion against her in small claims court. She said she didn't care. She wasn't gonna gimme one goddamn cent, no matter what. I was pissed. If a guy had done that to me, I woulda slugged him."

"So what did you do?"

"She had this beat-up car. Twenty-year-old Dodge. I had a baseball bat in my trunk. I keep it there all the time. You never know, right?"

"Right."

"I took out the bat and smashed all the windows in her car. She screamed at me and said she was gonna call the sheriff, and I told her to go ahead 'cause then I'd swear out a warrant for her arrest. I know guys in the sheriff's office. I woulda gotten outta the joint long before she did."

White and Hispanic trash America colliding with each other, Sheila said to herself. What have I gotten myself into?

"Do you have the name of the trailer park?" she asked.

"Blue Angels Estates," Jersey Guy said.

"Blue Angels? After the flyboys?"

"Pretentious, right? Just like her."

"Do you have any idea if she's still there?"

"No. But that place is the end of the line."

* * *

The website for Blue Angels Estates listed a number for the manager, so Sheila left a voicemail. It was early in the afternoon, and she had nothing to do. Inactivity felt weird. When the kids were small, she always planned family stuff for the weekend, but now Dylan and Bethany preferred their friends. On one level, Sheila understood, but on another, she felt rejected.

In the living room, Wesley was watching a Premier League match on the USA network, which struck her as a strange broadcasting outlet for soccer. Wesley was kind of, sort of, a Manchester United fan.

Outside, it was sunny, and the leaves on the curbside trees were beginning to turn. She looked at her Weather Channel app. Sixty degrees. No rain in the forecast.

"Let's go somewhere," Sheila said to her husband.

"You have any place in mind?"

"As a matter of fact, I do."

She carried her camera, and they rode a Bronx-bound No. 2 train to 96th Street in Manhattan before transferring to the 1, which they took to 116th. On the street, they were surrounded by college kids. Columbia. Barnard. City College.

"You should put a store here," Sheila said.

"A little far to reach," Wesley said. "I doubt I could supervise it the way I want."

"But all these students. What a market."

"Uh-huh."

"Dylan's thinking about Columbia. He could check in on things for you."

"Uh-huh."

They headed toward the Hudson. Afternoon sunlight glinted off the water. Riverside Park was a ribbon of green filled with toddlers, joggers, and bicyclists. Elderly people on benches gazed at the Palisades. It was impossible to believe something horrible could happen here.

They walked along the running path for five minutes before stopping. Sheila took out her camera.

"It happened here?" Wesley asked.

"She was heading south," Sheila said.

"She had earbuds."

"And her hood was up. She could only see straight ahead. The only thing she heard was music."

Sheila panned the scene.

"Is this what they call an establishing shot?" Wesley asked.

"Could be. Dunno if I'm gonna use it. But look around. It's beautiful. An urban oasis. I can contrast it to what happened to her."

She stopped filming but held the camera like a Wild West gunslinger ready for a quick draw, then pointed to a thicket about fifty feet from the path.

"Whoever attacked her dragged her there."

She aimed the camera at the ground. The assailant or assailants had grabbed Marie Antolini by the legs. Her backside created a thin, muddy trail through wet grass.

Sheila and Wesley stopped at the thicket. She turned off the camera. Wesley jerked his thumb at the trees and bushes.

"Shall we?" he asked.

"We've come this far," she said.

They stepped into the spot where Marie Antolini had been raped. Although Sheila wore jeans and long sleeves, she could feel the brambles trying to slice her skin. The space was only fifty yards long and twenty yards wide, but the leaves overhead blocked the sunlight, and she found herself blinking as her eyes adjusted.

"You really could get away with murder in here," Wesley said.

Sheila swept her camera in every direction and hoped she conveyed the site's seclusion. Finally, she pointed at the ground, which was strewn with leaves and branches.

"The attacker, or attackers, pulled her further in," she said.

"You're still using the plural?" Wesley asked.

"I'm trying to keep an open mind," Sheila said.

"Nobody does that anymore."

They stepped over a downed tree limb. Feet crunched on fallen foliage. They were in the middle of the thicket, where the attack had reached its brutal conclusion, and Sheila's breath came close to stopping because she saw a man sitting on a stump, looking up as if he were expecting someone.

"I thought I heard voices," he said.

The man was white and middle-aged and looked familiar. Sheila tried to place him, but Wesley spoke before she could say anything.

"I've seen you on television. CNN."

The man flashed a broadcast smile. "You've got a good memory. That was a long time ago."

"Your name is Seamus O'Toole," Wesley said. "You used to run around with Christiane Amanpour. The Balkans and Afghanistan and Iraq. Stuff like that."

"I was in Berlin when the Wall fell. A heady time. We all thought the world would be a better place." He shook his head. "Christ, were we naïve. Look at what just happened in the Middle East."

"I remember you now," Sheila said. "You used to wear a St. Christopher's medal."

"Even a foreign correspondent needs a gimmick," O'Toole said.

"You work for my brother now."

He looked at Sheila as if she'd just started speaking Mandarin.

"Michael Devine," she said. "He's talked about you. You're helping his campaign."

"Which needs all the assistance it can get, although it's not his fault." O'Toole stood and approached them. "You must be Sheila. That would explain the camera."

"I am, and it does." They bumped fists. She introduced him to Wesley. More fist-bumping.

"You're probably here for the same reason I am," O'Toole said.

"I'm not sure about that," Sheila said.

"The retracing-the-steps thing," O'Toole said. "Trying to see if anything's been overlooked. Your brother could lose the election if this thing isn't resolved PDQ. I don't like it when my clients lose. It's bad for business."

It had never occurred to Sheila that Michael might blow the election. It was obvious to her that Nelson Hernandez was an incompetent windbag, although his candidacy was well-financed, for reasons she could not understand.

"I just wanna get a sense of what it's like," Sheila said. "Stock footage. I might not even use it."

"The scene looks a tad different now," O'Toole said. "The trees are a little bigger. So are the bushes. I used to explore every inch of this place, back when I taught at Columbia." He pointed to a bare patch of ground about ten feet away. "There used to be poison oak there. One of the Parks people warned me about it."

"Columbia," Sheila said. Her mind made a connection. "Marie was one of your students."

"My best student," O'Toole said. "She would've been a star. It's such a waste. If only she hadn't…" He shook his head.

"If only she hadn't…what?"

"Gone running that night," O'Toole said. "None of this would've happened."

Some of it would've happened, Sheila thought. Those guys would've been arrested. But the charges would've been minor, and maybe their sentences would've been suspended, and, certainly, the city would've avoided a revenge frenzy.

"Can I talk to you about her?" Sheila asked.

"Not here. It's a little…creepy."

"More than a little." Sheila turned to Wesley. "Let's go."

Her husband shook his head. Dreads waved. "I'll stay a bit. I wanna look around." He flashed his charming smile. "But I'll be on the lookout for poison oak. Just in case."

* * *

She did a standup interview with the sun behind her and a bucolic park scene framing Seamus O'Toole in the background. He was a pro, so he knew exactly what was required.

"Tell me about Marie," Sheila said. "Something I don't know."

"The first time we put her in front of a camera, she glowed, and I said to myself, 'Sometimes you can just tell when a woman has it.'"

"Did she even need to go to graduate school? Couldn't she have landed a job with a station somewhere and worked her way up?"

"Columbia's a great ticket to punch. It stands out on your résumé, and it's easy to make contacts. It also gives you polish. Marie was from South Philadelphia. She had rough edges. That's not a bad thing in a print reporter, but if you're in broadcast, you have to hide it. So we worked on smoothing her accent."

"Anything else?"

"Despite her talent, she was provincial. Marie had never been outside Philadelphia all that much. I told her she needed to broaden herself, so I encouraged her to travel. Go to Europe. Things like that."

"How did she respond?"

"Enthusiastically. She was all in on her career." O'Toole shook his head. "I really enjoyed teaching her. It was like being the coach of a phenomenally talented player who's willing to work her butt off."

"How was she gonna get to Europe? What was she gonna use for money?"

"I offered to help her out. I knew people and places."

"I've talked to Rajeev Dalweet," Sheila said.

"Whenever I see him on CNN, I'm a little surprised. I did not predict great success for him." He sounded like an investor who'd passed on buying Apple in the Eighties. "I haven't talked to him in years."

He has the job you wanted, Sheila thought. How does the teacher feel when the student surpasses him?

"Was there anything going on between him and Marie?" Sheila asked.

O'Toole pursed his lips. "Was Rajeev obsessed with her? Did he want to sleep with her? Did she rebuff him? Could that explain what happened?" He shrugged. Sheila shrugged back.

"Then there's the boyfriend," Sheila said. "Seems he was in New York that day."

O'Toole spoke slowly. "If it can be proven beyond a doubt that he was in the city, he'll have to account for his whereabouts at the time of the attack."

Sheila stopped filming and swung the camera down to her side.

"They shoulda looked into all of this a decade ago," she said. Her vehemence surprised her. "There was a rush to judgment, but not to justice."

"Do you blame your brother for what he did?" O'Toole asked. "Or the police? The pressure was incredible. You remember what it was like. A classic media frenzy. The cops, prosecutors, and politicians all needed a quick resolution."

Sheila slung her camera back on her shoulder. "We're on the record again. Rajeev and Marie were friends with a woman named Gloria Estevez. Can you tell me anything about her?"

O'Toole sucked in some air, as if he'd just swallowed a particularly sour glass of lemonade.

"Wellllllllll…"

Out with it, Sheila thought.

"The problem with going through life with a chip on your shoulder is that you'll always run into people who want to knock it off."

"Was she difficult?"

"She thought that since she'd made it to Columbia, she could coast. I told her the school was a gateway, not a guarantee. It doesn't matter what your credentials are—there's always somebody behind you who is younger, hungrier, and willing to work harder."

"How did she react to that?"

"She accused me of disrespecting her because she was Latin."

"Did you?"

O'Toole blinked a few times. "You've got a pair."

"I've heard that before."

O'Toole forced a smile. "I admire your ability to pose the questions that

251

need to be asked." Slight pause. "No, I did not disrespect Gloria Estevez. I did tell her, on several occasions, that she should lose weight. She was deeply offended, but I also told her it was the reality of the profession. As you well know, the camera is merciless."

"What was her response?"

"She told me she was thinking of filing a complaint with the school administration. Accused me of belittling her and creating a toxic environment. So I informed her that if she thought I was tough, there was no way she'd ever last in a newsroom."

"Did she ever file that complaint?"

"I'm not sure. Columbia and I parted ways at the end of the school year. I'm not cut out for academia. I wanted to be around the action, not holed up in an ivory tower commenting upon it."

"How did Marie and Gloria get along?" Sheila asked.

O'Toole thought a bit. "They spent a lot of time together, but there was friction. Marie's future was bright, while Gloria was struggling. Sometimes two people like that graft onto each other." He paused. Thought some more. "They both liked Rajeev, and now I understand why. He was utterly calm. Nothing ever rattled him. They both regarded him as a stabilizing force."

Sheila stopped filming and thanked O'Toole for his time. He said it had been his pleasure and wished her luck with her project.

"I've been looking for Gloria Estevez," Sheila said. "I've tracked her to a trailer park in Nevada."

"It's funny you say that," O'Toole said. "I'd like to contact Marie. Your brother knows where she is, but he plays that card close to his vest."

"Michael woulda been a good spy. He never reveals much. Sometimes it's maddening. He told me she's at a medical center in Pennsylvania. She works with trauma victims."

"That's great to hear. Do you know which one?"

Sheila shook her head and said she didn't. Then she heard footsteps and knew they were Wesley's. He stopped beside her.

"Find anything?" she asked.

"No. After a while, it got unnerving in there."

O'Toole nodded. "I've always believed that parts of all of us who knew Marie were left behind in this place."

* * *

Sheila's phone vibrated as soon as she and Wesley got out of the Atlantic Avenue station. They were walking home, and she did not want the distraction, but when she glanced at the number she saw it was from Nevada.

"This is Sheila."

"You called me." A man's voice. Raspy. She imagined a cigarette hanging from the corner of his mouth.

"I'm looking for a woman who might be living at your park. Her name is Gloria Estevez."

No reply for a few seconds. Sheila was afraid she'd lost the connection.

"You from a collection agency?"

"No."

"'Cause I was gonna tell you not to waste your time. Getting money outta her is like getting blood from a stone."

"I'm a filmmaker working on a documentary," Sheila said. "I've got some things I wanna ask her."

"Is she gonna like them?"

"I doubt it."

She could almost see the guy smiling. "Here's her number."

Chapter Thirty-Four

Michael Devine

October 10, 2023

The 55-inch hi-def TV in his office was tuned to New York One. The station had switched live to the courtroom where Judge Iffath Khan was hearing Rolando Ortega's motion for a DNA sample from Rocco Cantone, Philadelphia police officer and former boyfriend of Marie Antolini.

"It's always a pleasure to see you, Señor Ortega," the judge said.

"The feeling is mutual, Your Honor."

The judge scrolled her laptop while addressing the court.

"You've filed an interesting motion, Señor Ortega. The problem is, you've already filed several interesting motions in this case. It seems as if you want to take DNA samples of half the male population in the Northeast."

Chuckles from the spectators.

"I would gladly do that, Your Honor, to rectify the injustice that has been done to my clients."

"We're not at trial, Señor Ortega. Skip the rhetoric and stick to the facts."

Michael had always respected Iffath Khan, the only judge in Manhattan who wore a hijab.

She asked Ortega why she should grant his motion.

"I have filed a deposition from Mr. DeMarcus Daniels, a driver for the

MaxiBus company. We believe the statement from Mr. Daniels raises legitimate questions about the activities of Rocco Cantone, the former boyfriend of the victim in the assault in Riverside Park. The court is aware—"

The judge interjected: "The victim had an order of protection against him. Keep going."

"We believe Mr. Cantone was in New York that day. We believe it is perfectly reasonable to get a DNA sample from him, to see if his semen matches that taken from the victim."

The judge swung her chair to face the prosecution's table. "How do you respond to that, Ms. Williams?"

Jackie Williams, Michael's top assistant, rose to her full height. Nearly six feet tall, she had played basketball at Fordham. Michael liked hiring former athletes because they understood how to handle both competition and adversity.

Call bullshit on him, Michael said silently to the TV screen. In polite, legal language, of course.

"As you yourself pointed out, Your Honor—"

Very good, Michael thought. Always praise judges for their acumen.

"—Señor Ortega has filed numerous motions in this case. The People's position is that he's engaged in the judicial equivalent of throwing pasta at the wall to see if something sticks."

Iffath Khan smiled. "That's how I always see if my pasta's done."

Jackie smiled back. "But that's when you're in a kitchen, Your Honor, not a courtroom."

More chuckles from the spectators.

Keep going, Michael thought. You're doing great.

"But there's a larger point, Judge Khan. Even if the DNA matches, it doesn't prove anything. Mr. Cantone and the victim had been engaged in a physical relationship and last saw each other only a few days before the attack. Even if the semen is his, it could very well be the result of a consensual encounter."

Iffath Khan nodded before looking at the lawyer next to Jackie Williams.

"Identify yourself, please."

The man rose. He was in his mid-thirties, shaved head, with a roll of fat on the back of his neck that sagged over his collar. His tie was violet, too wide, and a bit askew, and as Michael watched him stand, he asked himself, Is this the best they can do in Philadelphia?

"My name is Carmine Rizzo, Your Honor. I'm an attorney for the Philadelphia Fraternal Order of Police. As such, I'm here representing Officer Cantone."

"Mr. Rizzo, what does Mr. Cantone—"

"Officer Cantone, Judge."

For the first time in the hearing, Iffath Khan scowled, and Michael wished he was in the court so he could tell the greenhorn from the City of Brotherly Love that there was no way a New York Supreme Court judge was going to put up with his bullying crap, even if she was a five-foot-one woman with traces of Pakistan in her voice.

"He was Mr. Cantone at the time of the incident, Mr. Rizzo, so that's how this court will refer to him."

Let it drop, Michael pleaded silently to the man filling his TV screen.

"He is a police officer in the city of Philadelphia, Judge."

"And he's in a lot of difficulty there, from what I see in the media."

Titters in the courtroom.

"That matter has nothing to do with what's before this court," Rizzo said.

"True enough," the judge said. "Now stop arguing with me. What is Mr. Cantone's response to the deposition filed by Mr. Daniels?"

Rizzo's mouth worked a bit, but no words came out.

C'mon, Michael thought. You knew she was gonna ask this question. Don't you have something ready?

And then it occurred to him that Carmine Rizzo was flabbergasted by the reality that he had to make nice with a Muslim woman.

"Officer Cantone has no response, Judge."

Iffath Khan's eyebrows shot up toward her hijab. "What do you mean by that?"

"Officer Cantone has discussed this matter with counsel, Your Honor, and has decided he has nothing to say."

Iffath Khan closed her laptop and leaned forward. The woman's eyes grew fixed and hard, and as he watched her on TV, Michael could swear they changed color, from hazel green to steel gray.

"That's not gonna cut it, Mr. Rizzo. Not by a long shot. The deposition by Mr. Daniels raises serious questions, and Mr. Cantone must answer them."

The day before the hearing, Michael and Jackie had war-gamed every possibility. Now, he wondered what the Philly lawyer had done to prepare, and he decided the answer was simple: Nothing. Attorneys for the police union in Philadelphia were used to judges letting their clients skate on everything.

"If you order a DNA test, Judge," Rizzo said, "we're gonna file an appeal."

"I know that—I'm not an idiot. Moreover, I'm inclined to agree with Ms. Williams, who pointed out in a thoroughly professional manner that even if his DNA matches the sample taken from the victim, it's unlikely to prove anything." Iffath Khan turned to Ortega. "Sorry, Counselor, but I'm gonna deny your motion. Nice try."

Ortega nodded at her in a sign of respect. The judge swiveled back toward Rizzo.

"As for you, I'm ordering you to produce Mr. Cantone before this court at nine a.m. on Thursday. I've got some questions to ask him, and he better be ready. So should you."

"But, Judge, that's just two days—"

Iffath Khan slammed her gavel. "Philadelphia's only ninety minutes away. He can get here."

"He's a family man—"

The gavel again. Louder.

"He's been suspended with pay. He has time on his hands, and he can afford the trip."

"But there's no evidence—"

The judge cracked the gavel so hard Michael was afraid it would break in her hands.

"I've looked over the transcript of the interview that Detective Haggerty

257

conducted with Mr. Cantone shortly after the attack," she said. "There's plenty of evidence that your client may have lied to a police officer, and he'll have to talk about that, whether he likes it or not."

Chapter Thirty-Five

Sheila Devine

October 11, 2023

The landscape was dry and dusty and barren and brown, and Sheila found herself seething with resentment at everybody and everything that had led her here. She reserved most of her ire for Gloria Estevez, who had insisted she would only talk to Sheila in person, at her home in Nevada, and her demand was non-negotiable.

Sand blew across the two-lane road. Sheila cruised slowly, like a kid taking driver's ed. Some sections of the desert are beautiful, she told herself. This part isn't.

At the trailer park, she turned down the dirt path Gloria had told her to take. Sheila stopped her econo-rental behind the beat-up Dodge that Jersey Guy had told her about. Gloria's mobile home looked battered and dingy.

Sheila texted **I'M HERE**.

No response. She walked to the door and rang the bell. No answer. Rang it again, louder and longer. Still nothing. Bad thoughts flooded Sheila's mind. She pushed on the door, which creaked open, then felt the bottom of her bag and caressed her can of Mace.

It was dim inside, and crap was strewn all around—clothes, newspapers, magazines, DVDs, CDs, rags, plastic bottles, metal cans. The air stank of tobacco.

Sheila reached into her bag, gripped the Mace, took another step. She heard a rustling sound and let out a small shriek of surprise as a four-legged, khaki-colored critter skittered into a crevice in the wall.

Friggin' lizards, Sheila thought. Why in the world does anyone live here?

She breathed deeply and detected the odor of alcohol, then told herself to be absolutely still. She thought she heard light snores. Next to the wall, she saw a sagging sofa topped by shredded blankets that moved up and down. Sheila stepped toward the spot…thought about putting away her Mace…decided against it. When she lifted the blankets, she saw a short and plump Latina with stringy hair that bent in five directions. The woman wore a white T-shirt and Eddie Bauer shorts, and her face bore the prematurely aged look that comes to those who see their dreams die.

Sheila tapped her on the back. Nothing. She lifted the woman's arm and let it fall back onto her side. No response. Finally, she shook the woman's shoulder as violently as she could. No movement at all. On an end table right by the woman's head, Sheila saw a bottle of Zapopan and a box of Ambien.

Booze and sleeping pills, Sheila thought. What could possibly go wrong?

She took out her iPhone and set the alarm for one minute away. She ratcheted the volume as high as it would go and put the device in the woman's ear. When it went off, it sounded as if someone was trying to rob a Brink's truck.

The woman's eyes opened a millimeter. "What the fuck?"

"Ms. Estevez?" Sheila said.

The woman tried to swat at the phone, but her hand fell back to her side. "Who the fuck are you?"

"Sheila Devine. We talked on the phone. Remember?"

"Shit. What day is it?"

"Wednesday."

"Shit."

"I flew here from New York to interview you, Ms. Estevez. And that's what I'm gonna do."

"Shit."

"Do you have a coffeemaker?"

The woman waved toward the back of the trailer. Sheila headed that way, sniffed cat piss, started breathing through her mouth. She stepped over a poop-filled litter box and was grateful the machine on the counter was black, so she couldn't tell how dirty it was.

"You need a cup of coffee?" Gloria asked.

"No, Ms. Estevez. You do."

As a peace offering, Sheila had brought a pound of Wesley's best. She found a filter and filled it, then poured in water from the two-liter bottle of Poland Spring she'd bought at the airport. As the coffeemaker creaked to life, she hoped the aroma would mask everything she could see and smell.

When Sheila turned, she saw Gloria swigging the Zapopan. Sheila walked straight to her, grabbed the tequila, and thrust the remaining Poland Spring into her hands.

"What the fuck?" Gloria said.

"You're gonna be sober for this interview," Sheila said.

Gloria lunged for the tequila like a toddler at a birthday party, reaching for a balloon. "Gimme that."

"You want me to pour it down the sink?"

Gloria stopped, then looked at the water as if it were radioactive.

"Drink that," Sheila said. "Get hydrated."

Gloria's face scrunched in distaste as she sipped the Poland Spring. When the coffeemaker stopped, Sheila found a dusty mug that she wiped with a paper towel.

"How do you take your coffee?" she asked.

"Black." Gloria cackled. "Like my men."

Spare me, Sheila thought as she brought the mug to the woman, who raised it to her lips.

"This smells good," she said.

"Best coffee in the world. It's from my husband's store."

Gloria sipped. "You're married, huh?"

"With two kids."

"Must be nice."

"It usually is."

Sheila looked for a place to sit. Nothing.

Gloria said, "I've been drinking tequila because I ran out of Percocet last week. You have any?"

"No."

Sheila reached into her bag and took out her Sony. Gloria grunted before pointing at the camera.

"I haven't seen one of those in a while."

Sheila decided against asking for permission and just started filming. "You used to be in TV. Why'd you leave?"

"Kept having run-ins with my bosses. Eventually, I figured I'd be better off working for myself."

Sheila panned the trailer and thought, *Look how well that's turned out.*

"As I told you over the phone," she said, "I wanna talk about Marie Antolini."

"Little Ms. Perfect."

"Why do you say that?"

"Oh, they all thought she was gonna be a star. Especially that guy—whatshisname?"

"Seamus O'Toole?"

"That's it. He worshiped the ground she walked on, and she liked being worshiped."

Sheila hated the question she was about to pose, but she had to ask: "Was something going on between them?"

"There were rumors." Gloria cackled again. "I started most of them."

God save us all from frenemies, Sheila thought.

"You spent a lotta time with Marie," Sheila said.

Gloria shrugged. "We worked on stuff together. And with Rajeev. We were assigned to be a team, and we did well. We split the work evenly, but O'Toole thought Marie did all the heavy lifting."

Gloria sipped some coffee. Sheila liked the direction the interview was taking. Gloria obliged by continuing to talk.

"The way they looked at each other—Marie and O'Toole. Whenever we had an appointment with him, she'd show up five minutes early. We'd walk into his office, and they'd be making goo-goo eyes at each other."

"I've talked to Rajeev. He said nothing about that."

"Men are oblivious."

"I've talked to O'Toole. He said you threatened to file a complaint against him."

"He's an asshole," Gloria said.

"Why do you say that?"

"He kept telling me point-blank that I had to lose weight. He said viewers didn't wanna see fat women delivering the news. He asked why I couldn't be more like Marie."

"Did you file that complaint?" Sheila asked.

Gloria shook her head. "This was before #MeToo. I was a student, a Latina, a nobody, and he'd been a correspondent for CNN. Who do you think the administration woulda listened to?"

Sheila resisted the urge to nod.

"Besides," Gloria said, "I decided to leave. I didn't like school, and I hated New York. I thought the best thing to do was go home and get a job. And after what happened to Marie…" She shuddered.

"It musta been traumatic."

"I dunno if I'd put it that way. Sometimes, when people are perfect, and they like to remind you that they're perfect, when something bad happens to them, you feel a little…oh, what's that word…it's German."

"Schadenfreude?"

"That's it."

Sheila reminded herself that eventually, deep down, even if they refuse to acknowledge it, almost everyone believes that people deserve the bad things that happen to them.

"Have you been following the news?" Sheila asked.

"Sometimes I watch cable." Gloria gulped some water. "I could do better than those airheads. Never got a chance."

"There's a bus driver who swears he dropped off Marie's ex-boyfriend in New York the day of the attack."

"Rocco," Gloria said, and in that single word, she conveyed the longing of a woman who had never gotten anything she wanted.

"I heard that he and Marie had a—" Sheila searched for the right term. "—complicated relationship."

Gloria looked around the trailer. "I wish I had a drink."

Sheila flashed back to when her children were little. Extracting them from the playground was always excruciating. Eventually, she hit on the idea of promising a small piece of chocolate if they left quietly.

"Maybe when we're done. Not before."

Long sigh from Gloria. "Marie talked about this guy she'd been dating on and off since high school. She couldn't figure out why she kept going with him. I tried to be sympathetic, but actually, I didn't understand why she stayed with him if he was such a jerk."

Gloria chugged both coffee and water.

"Then I met him."

Chapter Thirty-Six

Gloria Estevez

1

March 25, 2012

Gloria and Rajeev waited for Marie and her boyfriend in a Starbucks on Amsterdam Avenue near the Cathedral of St. John the Divine.

"It's like we're in friggin' *Friends* or something," Gloria said.

"You think he sounds like Stallone in that movie?" Rajeev tried a Philadelphia accent. "'Yo, Adrian.'"

Gloria laughed, looked at the cappuccino and ginormous brownie she'd ordered, told herself she should cut back on the sweets. Professor O'Toole kept saying the camera amplified every imperfection, especially excess weight.

He was right, but she was under so much stress. Everybody at school was under so much stress.

"I see her," Rajeev said.

Gloria's back was to the door. "What's the boyfriend like?"

"Can't tell. He's wearing a hoodie."

Gloria turned to look. Marie was coming toward them, and it was hard to tell if her smile was genuine or forced. Sometimes, Gloria caught her practicing that grin before mirrors. Professor O'Toole kept telling them it was important for newscasters to have a nice smile and doubly important for women. He didn't mean to sound sexist, but that was the reality of the business. Gloria resented it, but Marie was determined to go places, and she was one of those people who worked on everything until it was flawless.

Maybe I should make my career behind the scenes, Gloria said to herself. Become a producer or something.

She thought some more, then shook her head. Nah, I really wanna be in front of the camera.

Marie led the boyfriend by the hand. The floor was slick with melted snow. Marie was petite, but she always stood straight, and her face glowed, and people paid attention to her.

The hoodie drooped over the boyfriend's forehead. Gloria was reminded of drawings she'd seen of medieval monks. Marie made the introductions and Gloria shook his hand lightly, the way men and women do. He reached for his hood.

Time for the reveal, Gloria thought.

When it occurred, she tried not to swoon.

Rocco was nearly a foot taller than Marie and solidly built, a guy who enjoyed his hours in the gym. His skin was smooth and olive, his hair was dark, his lips were full, his jaw was square, and he was, by far, the best-looking guy Gloria had ever seen in person.

I get it now, she said to herself. Oh, boy, do I get it.

Marie asked Rocco if he wanted anything. He grunted. She went to the counter, and Gloria figured they had the kind of code that couples acquire after they've been together a long time.

Gloria noticed Rocco looking over Rajeev the way a lion king on the Serengeti would regard another male who was trying to infiltrate the pride.

"So," Gloria said to Rocco, "Marie tells us you two have been together a while."

He gazed at her. Brown eyes smoldered.

"Uh-huh," he said.

Rajeev took a turn. "What do you do? Back in Philadelphia?"

He only half succeeded in keeping his disgust out of that last word. Rajeev had once told Gloria and Marie that he'd rather clean toilets at New York One than work as an anchor in Philly.

"I got a job," Rocco said.

Marie came back with two cups and placed one in front of Rocco. Marie had a latte. Marie drank one latte a day and never ate sweets, and was seriously thinking about training for a triathlon. She was awfully fit anyway.

"I just got an email from Professor O'Toole," she said.

Of course you did, Gloria thought. Teachers like to stroke their pets.

"What does he want?" Rajeev asked.

Just like Rajeev, Gloria thought. Always focused on the next thing. Can't you rant with indignation every once in a while, just like the rest of us?

"He wants us to do something on stop-and-frisk," Marie said.

They kicked around the idea of asking cops whether they thought the policy was effective, but after a while, Gloria started glancing at Rocco, who was alternating between drumming his fingers on the table and folding his arms across his chest. He returned her looks, and she could tell he was measuring her from head to toe.

She wished she'd worn something more revealing. She wished she was twenty pounds lighter.

When she glanced at her brownie, she realized she'd eaten only half of it, so she flashed her best smile at Rocco and asked if he wanted any of it.

He gazed at Gloria, at the brownie, and at Gloria again.

"Yeah. Thanks."

She broke off a piece and gave it to him. Marie's eyes turned to daggers.

"You shouldn't be eating that," she said to her boyfriend.

2

April 7, 2012

Gloria was walking back to her room in Graduate Housing and telling herself she was twenty-six years old and it was time to stop living in a cubicle and going to classes as if she were still a schoolgirl. She was an adult. She should work. She should meet a man and get serious about him.

As she crossed Amsterdam, she noticed a guy in a hoodie moving with the easy grace of an athlete. Something about him seemed familiar, but it was dark, and she thought about keeping on her way, but she wanted to be a journalist, and the first rule of the profession was to check things out; and, besides, if she went back to her warren, she'd just drink warm milk and eat Oreos and feel sorry for herself.

She approached him from behind and began to get a feeling. He was looking at the ground and trudging along like a dude who'd just heard that his best friend had died.

"Rocco?" she asked. She still wasn't sure.

He turned. She swooned. And then she thought: *Oh shit, what if he doesn't remember me?*

"I'm Gloria. Marie's friend. We met a couple weeks ago. At Starbucks."

He looked at her blankly. Her heart collapsed.

"Oh yeah," he said. A pause. "Hi."

Gloria smiled as widely as she could. "I guess you're here to see Marie."

He blew out some air and thrust his hands deep into the pockets of his hoodie.

"Is something wrong?" Gloria asked.

Rocco looked away but asked, "You're a girl, right?"

She was unsure how to answer this. "I think so."

"Why can't I make her happy?"

Because she's ferociously ambitious, Gloria felt like saying. The only person who will ever make Marie happy is herself, and if you wanna be with her, you better strap in your butt for the ride.

"Well," Gloria said, "Marie is…complex."

For the first time since she'd met him, Rocco laughed.

"You can say that again."

Gloria laughed, too, then told herself she had an opening.

"I don't mean to pry, but did you two have a fight or something?"

"It was huge." He grunted. "I guess we were loud. The cops came."

Gloria searched for a positive spin. "At least you weren't arrested."

"She says she never wants to see me again."

"Has she ever said that before?"

"She might mean it this time." He sighed long and loud, an ordinary guy with ordinary hopes who'd just seen them vanish.

Say something, Gloria told herself. Anything.

"You wanna talk about it?"

He turned to her and smiled, and his teeth were white and dazzling, and Gloria couldn't believe she was alone with a guy like this.

"Sure," he said. "As long as it ain't at a friggin' Starbucks."

She laughed and steered him to Mulligan's. It was popular with grad students and Gloria was hoping somebody she knew would see her with this really hot guy. They ordered beers and found a booth in the back. The alcohol worked its magic as the taciturn Rocco turned into Bill Clinton while he talked about Marie:

Nothing was ever good enough—Philadelphia wasn't good enough, that movie wasn't good enough, he wasn't good enough—and as he went on, Gloria realized that whenever they went out to eat, even if it was only for a slice of pizza, Marie always found something to criticize.

Eventually, Rocco slowed down. Speaking had made him weary, and his normally sloping shoulders slumped. When he looked at his watch, Gloria was afraid he'd grown bored with her.

"Do you have a boyfriend?" he asked.

She blushed. Stammered. Said no.

"I'm surprised. A good-looking girl like you." He shook his head. "I guess I should call you a woman. Politically correct and all that bullshit. That's important at colleges, right?"

"You can call me whatever you want," Gloria said.

He looked at his watch again. Gloria was on the verge of asking him back to her room.

"Shit, I gotta go."

She wanted to scream, *Noooooooo!!!!!!*

"I gotta catch a bus. I already paid for the ticket."

"Back to Philly?" she asked.

He nodded. "Tomorrow's Easter. I gotta be at work at six in the morning. Gonna be a long day. I only came up here 'cause Marie couldn't make it back home."

"Sounds tough."

"It's all right. I like to work, and then I'll have dinner with my family. It's a lot better than this." He waved his arm, dismissing the Ivy League with one motion. "That's what Marie don't get. I work hard. I can provide. I dunno why that ain't good enough."

"She's headstrong," Gloria said. "Maybe she doesn't realize what she has. It's always easy to take things for granted."

They put on their coats and walked out of the bar. On the sidewalk, the streetlamps backlit Rocco Cantone, who glowed with the aura Gloria associated with movie stars.

"She's got something going on," he said.

"Marie? What're you talking about?"

"With some guy. She's gonna go to Europe. She let it slip. She thinks I'm dumb, but I figured it out."

Gloria searched her head. All of her classmates wanted to travel, but it was so expensive. Gloria ran through her conversations with Marie and remembered one night when they'd opened a bottle of cheap wine, and Marie said she might've found a way to go abroad on somebody else's dime. Gloria asked if she had a fellowship—she was just the type to land one— and Marie giggled before saying it wasn't like that. Gloria had done most of the drinking, but she realized what Marie was implying and shot her a withering look. Marie suddenly sounded completely sober and said nothing was definite and everything was tentative, and she'd probably talked too much already.

Chapter Thirty-Seven

Michael Devine

October 12, 2023

J udge Iffath Khan, light blue hijab contrasting with jet black judicial robe, gaveled court to order at two minutes past ten. Michael had considered asking her to close the hearing to the media and public, but he feared she'd say No, and then he'd look both weak and secretive. Besides, Iffath Khan liked attention. TV producers had approached her about doing a legal reality show.

"To what do I owe the honor, Mr. Devine?" she asked.

Michael rose. "This is a matter of great public interest, Your Honor. My obligation to The People compels me to be here."

He sat. Jackie Williams and Carmine Rizzo flanked him. Rizzo leaned over a few millimeters.

"What should I say?"

"As little as possible."

Judge Khan spoke. "The purpose of this hearing is informational. Señor Ortega—"

She motioned toward the lawyer, who nodded in response.

"—has filed a motion on behalf of his clients. I rejected the motion for reasons that are already a matter of public record. Nevertheless, in my examination of the evidence, I have become deeply concerned that a man who was questioned by the New York Police Department in connection with the events of April Eleventh, Two Thousand Twelve, was not entirely forthcoming in his statements. To put it bluntly, he may have lied."

Rizzo started to rise to his feet. "Judge, I—"

Michael put a firm hand on the guy's shoulder, drove him back into his chair, and whispered, as fiercely as he could: "You hafta take it. Siddown and shuddup."

Iffath Khan looked at the prosecution table. "Is there a problem, Mr. Devine?

"Not anymore, Your Honor."

The judge went on. "Whenever this court learns that an untruth may have been uttered while law enforcement officers are trying to discharge their duties, it has an obligation to explore the matter to the fullest extent possible, as quickly as possible. I am troubled by my suspicions that, during the investigation into the events in Riverside Park on the night of April Eleventh, Two Thousand Twelve, deliberately misleading information was given to a New York City police detective. If an accurate account had been given to the NYPD, this case may have unfolded differently. So, I want to delve into all of this as deeply as I can to resolve these questions, and I want to do it today. To that end, I'll begin by calling New York City Police Detective Brendan Haggerty to the stand."

Haggerty left his seat in the front row of the spectators' gallery and strode toward the witness box with the confidence of Yul Brynner doing *The King and I* for the five thousandth time. Haggerty raised his right hand, swore to tell the truth, and sat in the chair, then stated his name, job title, and shield number.

"Detective Haggerty," the judge asked, "during the course of your investigation into the attack on Marie Antolini, did you question her former boyfriend, Rocco Cantone?"

"I did, Your Honor."

"Is Mr. Cantone in the courtroom today?"

"He is, Your Honor."

"Identify him for the record, please."

Haggerty pointed to Cantone, who was seated next to Rizzo.

"Did you ask Mr. Cantone about his activities the night Ms. Antolini was attacked?"

"I did, Your Honor."

"And what did he say?"

Iffath Khan possessed the remorselessness of a warrior for Saladin. Michael had always appreciated Haggerty's appraisal: "The judge is a total bitch, and she's unapologetic about it. That's why I like her."

"He told me he was at home that night. He said he ate dinner with his parents, and then they watched *Law & Order* together. He went to bed, got up early the next morning, and reported for his job at a delicatessen in South Philadelphia. He was there at six in the morning. The owner of the store confirmed he was at work on time that day."

"Did you talk to Mr. Cantone's parents?"

"I did, Your Honor."

"What did they tell you?"

"They ate dinner together, watched *Law & Order*, and went to bed."

"Did you believe them?"

In the witness seat, Haggerty shifted around as if his underwear had developed a wedgie. "Well, Your Honor…"

"You're under oath, Detective."

Michael studied the man, who looked like a teenager wondering if he should tell his parents exactly what had happened at that party last night. Michael and Haggerty had worked dozens of cases together. As far as Michael knew, Haggerty had never testi-lied although, like all cops who appeared in court regularly, he often slanted his presentation to make his evidence look stronger than it actually was.

"I uncovered no information that indicated they weren't telling the truth," Haggerty said.

Michael was impressed by the skillful use of the double negative.

"When you investigated the case in Two Thousand Twelve, did you receive any information from Mr. DeMarcus Daniels?" the judge asked.

"No, Your Honor."

"What would you have done if he had talked to you?"

Haggerty smiled. "I've spent a lotta time in courtrooms, Your Honor, and that question is, as the lawyers like to say, speculative."

A few titters from the audience. The judge remained stone-faced. She's jury and executioner, too, Michael thought.

"Since I asked the question, Detective, you are free to speculate as much as you'd like."

Haggerty shifted again. Likely, this was the first time he had considered the possibility of what might have happened if he'd talked to the bus driver. When the detective spoke, he sounded like a guy who was trying to hide some of his income from an IRS auditor.

"If Mr. Daniels had presented me with the information he provided in that deposition to Mr. Ortega, I woulda gone back to Mr. Cantone and his parents, and asked them more questions."

"Thank you, Detective. That is all."

Haggerty left the stand. Michael noticed a few beads of sweat on his upper lip and around his hairline. Facing Iffath Khan was like defending yourself in catechism class against the toughest nun in the school.

"Mr. Cantone, I'd like you to take the stand now."

Rocco Cantone buttoned his Men's Wearhouse jacket as he walked toward the witness box. Behind him, Michael heard a couple of female sighs. There was already a handle on X—#sexyRoccoCantone—with more than twenty thousand followers.

Cantone raised his right hand and swore to tell the truth. As he sat down, Michael tried to read him. A decade earlier, he'd been a surly and uncommunicative stock clerk. Now he was a police officer, an occupation where being surly and uncommunicative were often assets. He had three children, so at some point he must have gotten over Marie Antolini.

Cantone gave his name and current occupation. His voice sounded like cheesesteaks and rowhouses.

"You know why you're here, Mr. Cantone?"

At the sound of the honorific rather than a title, Rizzo clenched and unclenched his fists, and his butt lifted an inch off his chair. Michael kicked him in the shins.

"I do, Your Honor."

Cantone seemed unruffled. He was a cop, and all cops got used to taking the stand, and Michael had no doubt this guy would tell whoppers if he believed he could get away with them.

"Mr. DeMarcus Daniels has sworn out a deposition, on pain of perjury, that you were on a bus he drove from Philadelphia to New York on April Eleventh, Two Thousand Twelve. Do you have any response to that?"

"I do not, Your Honor."

Judge Iffath Khan stared at him with steely eyes, as if she couldn't believe he'd just stonewalled her. She tried again:

"Were you on that bus?"

Cantone glanced at Rizzo, who nodded a centimeter.

They've worked it out, Michael said to himself. At last, a sign of professionalism.

"With all due respect, Your Honor, I am invoking my right under the Fifth Amendment, and I decline to answer that question."

Murmurs. Whispers. Gasps. The judge banged her gavel.

So help me God, Michael thought, you were on that fucking bus.

Iffath Khan glared at the man in the witness box.

"Were you in New York on April Eleventh, Two Thousand Twelve?" she asked.

"Once again, Your Honor, with all due respect to you and the court, I am using my right under the Fifth Amendment, and I decline to answer that question."

Michael had a flash of a hooded Rocco Cantone lurking in Riverside Park, waiting for Marie to run by.

Judge Khan pursed her lips and narrowed her eyes. She looked ready to engage in a jihad against Rocco Cantone.

"During the investigation into the attack in Riverside Park on April Eleventh, Two Thousand Twelve, you told a New York City police detective that you were at home in Philadelphia that night with your parents. Was that statement accurate?"

"Upon the advice of counsel, Your Honor, I respectfully decline to answer that question, given my Fifth Amendment rights."

"Did you have dinner with your parents that night? Detective Haggerty's notes even break down what you supposedly ate."

"I'm sorry, Your Honor, but I decline to answer under the Fifth Amendment."

"Did you watch *Law & Order*?"

"Fifth Amendment."

Michael felt his iPhone vibrating in the inside pocket of his suit.

"Is there anything you are willing to say regarding the events of April Eleventh, Two Thousand Twelve?" Judge Khan asked.

"Once again, Your Honor, I must invoke my rights under the Fifth Amendment."

Michael's phone vibrated again.

"I could immunize you," the judge said. "If I do that, and you continue to refuse to answer my questions, I could hold you in contempt and order you jailed until you have a change of heart."

Michael's phone was rattling nonstop. He knew he was risking the judge's wrath, but he had to look. As discreetly as he could, he reached into his jacket, took out his phone, put it on the table, and unlocked it.

Calls from Sheila. Voicemail from her he couldn't listen to. And, finally, a text from his sister, in capital letters:

I KNOW WHY HE'S STONEWALLING

As the judge berated Rocco Cantone, Michael texted back:

WHERE R U

Two seconds later:

OUTSIDE THE COURTROOM

Beside him, Rizzo had risen and was saying something about how the judge was browbeating a fine and upstanding police officer. Michael shot to his feet and spoke over him.

"Your Honor, The People request a fifteen-minute recess."

Judge Khan pointed to the phone on the table. "Is it because of those texts you've been exchanging?"

Michael looked at the black device. The best thing to do when you're busted, he reminded himself, is just admit it.

"Your Honor," he said, "we may be on the verge of a *Perry Mason* moment."

For the first time since the hearing began, Judge Khan smiled. "I've always wanted one of those," she said.

* * *

Sheila looked fried and frazzled, and before Michael could say anything, she began talking about how she'd spent the last eighteen hours in shitty airports with lousy WiFi and then in fucking planes with no food, and when she landed at Kennedy the first thing she tried to do was call him but she went straight to voicemail so she tried his office but went to voicemail again and it took close to half an hour to reach a live person and when she finally did she found out he was in court.

"So I asked what it was about," Sheila said. "I mean, when was the last time you were in court?"

Michael had his hand on his sister's back as he searched for a room he could commandeer. Sheila was sweating and breathing rapidly, as if she'd just gotten out of a Zumba class.

"Anyway, they told me, and I said, 'Holy crap, that's what I've gotta talk to him about,' so they told me where I could find you and here I am."

Michael guided his sister into a dark and empty warren. Jackie Williams was right behind. Michael shut the door tight, locked it, flicked on the fluorescent light.

They sat close together at a small wooden table. Hard chairs scraped linoleum. Sheila flipped open her laptop.

"I was in Nevada," she said. "I thought I could get a direct flight to New York. No such luck. So, I thought I'd change planes in Atlanta. It's a hub, right?" She shook her head. "Weather. We landed in Birmingham, Alabama. Then I started scrambling. I managed to get a plane to Louisville, Kentucky. I slept in the waiting area there. At six this morning I boarded a flight to JFK, but we sat on the goddamn runway for close to an hour, so of course when

I landed it was rush hour, and I fucking hate the fucking airline industry."

"Why were you in Nevada?" Jackie asked.

The door rattled, and the knob turned, and they all heard a hand with a wedding ring knocking against the smoked glass.

Michael used his barking voice: "We're in conference."

"I'm aware of that, Mr. Devine. But I want to ask your sister if she would like to share this seemingly explosive information with the man who commissioned her film."

Rolando Ortega never misses a thing, Michael said to himself.

He looked at his sister. "I'll leave this up to you."

Sheila sagged. Michael sensed her adrenaline surge was fading.

"Let him in," she said. "He'll see this eventually anyway."

Michael unlocked the door. Sheila motioned Ortega to the only unoccupied chair in the room.

"Pull up a seat," she said. "It's showtime."

She booted up her laptop.

"Yesterday, I interviewed Gloria Estevez at a trailer park in Nevada. I transferred the recording from my camera because it'll be easier to show the footage this way. Here goes."

A sharp image of a ravaged woman filled the screen. Michael heard Sheila's voice:

"So you and Rocco Cantone started texting each other?"

"That's right."

"How did that turn out?"

"Well…" Gloria giggled. "Texting turned to sexting. Now, I couldn't go to Philadelphia—he lived with his parents and stuff. So I suggested he come to New York to visit me. Which he did."

"On April Eleventh, Two Thousand Twelve?"

"That's right. He got to my room around six p.m. He left about midnight."

She giggled again. When the captain of the football team notices a zaftig girl with braces, she remembers it the rest of her life.

"He was in your sight the entire time?"

"He was in me the entire time. God, he was great in bed."

Chapter Thirty-Eight

Sheila Devine

1

October 12, 2023

She needed sleep, but there was too much to do, so she binged on caffeine. She talked to New York One, CNN, and MSNBC. Joel Moscowitz texted that the publicity was invaluable; everyone wanted to see the movie; Netflix, Amazon, Hulu, and Apple had all been in contact; when the film reached the theaters, it would break every box-office record for documentaries.

"This is excellent."

Thought-chain broken.

She'd forgotten that Rolando Ortega had accompanied her to Brooklyn.

"My father," he said, then stopped. The lawyer had loosened his tie in what Sheila regarded as an acknowledgment of the day's breathless events.

"What about your father?"

"While I was growing up, he contrived ways to get beans from Cuba, which he ground himself every morning. I never asked how he acquired them. Perhaps I should have. I might have learned something." Ortega sipped his drink. "This reminds me of what my father used to make."

"My husband is the Coffee Whisperer," Sheila said. "He finds this stuff in

280

Jamaica. It's always the best."

She put her cup on the table. She knew she'd need a fourth or fifth wind, but she was grateful to be in Wesley's place, which was calm and comforting and felt almost like home.

Just a few minutes, she said to herself. I need a few minutes where I don't think about anything.

Ortega leaned forward.

"Today's events do not resolve the question of who attacked Marie Antolini."

Sheila knocked back a big slug. I'll have to keep thinking all friggin' day, she thought.

"My brother's theory is that Marie was assaulted by one of the perps who got away. There were up to twenty guys in that pack, which scattered in every direction as soon as the cops got close. Only five people were apprehended. Only four were brought to trial. My brother believes it's most likely that one of the other kids in that gang saw Marie and attacked her, and he argues that since the attack grew out of the rampage, the guys in prison are still culpable for what happened."

And then there's Felipe Huerta's story, Sheila said to herself. Even if it's accurate, there's no way it would stand up under questioning. No judge or jury would believe him. I'm not sure I believe him.

"I take issue with your brother's scenario," Ortega said.

Of course you do, Sheila thought. Your possible payday depends on it.

"I think the man who violated Ms. Antolini was not there by chance," the lawyer said. "He knew her habits. He assaulted her when he knew she'd be vulnerable. And the way he beat her—he was enraged. He wanted to punish her for something she had done to him."

"That's plausible, too," Sheila said. "But you hafta prove it. As things stand, an appeals court will side with my brother. You know that better than I do."

Ortega emitted a yammering sound that indicated his reluctant agreement with her analysis.

"Rocco Cantone didn't attack her," Sheila said. "He was my prime suspect. Yours, too."

"Perhaps Ms. Estevez was lying to protect him."

Sheila shook her head. "Did you see how red his face got when I showed that footage to the judge? You need to come up with somebody else."

Ortega drummed manicured fingers on the table. "How about that young man she hung out with at Columbia? The CNN anchor?"

"Rajeev Dalweet was in the editing lab that night, then went back to his room. Surveillance cameras back up his story."

Ortega sipped more coffee. Sheila was tempted to ask if it was okay to start filming. The scene could be excellent, she told herself—the unruffled legal giant, finally flustered.

"The footage you showed..." he said.

You're thinking out loud, Sheila said silently, because you need to pull a *Harvey*-sized rabbit out of a fez.

"Ms. Estevez mentioned Mr. Cantone's fixation with a trip to Europe that Ms. Antolini was planning to make."

"Rocco was venting to her. He never did anything about it."

"You're missing the point."

"Enlighten me."

Ortega slugged more caffeine. The gears in his lawyerly mind were beginning to mesh.

"Who was she supposed to go with?"

2

October 11, 2023

She had packed the camera. Ready to go and happy about it. Sheila feared she was shortening her lifespan by a week every time she inhaled the crap floating around Gloria Estevez's trailer.

What do I say to this woman before I run outta here? she asked herself.

"I wanna thank you for your time. It's been...interesting."

Gloria waved her off with her left hand and brought the bottle of Zapopan to her lips with her right.

"Friggin' Rocco," she said.

"What about him?"

"An experience like that. It was unforgettable."

Sheila tried to recall her one-night stands. Most were alcohol-fueled, and she regretted them for days. Meeting Wesley was the best thing that ever happened to her.

Gloria swigged more tequila. "But whenever we came up for air, all he wanted to talk about was Marie. God, he was in love with her."

Silent observation from Sheila: He loved her so much he was happy to screw one of her classmates.

"I'd tell him to shut up. That turned him on. We'd start doing it again."

Porn star stuff, Sheila thought. Maybe you both picked the wrong careers.

"He was really upset about that trip to Europe." Another swig. "Said he couldn't believe Marie was turning into a whore, but maybe that's what it took to get ahead in the news business."

Sheila considered taking out her camera. This was good stuff, but she wanted to leave.

"The night after she broke up with Rocco, Marie came clean with me." Gloria was beginning to slur her words. "She said a guy had told her he was gonna make a summerlong trip through the E.U. He thought there was a great story brewing about migration and how all these countries with no history of accepting immigrants were gonna deal with it, or not deal with it."

"That was a good call in Two Thousand Twelve."

"The guy needed an assistant, and he'd sounded her out. She was definitely interested."

"An older man?"

"That was my impression."

"Traveling around Europe with a young and attractive female assistant?"

Gloria came close to draining the bottle. "Doesn't take much of an imagination to figure out what could happen."

"Did Marie tell you who the guy was?"

"No, but here's the funny thing." Gloria cranked down the dregs of the

Zapopan. "The day before Rocco saw me, Marie and I had lunch. Obviously, I didn't tell her anything about the plans I'd made with Rocco."

Obviously, you drunken bitch, Sheila thought.

"And she told me, outta the blue, that Rocco had said something to her that made her think. And Rocco had never made her think before."

"What was it?"

"She said that if she went to Europe with this guy, he'd expect her to sleep with him, and she probably would, and then, when you got right down to it, no matter what kind of work she was doing, she'd be little more than a hooker. And if that was the case, then she wouldn't be able to look at herself in the mirror. So she told the guy she appreciated the offer, but in the end, she had decided against it, and boy, was he pissed."

With that, Gloria Estevez toppled to her side and passed out.

3

October 12, 2023

Wesley carried something frou-frou toward Sheila and Ortega. His smile was impish, and his eyes twinkled, as if the food he was bringing was the world's most closely guarded secret. Sheila pointed at the plate and asked what it was.

"Jamaican black cake," he said. "My auntie's recipe. I'm thinking of putting it on sale. You two are my guinea pigs."

"How many aunties do you have?" Sheila asked.

"I've lost track."

He doled out forks. Sheila and Ortega both took bites and said it was delicious.

"I watched what happened today in court," Wesley said. "I figured you two could use a treat."

"That is an accurate assessment, Señor McBride," Ortega said.

Wesley rubbed his hand over his wife's back.

I could use a massage, she thought. Maybe something more.

"What's your next move?" he asked Sheila.

She jerked her thumb at Ortega. "Depends on him. But if this isn't checkmate, we're close to it."

Ortega said nothing.

The counselor is keeping his own counsel, Sheila said to herself.

Wesley's fingers dug into a knot near Sheila's shoulder. She grimaced before saying "ouch" as softly as she could.

"You're tense," he said.

"I've been on TV all day," she said. "But I can't figure this thing out."

"What do you keep telling me?" he asked.

"Pick up a bottle of wine for dinner."

Wesley smiled before correcting her. "Several times, as we've discussed this, you've said, 'Felipe Huerta is the key to this whole mess.'"

Sheila told herself that her husband had a point. She opened her laptop and found the interview with Huerta. The two men pulled their chairs close beside her. If you listened closely, Huerta's rants made sense. By now, Sheila had memorized everything he'd said.

What am I missing? she asked herself.

As if to answer her, Wesley pointed to the image of Huerta on the screen. "What's that thing around his neck?"

Chapter Thirty-Nine

Marie Antolini

October 12, 2023

She walked out of the medical center and headed for her car. Sometimes, she had trouble remembering things, so she was glad she had an assigned space in the lot. Still, it felt reassuring when she wielded her key chain and heard the blip of doors unlocking.

She'd play classical music on the way home. The sounds soothed her. Vivaldi was the best.

"Marie?"

She turned. The voice was male and seemed familiar, but she couldn't quite place it. That happened to her occasionally, all these years after the incident.

"Yes?"

She smiled. It was a tic that women had been trained to employ so they could ingratiate themselves with men, and she kept telling herself she should do it less often, but it was a difficult habit to break. Besides, she could remember someone, somewhere, telling her it was important for women to smile to soften their appearance. Yes, it was sexist, but that was the way of the world.

"I've been trying to find you," the man said.

Chapter Forty

Sheila Devine

October 12, 2023

"That is an awfully thin reed to lean on," Michael said.

"After the attacker fled," Sheila said, "Huerta saw something on the ground next to Marie. He snatched it because that's the kinda guy he is. He said it looked nice, and I bet he decided to keep it. His own version of bling."

Michael flicked away her words with a dismissive wave, as if she were heckling him from the last row in the auditorium.

"I wanna talk to your media adviser." Sheila hoped this sounded like a demand.

"I don't know where he is."

"Waddya mean, you don't know? He works for your campaign."

"He's a consultant. When I need to consult him, I call."

"Then gimme his number. I wanna talk to him ASAP."

Michael pointed to the image on the laptop that Sheila had placed on his desk after barging into his office the way a tornado rampages through an RV park.

"Because of that? Are you outta your mind?"

"I've already interviewed him. I'll tell him some things have come up, and I wanna ask him a few more questions. That's even the truth."

"Have you talked to Ortega about this?" Michael asked.

Always worried about Rolando Ortega, she thought. They're like aging athletes who can't stop competing against each other.

"He was right there when I zoomed in on that medal."

"And what did he say?"

"It was intriguing."

"Anything else?"

Sheila shook her head.

"You like to talk about dogs that don't bark," Michael said. "Well, Rolando Ortega is doing nothing with this information. Which should tell you a lot."

Michael looked at his sister like a father who feels he has overindulged his favorite child, but he took out his iPhone and hit some keys.

"I texted you the number you want."

Sheila hunched herself in a chair in a corner of Michael's office while listening to the furious plupplupplup of an angry man pounding out emails. She sent a text and looked at her phone for a minute, silently willing a reply.

Nothing.

She punched in the number her brother had given her and it went to voicemail on the first ring. She listened to the message, which was delivered in the practiced and modulated cadence of a man who once spoke to a camera for a living.

"I'll be away for a day or two, but I'll be checking messages and emails periodically. It may take me a while to get back to you. I promise to catch up with everyone and everything when I return."

Sheila powered down her phone and looked at her brother, who sensed her staring at him.

"What is it?" he asked.

"He's out of town."

Chapter Forty-One

Marie Antolini

October 12, 2023

He said they had known each other, way back when, and asked if she remembered. She said she recognized him, sort of, but much of her life before the incident was a blur. He said he used to visit her in the hospital. Her recovery had been remarkable.

"I just did what I had to do," she said.

"You always had that spirit," he said. "I admire that."

"Thank you."

"I read your book, too. It was terrific."

"To be honest about it, I had help."

"You were always straightforward. So few people are like that, even in a business where you're supposed to be accurate and truthful."

He reached into the tote bag he was carrying. She noticed the CNN logo.

"I was wondering…"

It was a copy of her book.

"Could you sign this for me?"

"Of course."

She took a pen from her purse while he opened the book to the title page. She asked his name again, and then she wrote it down before scribbling a few anodyne words followed by her signature. Before handing the book back she lingered on the dedication. She always liked seeing Michael's name.

"I'm working for him," the man said.

Marie looked up. "Excuse me?"

"Michael Devine. I'm a consultant on his campaign."

This time, her smile was wide and genuine. "How's he doing?"

"He's hit a tough patch. Personally, he's holding up as well as a man can under the circumstances, but he's not a shoo-in anymore." The man shook his head with a seriousness she vaguely recalled from watching correspondents on TV when she was young. "I thought his campaign would be an easy gig. Now I have to earn my money."

She thrust the book into his hands and looked him straight in the eye.

"Please give Michael my best. And tell him I'll do anything to help him. During my recovery..." She stopped. The process had been long and painful, and she tried to avoid thinking about it. "He was so kind and generous. He really cared what happened to me."

"Michael is like that. His opponent is an opportunist." The man paused before gulping in some air, as if he were about to say something he knew he should keep to himself. "I have a confession to make."

"Go ahead."

"I've spent days tracking you down. Michael wants to be protective, and I understand that, but I know you can handle whatever happens."

"Have you told that to Michael?"

"I've tried. He won't hear of it. That's where you come in. I truly believe you'll be able to assist him. Can we discuss what I have in mind?"

Although she had no desire to ever again set foot in New York, she admitted to herself that she'd enjoy spending time with Michael Devine.

Chapter Forty-Two

Sheila Devine

October 12, 2023

Going eighty on the Jersey Turnpike past rest stops named for Joyce Kilmer and Molly Pitcher. Michael beside her. Haggerty in the backseat, at Michael's insistence. In the one-in-a-million chance that this thing panned out, he said, they needed somebody unrelated who could corroborate what had happened.

"Wild fucking goose chase," Haggerty muttered.

He had agreed to go because of Michael. He wouldn't have done this for any other prosecutor.

"Have you reached her yet?" Sheila asked as they sped over the Delaware.

"Nope," Michael said.

"You've called?"

Sheila sensed him rolling his eyes. "Yes, Sis, I've called. Numerous times. I've also sent emails and texts. No response."

"Fuck," Sheila said.

"I'll admit that's not like her," Michael said. "Whenever I reach out to Marie, she usually gets back in a few minutes."

"I'm worried," Sheila said.

From the backseat, she heard Haggerty mumble something about women always worrying too much. She kept her response to herself:

We worry because we have to.

Chapter Forty-Three

Marie Antolini

October 12, 2023

She wasn't used to having private conversations with strange men, so she had no idea where they should talk. She decided on a Starbucks because it was public but quiet. She ordered green tea. The man got a cappuccino and asked if she still worked out. She said she went to the gym six times a week. He said that was another thing he admired about her. As he paid for their drinks at the counter, he said he tried to watch what he ate, but he had difficulty summoning the will to exercise regularly.

They took a table in the corner. The place was almost empty. The man grinned at her. He said it really was great to see her again after all these years.

"How closely…" Marie started to ask. Then she stopped. Sometimes, she had trouble inquiring about matters that truly touched her.

"How closely what?" the man asked.

Go for it, she told herself. "How closely do you work with Michael?"

"When I started on his campaign, I didn't see him that much. He was far ahead. But lately, with everything that's going on, we talk several times a week. He's a cool customer. Nothing rattles him."

Marie sipped her tea. "He's always been like that."

"Some of us…" The man shook his head as his voice trailed off.

"Some of us what?"

The man licked his lips. Marie sensed he had rehearsed what he was about to say.

"Some of us think he should be rattled. At least a bit. The polls are getting tight. We're getting hammered on social media, and even the legacy publications are starting to give us a hard time. When *The New York Times* says, 'Legitimate questions have been raised,' you're in deep shit." The man stopped. "Sorry. I don't know if I should've used that word."

"I've heard it before."

"The election's only a few weeks away," the man said. "We've got to turn things around."

Marie asked what he wanted her to do.

"Make a statement on Michael's behalf," he said. "Everybody's complaining about how he handled the case and whining about due process and all that nonsense. The creeps who were marauding in the park that night have a great lawyer, so they're getting the attention. We need to change the narrative. You were the one who was attacked. We need to remind the voters of that."

Marie remembered why she disliked politics—a rough business where winning was the only thing that mattered.

"If I make this statement..." Her voice trailed off again. "How will it get out to the public?"

"You can post it on Facebook or Twitter. I mean, X. Like everybody else, I'm having trouble with the change."

"No matter the name, I don't use them. Social media is a cesspool."

"Unfortunately, it's a cesspool we all have to live in." The man glanced outside, as if he were looking for inspiration in the setting sun. "Tell you what—you could email the statement to me, and I can put it on my website, as well as my social media feeds. Then, I'll contact the people I know in the traditional media, just to make sure they're paying attention. We should get some traction if we do it that way."

"But you're not gonna tell Michael about it?" She knew she sounded like a sixth-grader who was afraid of defying the teacher.

"If I mention this to him, he'll order me not to do it. This is one of those occasions where it's better to ask for forgiveness than permission."

"I wanna help. I'm just not sure this is the right way to do it."

The man leaned toward her. They were almost touching. "If you do what I suggest, I'm sure Michael will reach out to you. To be honest about it, I picture the two of you making an appearance together on the courthouse steps in Foley Square. The visual would be so powerful, it wouldn't even matter what either of you said."

She sipped her tea, which was getting cold. "I'd need help."

"Help doing what?" He sounded solicitous. His tone reminded her of the way Michael always talked to her.

"Composing the statement," she said. "I'd wanna make sure I said the right things."

"That's why I'm here."

Chapter Forty-Four

Sheila Devine

October 12, 2023

The two-lane asphalt road led past silos and cows and sagging farmhouses.

"Where do we start?" Haggerty asked.

"The medical center," Michael said. "She might be at work. Sometimes, she puts in long hours. That could be why she hasn't gotten back to me. Maybe something's come up, and she hasn't had a chance to respond."

GPS talked Sheila to the hospital's parking lot.

"What now?" Haggerty asked.

"When in doubt," Michael said, "play it straight. We go to the information desk and tell them we're looking for Marie Antolini. She works in occupational therapy. They call there and we talk to her, and Sheila can relax."

The information desk was staffed by a pleasant-looking woman in a bonnet who wore a plain and formless dress. The New Yorkers stopped over her. The woman asked what she could do for them.

"We're looking for Marie Antolini," Michael said.

"Gee," the woman said, "it's late. I don't know if she's still here."

"Could you check for us?" Michael asked.

"Of course." The woman picked up her phone and tapped a few digits.

"Hi, Darlene, it's Betty at the information desk. How are you?" Pause. "Oh, I'm fine, just fine, thanks for asking. How are your cats?" Another pause. "Oh, that's too bad. I'm really sorry to hear that."

Sheila resisted the urge to grab the receiver from this polite woman's hand and scream that they were looking for Marie Antolini because it was a goddamn emergency.

The pleasant woman seemed to sense Sheila's vibe. "Some people are here looking for Marie. Is she still there?"

Another pause. The woman nodded. "I see." Pause. "I see. Yes." Pause. Nod. Licking of lips. "Okay. Thanks. And I hope Fluffy feels better."

The woman looked at the people standing over her. "Marie left about an hour ago."

Chapter Forty-Five

Marie Antolini

October 12, 2023

She rarely drank alcohol, but tonight, she wanted some. She kept a bottle of zinfandel in the fridge for occasions like this. She'd pour herself a small glass and sit at the kitchen table and try to let her mind unwind.

Something about the encounter was disquieting. The man seemed nice, and his request was reasonable, and she sort of, kind of, recalled who he was, but still...

She opened the refrigerator, looked at the wine, decided to skip it. Instead, she went into her bedroom and booted the desktop while she changed into sweatpants and T-shirt.

She had told the man she needed to think about it. She wanted to help Michael, but she was unsure what to say. The man had suggested finding someplace quiet and private where they could work on her statement. Maybe her apartment? Or maybe another spot, if she knew one?

Marie said she lived in a house. A small one, but it was hers. She liked the privacy. He said it sounded nice. He'd like to see it, to tell the truth.

She shook her head and said she wanted to be by herself for a while. The man said he understood, but time was precious. It was important to get something out as soon as they could.

Marie promised to contact him in the morning. He looked disappointed while they exchanged phone numbers. As she looked at her device she said it might be a coincidence, but Michael was trying to reach her. His texts asked if she was OK. The man looked concerned and told her to hold off on replying. It would be better if they both responded to him, preferably with her declaration of support.

Sometimes, the man added, candidates don't know what's in their own best interest.

Alone in her room, she looked at the computer screen. No words came. She wondered if she could go through with it. She wouldn't do anything like this for anyone but Michael. She felt antsy, so she walked through the house, got ice from the freezer, poured water from the tap. Often, when her mind got cloudy, she realized it was because she was dehydrated and hungry.

She looked at the kitchen table, where she ate most of her meals, and realized she'd think better if she ate something. She half-filled a pot with water and started the stove. She threw in a pinch of salt, then looked in the fridge to see if she had enough lettuce for a salad, and was happy to see that she did. She also had tomatoes, celery, and carrots. She'd reheat the homemade marinara she had prepared a few days before. It was her mother's recipe. She wished she remembered more about her parents and the life she'd led while she was growing up, although Pasquale and Regina were awfully sweet.

As she took out the vegetables, she gazed at the bottle of zinfandel. Maybe she'd have a small glass with dinner after all. She had half a loaf of bread, too. She'd cut a slice or two to soak up the sauce.

As she opened the drawer where she kept her knives, she wondered what it would be like to see Michael again. To actually spend some time with him. He always made her feel better.

She heard a noise at the door.

Chapter Forty-Six

Sheila Devine

October 12, 2023

Michael knew her address. Sheila punched it into the GPS. Even for a rural area, she lived in the sticks. No lights on the roads. Sheila flipped on the high beams and ignored the speed limit. From the backseat, Haggerty muttered that they were gonna look like fucking idiots when they screeched to a halt in front of a house straight outta *Green Acres*. Beside her, Michael said he'd never been so glad for seat belts.

The house was down a long driveway flanked by pines—the type of place you couldn't find unless you were looking for it. Gravel crunched underneath the tires. The place was one story, with a small attic, very *American Gothic*. The moonlight was weak, so it was difficult to tell the color, but the place blended into the night, and Sheila had the feeling this was a home that few people visited.

The house was unlit. A late-model Kia was parked by a small porch that had a swing and two deck chairs. Sheila veered off the driveway, stopped under some trees, and cut her lights.

They got out of the car and closed the doors as quietly as they could.

Sheila, in a murmur: "Why are all the lights out?"

A soft reply from Haggerty: "Maybe she went to bed."

"It's only a little after eight."

They crept toward the front door. The sound of their feet against pine needles was like an effect in a Dolby movie.

Up wooden steps. Across the porch. A whisper from Michael: "Should we enter?"

Haggerty, the veteran of raids and surveillance: "You're the one who knows her."

Michael turned the knob. The door creaked open. Sheila wanted to move stealthily, but she felt like a member of a herd of giraffes.

Stepping inside. Pitch black. She noticed clumps that she assumed were furniture, but she was afraid to turn on the light. Beside her, she sensed Haggerty reaching into his jacket for his service revolver.

She heard a sound. The men tensed. The noise came from the back of the house, and Sheila held her breath so she could listen more closely. In a few seconds, she detected the sound of erratic gasps.

They took off. Haggerty pulled his gun. Sheila bumped against chairs. The gasps grew louder. Sheila surged through a small dining room, then felt her shoes hit kitchen linoleum.

Reaching for the wall. Feeling a switch. Fluorescent light flickering on. The glare revealing her fears:

Blood on the floor and the counter and the stove and the fridge. Sheila looked left, right, up, down. No one in sight. Louder and more frequent gasps from an unseen source.

In a nook, a small table nestled against a back wall. Sheila took cautious steps. Haggerty took out his cell and said this looked like a crime scene, and they had to be careful. He punched in three numbers.

When Sheila peered into the nook, she tried not to scream.

Marie Antolini was propped against the wall. Her eyes were glassy, and her mouth was open, as if she wanted to yell. Her body heaved with every breath. Her clothes were torn. Red smears covered her face and arms and the long breadknife in her right hand.

At her feet lay the body of Seamus O'Toole.

Chapter Forty-Seven

Rolando Ortega

November 10, 2023

Sheila Devine strode into the lawyer's office, introduced Ortega to her son, and said the young man would film the interview while she asked questions. She chuckled as she said this was a way to keep her costs down.

"Where do you go to school, Dylan?"

The interests of young people always intrigued Rolando Ortega. The world had yet to limit their hopes.

"Brooklyn Tech."

"What year are you in?"

"I'm a senior."

"You must be looking at colleges."

"I am."

An interjection from his mother: "Another reason I'm trying to cut expenses."

She opened her laptop and ran her fingers over the screen. He figured she was searching for the questions she had prepared. The woman was always prepared.

"Do you have any idea what you might study?" Ortega asked the boy.

"For a while, I was thinking about architecture. But lately, I've got interested in film again."

"They're both good fields. You have plenty of time to figure things out. Do you know where you want to go?"

"I dunno if I wanna go far away. I'd miss New York."

Ortega smiled. "This is an exciting period in your life. Enjoy it."

Dylan finished the set-up and turned to his mother, who seemed engrossed in whatever she'd called up on her screen.

"I'm ready, Ma."

Sheila Devine looked straight at the lawyer. "Gracias, Señor Ortega, for giving us the time to do this."

"No problema, Señora."

"The men you represent in the Riverside Runner case are all out of prison now."

"Sí. They've been reunited with their families. They are doing their best to readjust to society."

"What do you do now?"

"Our legal action continues. They were unlawfully imprisoned."

"How much are you asking for?"

"One hundred million dollars."

Ortega heard Dylan whistle, so he turned toward the teenager.

"It's not that much money, mi amigo. Four men were incarcerated for more than ten years for something they didn't do. It's a little more than two million dollars a year for each of them."

"There are still some people who believe they did it," Sheila said. "Or were somehow responsible."

Ortega repressed an urge to grin. "Detective Haggerty's theory is that the youths attacked Ms. Antolini and left her dazed and helpless before the rapist came along to finish the job, so to speak." The lawyer shook his head as if he were conveying a sad truth to a jury. "There's no physical evidence to back that up. The DNA from the semen matched Seamus O'Toole. Nothing recovered from the crime scene can be linked in any way to my clients."

"Detective Haggerty says he intends to write a book about the case."

"It's a free country." Ortega shrugged. "I will say this—I think it's good for everyone involved, and for the city as well, that Detective Haggerty has filed his retirement papers."

The bloodbath in Pennsylvania shattered the internet. Calls for the exoneration of the Riverside Four flooded every form of social media. Michael Devine went before Judge Iffath Khan and asked for the immediate release of the men who'd been imprisoned in the case, and the vacating of their convictions. The judge agreed before excoriating the district attorney's office for dragging its feet on the matter. In an unprecedented move, the *Times* rescinded its endorsement of Michael's candidacy and instead backed Nelson Hernandez, who wound up winning with sixty percent of the vote.

"I am sorry about the effect all of this had on your brother," Ortega said. "He made mistakes, but he is better suited for the DA's office than his opponent. The voters made an emotional decision, rather than a rational one."

Sheila pursed her lips. Ortega recognized the signs of a client or witness who did not wish to discuss a sensitive issue, so he decided to say nothing more about Michael Devine unless he had to.

"Have you reached out to Marie Antolini?" Sheila asked. "Have you talked to her at all?"

"I have not."

"Will you?"

Ortega stroked his chin and glanced at the popcorn ceiling. He'd been meaning to smooth it out for years.

"I would prefer not to, Señora, given everything that has happened. But if the lawsuits remain unresolved, she will have to give a deposition. That's why I hope the mayor is sincere in his statements that he wants to settle this case without spending years in litigation."

When she was attacked in her home, Marie Antolini sustained physical injuries, but by far, the worst effects of the assault were psychic. She was barely able to speak, although investigators stitched together an account:

Seamus O'Toole had discovered that Marie was working in a medical center in rural Pennsylvania. Phone records indicated he called a number of them until he discovered the one that employed her. During what he believed was a lull in Michael Devine's campaign, he drove there and contacted her before talking to her at a Starbucks. Then he followed her to her home.

Now, Marie Antolini was a patient in the facility where she had worked for a number of years. At least the care was top-notch.

"In a way," Ortega said, "she was fortunate she had a knife in her hand when he broke into her house."

Investigators said she struggled with the intruder as he attacked her. Although she was petite, she was physically strong, and she slashed and stabbed him numerous times.

"There was nothing fortunate about what happened to Marie Antolini," Sheila said.

A long pause. Ortega waited for her to continue.

"Let's return to the night in the park," Sheila said at last. "April Eleventh, Two Thousand Twelve. What's your theory about what happened?"

"I try to avoid theories," Ortega said. "Let's look at the evidence. Ms. Antolini and Mr. O'Toole were in contact. That's no surprise—she was his star student. That night, she sent him an email saying she had almost completed her project, but she was going for a run. That occurred about eight-thirty. He knew her routine, so he went to the park and lay in wait before attacking her from behind. She fought as best she could, and during their struggle, she tore off his St. Christopher's medal, which Felipe Huerta grabbed before he fled the scene. It was quite observant of your husband to notice the object Señor Huerta was wearing around his neck."

Ortega recalled the moment at Wesley McBride's coffeehouse. Sheila was staring at the image on her laptop in a silent plea for it to tell her something. When Wesley pointed to the pendant, Sheila zoomed in on it. Crud covered the thing, but she got in real tight and noticed the image of St. Christopher carrying the Christ child. After staring at it for close to a minute, she leapt to her feet and let out a string of expletives that revealed her roots in the working class.

"Is it fair to say that O'Toole was obsessed with Marie?"

Ortega snapped back to the present. He was on camera for a documentary that was likely to fill the arthouses.

"I keep my speculations to a minimum," he said, "but that woman in the desert had a few observations."

After the attack in Pennsylvania, Gloria Estevez emerged from her trailer to sell a story to TMZ:

Toward the end of the semester, Marie told her that Professor O'Toole's attitude had shifted from mentoring to harassing. He made it clear he wanted to sleep with her. He made it clear he expected her to comply. Marie did not want to alienate a man who could help her career, but his behavior had become intolerable. Still, the academic year would soon be finished, and everyone had heard that O'Toole would leave the university, so Marie hoped the situation would sputter to a neutral conclusion.

"All of this fits in with what we know about Mr. O'Toole's activities around that time," Ortega said. "He had laid the groundwork for his overseas assignment, and he thought Ms. Antolini would accompany him. He would do his reporting during the day and sleep with her at night. But then she backed out."

"When I was young, trying to make it in a field dominated by men, you wouldn't believe the crap I had to put up with."

"Unfortunately, Ms. Devine, I would."

Ortega shook his head. He hoped he looked and sounded sincere, and decided his best option was to maintain a professional pose.

"Let's return to the night of the attack," he said as if he were addressing judge and jury. The case was now being tried before the public. "A police report recently surfaced that everyone skipped over in Two Thousand and Twelve. Undoubtedly, you've seen it."

"I have."

Late on the night of the attack, police officers in Riverside Park stopped a man who looked disheveled, with scratches and marks on his face. He sounded out of breath. The officers asked if he'd been assaulted by the marauding gang of youths in the park, and after a few seconds, he said he had been. The officers asked if he'd like to talk to the police so they could press charges, and he replied that he just wanted to get the hell out of there.

The report noted that the man, who was white, wore a hoodie and had a foreign accent.

"Institutions," Ortega said, drawing out the word as if it were painful, "are always more worried about their own reputations than they are about the people whose lives they affect."

"After January," Sheila said, "for the first time in his career, my brother won't be working for an institution."

Despite everything that had occurred, Ortega was concerned about the most worthy adversary he had ever faced, and now his sister had given him an opening.

"I've had many differences with Michael, but I've always respected him. How is he doing?"

"He's been in Pennsylvania the past few days. He spends a lot of time with Marie. The people at the hospital say his presence lifts her spirits, although she still can't say much."

"Your brother is a good man, even if he has not always done good things. Have you talked to him recently?"

"Not for weeks. I've texted. Called." Sheila sounded like a tire losing its air. "He's ghosting me. I wonder if he blames me for the outcome."

"He should blame himself," Ortega said. "He sought to protect his office and the police instead of following the evidence."

Sheila looked away. He thought he detected the beginnings of a tear in the corner of this strong woman's eye.

"Thanksgiving's coming up." Her normally firm voice grew faint. "We've always spent it together."

Acknowledgements

I'd like to thank Harriette Sackler for her advice as I got this manuscript into shape, and I also want to thank Charles Salzburg and Tim Wendel for their continued friendship and support. I'm grateful to the team at Level Best Books—Shawn Reilly Simmons, Verena Rose and Deb Well—for all their hard work in getting this novel published, and for their belief in this project. Most importantly, I want to thank my wife, Jill, and our daughter, Skyler, for putting up with me while I worked on the book. I have been fortunate for many things in my life, but most of all for my family.

About the Author

Tom Coffey grew up on Staten Island, where he attended Catholic schools. His first novel, *The Serpent Club*, was published in 1999 by Pocket Books and received a starred review from Publishers Weekly. His second novel, *Miami Twilight*, came out two years later. In 2008 Toby Press printed *Blood Alley*, which also earned a starred review from PW. In 2015 the independent Oak Tree Press published *Bright Morning Star*.

Tom graduated from the Newhouse School of Public Communications at Syracuse University and attended film school at the University of Southern California. After a long career in journalism that included stints at *The Miami Herald*, the *Los Angeles Herald Examiner* and *New York Newsday*, Tom retired in 2023 from *The New York Times*. That same year, he signed a deal with Level Best Books for The Devine Trilogy, which traces the arc of law enforcement in New York City from the 1980s to the present. The first book in the series, *Public Morals*, was published to wide acclaim.

Tom lives in Lower Manhattan with his wife and daughter.

AUTHOR WEBSITE: tomcoffeyauthor.com

SOCIAL MEDIA HANDLES:
Instagram: tomcoffeywrites
Facebook: https://www.facebook.com/tom.coffey.311/
LinkedIn: https://www.linkedin.com/in/tom-coffey-506a4816/

Also by Tom Coffey

The Serpent Club (1999)

Miami Twilight (2001)

Blood Alley (2008)

Bright Morning Star (2015)

Public Morals (2023)